HER SELFLESS WARRIOR

OMEGA SKY, BOOK ONE

CAITLYN O'LEARY

Family is funny. Sometimes you're born into it, sometimes you make your own. Sometimes you're lucky enough to be blessed with a person who you would CHOOSE to have in your life, and they actually ARE your family. I was lucky enough to have my Uncle John (Jack) Marti who was my real uncle and someone I would choose again and again to have in my life. My first memory of him was when he brought two big red table candles to our house to put on my birthday cake, to wish me a happy second birthday.

I was four.

I stamped my foot and threw a fit, and argued with this strange man all day. He insisted I was two, and I insisted I was four. He told me I wasn't going to get the present he brought me unless I agreed I was two. I never gave in. I wouldn't blow out those darn big candles on my chocolate birthday cake either, even though he said I wouldn't get a piece, and chocolate was my very favorite. (He lied about that too; Mom let me have my birthday cake, but boy did her brother wind me up.)

Yep, that was Uncle Jack. He and my Aunt Micki and Cousin Carrie would come up from California to visit us in Seattle every year. He'd go to play golf and bet on the horses with my dad, and then come back to the house with me and my four siblings and get us going. It was always a battle of wills and I loved every minute of it because I was determined to beat him.

I learned how to tease and be teased, I learned how to be a good sport because of my Uncle Jack.

When I first became an author, he was a voracious reader, who read many of my books, and he was one of my biggest fans. Did I still get teased by my Uncle Jack? Hell yes! I wouldn't have it any other way.

I was lucky to have had a man like him in my life.

Uncle Jack, don't just rest in peace, you continue to have fun and give 'em hell.

1933 - 2022

SYNOPSIS

Will they get their second chance at love, before fate rips it away?

As a child, Kostya (Konstantin) Barona saw his father dragged off and his mother brutally murdered by the Russian secret police. He barely escaped the former Soviet Union with his own life. Now that he leads a Navy SEAL team, his whole life is based around rescuing those in need.

Lark Sorensen is an investigative journalist. There has never been an injustice that she didn't want to scrutinize and throw a spotlight on so the world would know about the atrocities going on around them.

Months ago, Kostya and Lark worked together in Afghanistan to help save a mother and her two little girls, and now they've met up again. The fiery sparks everyone expected to fly seem to sputter, but Kostya is intent on fanning the flames.

Now as lives are on the line, can these two work together, or will the injustices of the world finally drag them under?

This is an action, adventure, romantic, stand-alone novel.

PROLOGUE

"POLINA, YOU HAVE TO LISTEN TO ME."

Papa sounded scared. His Papa was never scared. Little Konstantin pressed his ear closer to the thin wooden door, trying to block out the sound of his older brother's questions from across the room. Their Papa had told them to hide with the baby in the ancient cupboard, but Kostya was too curious, so he was at the bedroom door.

"Polina, they're coming tonight, and when they do, I will go outside and meet them. I need you to stay inside and hide in the bedroom with the children. No matter what happens, stay inside and don't say a word. It's up to you to protect our children."

"You keep saying that. But who's coming? What are you talking about?"

Mama's words were loud and she sounded even more scared than when his friend Ivan had almost been eaten by the wild boar!

Even though it was really cold in the bedroom he shared with his brother and sister, fear crawled up his back, heating his skin. Kostya wanted to cry, but he forced the tears back. He was seven, he was too old to cry. He sucked in a deep breath and continued to listen.

"Wife, listen to me!" Papa yelled. "The second they take me away, you need to leave here and go to your brother's house, he will take care of all of you."

"That's impossible," she whimpered. "Vasily, you know his house is too far away; we won't make it in winter, not with a sick child and such a young child. It's impossible." Kostya watched as his mother threw herself at his father, grabbing at the lapels of his threadbare coat, her face red with tears.

Kostya ached to run out into the little common room and comfort her, but Papa would be the maddest if he thought Kostya wasn't hiding in the cupboard where he'd put his three children. His Papa didn't smile anymore—lately, he was either sad or angry.

"Polina, you are a strong woman," Papa said, gripping her wrists. "You can do this. You have to protect our children. Be brave!"

"Vasily, I'm begging you to come with us! Please, I'm begging you."

This time it was hard to understand his mother because she was sobbing so hard.

Kostya straightened his shoulders. He knew that he was the one who needed to be strong and brave. He was the most like Papa; his older brother Roman was sickly, and Irina was just a baby.

"*Myshka*, my love, there is no time left." His Papa lifted one hand and stroked his mother's cheek and she shuddered. "After they take me, get my mother's diamond brooch from the children's mattress and go to your brother's."

"Vasily, it's too far, little Irina will never make it to

Mikhail." This time his mother sounded sad, almost broken.

Kostya looked over his shoulder at the cupboard. Roman had the door open. His black eyes were dark as pitch as he stared at him. Roman couldn't hear what was going on, but somehow he knew. He might be sickly, but he knew things were bad...desperate. He gave Kostya a nod and Kostya felt himself settle. He and his brother were in this together.

His Mama started to talk again and his head swung back to the crack in the door.

"What you're asking, it's too much. It's an impossible task. I'm not strong like you. I'm not brave like you. We will all die, Vasily." This time she didn't sob. Her words were sad and hopeless. Kostya saw his father's expression change as he hugged his Mama tight.

"All right, *Myshka*. All right. I didn't want you to do this because you'll be left with nothing. No money, no security, but you can go to Fedor instead."

"Fedor?"

"The butcher's helper in town," his Papa explained. "I have heard that he knows ways to cross the border. It is a rumor only, but it's your only chance."

Kostya watched as his mother threw her arms around his father's waist. "Please come with us," she begged again. "We can hide with a neighbor. Whoever is after you will forget in time."

"It's too late for that. They found out I was working on distributing flyers with Pavel, you know he disappeared, and look what happened to his family. I can't take that chance with you and our children."

"It was an accident when their house burned down.

Nobody would have left Anna Popov and her children to die in that fire," Kostya's mother gasped in horror.

His father stroked the hair back from her face and kissed her forehead. "It was a message to the rest of us."

Kostya wiped away his tears. A month ago his friend Sergei Popov and his mama and all of his sisters had died when their cottage had burned down. Everyone but his father. Is that what was that going to happen to them?

"I've got to go, Polina," his Papa said as he pulled away from his Mama. He turned to the door.

Kostya jumped at the thunderous crash as the front door of their home was slammed off its hinges. Kostya quickly pushed the bedroom door shut.

"Vasily Baronavich! You are under arrest for crimes against the state!"

His mother screeched out in terror.

Kostya thought he heard his sister whimper. He whipped his head around and saw Roman holding a squirming Irina with one hand over her mouth and the other motioning him to get into the cupboard. Kostya shook his head and turned back to the door. He opened it a couple of millimeters so he could see what was going on. His blue eyes went wide. In the dimly lit, cramped room he saw giant figures in all black—even their heads were covered in black!

Two of the monsters grabbed his father and started to drag him toward the door.

"Don't take him!" his mother shrieked.

"Silence!"

Who said that?

"He's a good man, don't take him," Kostya's mother continued to plead.

"Polina, hush—" his father started to yell.

Did Kostya just hear Irina? *Please no.*

Flashes of light and the loud crack of bullets rent the air, mixing in with his mother's screams, cries, and pleas. Kostya was dizzy and stunned as he tried to focus on anything that he could make sense of.

His mother's blue eyes were wide with horror, then she raised her hands up in front of her face.

"Please! No! Please, I—"

Kostya saw a yellow flash of gunfire, then red—so much red as his mother's stomach burst open, her blood spraying across the walls and ceiling and finally landing across his father's stunned face.

"*Myshka!*" was the last word his father uttered before one of the men punched a rifle butt into his temple. Then they dragged his body out the door.

"Dammit!" one of the monsters said as he pulled a black mask off his head and wiped Kostya's mother's blood from his eyes. "These goddamn villagers need to be taught a lesson again. I want this house burned to the ground, and this time I don't care if all the houses next to it burn with it." He pointed at another masked man who started pouring petrol on the kitchen table. "Do you understand me? Make it burn bright!"

The monster nodded. Kostya thought he heard him laugh.

Then Kostya's eyes widened in horror as one of the other demons headed toward his parents' bedroom door. "I'll see if there's anyone else here," he said as he slammed Mama and Papa's door open.

Kostya closed his bedroom door and started running to the cupboard. Their bedroom door started to open as Kostya climbed into the cupboard.

"Boris, stop!" someone yelled. "Who gives a fuck if

they have some brats? We'll burn them all. Come on, we need to go."

Kostya looked over at his brother and sister. Even in the dim light, he could see the whites of their frightened eyes. Roman clamped his hand firmly against Irina's mouth. The toddler looked terrified. Roman looked resigned as he looked to Kostya for direction. Even though Roman was older, Kostya had always been the leader.

Kostya opened up the cupboard door just a little bit. When he didn't hear any voices, he shot out of the cupboard to the bedroom door and peeked out.

The kitchen table was on fire.

He looked for his Mama, but couldn't see her. He slammed the door shut. He needed to save Roman and Irina.

When he turned around, Roman was out of the cupboard. He still held Irina, but now she was no longer struggling. She was limp, her eyes glassy.

"What now?" Roman asked.

"We have to go out the window. Fast. Roman, you go first," he commanded. "I'll push Irina out to you afterward."

"Our parents?" Roman asked.

Kostya shook his head and Roman winced. He handed Irina to Kostya who gratefully cradled his little sister; it felt good to feel her warmth, her living body.

Kostya watched as Roman climbed on the bed, then shoved open the bedroom window and shimmied out. As soon as Roman was through, Kostya climbed on the bed and looked down at Irina who was still limp in his arms.

"Ah, my little *milaya*," Kostya said as he kissed the top of Irina's head. Her expression changed and she looked up at him. "Kostya?" she asked in her three-year-old voice. Then she started to struggle.

"You're going out to play with Roman, *Irinushka*. You get to go outside through the window," he said with a big grin, hoping she would think the whole thing was fun.

"Roman?" she asked.

"Yes. Now, let's hurry. He's waiting for you," Kostya lifted her up to the window and carefully lowered Irina down to Roman. As soon as his brother took ahold of their sister, Kostya hissed at them, "Quick, run to the church steps. I'll meet you there."

"No, come with us now," Roman insisted.

"I can't. I have to find Grandmother's jewelry. You've got to go now," he said angrily.

Roman held his ground despite the fact his thin body was shivering in the snow.

"Just go!" Kostya shouted. He waited until he saw Roman turn and start walking, then he ducked back into their room.

I have to find the brooch!

Kostya smelled smoke. He didn't have much time.

He yanked the blankets off of the flimsy mattress, frantically trying to remember what his Papa had said. Something about his grandmother's diamond brooch being in the children's mattress. Kostya wiped the tears and snot from his face as his small hands fumbled to see where the jewelry might have been sewn in. Roman sometimes helped Mama with the sewing, he would have known where to look.

Derr 'mo Konstantin swore. He should have thought of that before having Roman go out the window!

Kostya started to cough. He wiped his eyes when they started to sting.

Struggling, he was finally able to pull the mattress off the wooden frame and shove it over. He saw a spot on the back where there was a different kind of thread. It was like when Mama mended his socks. He pulled at it, trying to tear it open with his nails, but it wouldn't come loose.

I need Mama's scissors!

Kostya thought desperately for another few seconds, then let out a roar of satisfaction. He ran to his dresser and pulled out the hunting knife his father had given him and hacked at the mattress until the outer layer ripped open, then he dropped the knife and dug inside the stuffing. Finally, his fingers gripped something solid and he pulled it out. It was a velvet pouch with something in it. He fumbled with the string until he could peer inside.

The smell of smoke was overwhelming. He looked over his shoulder and saw the bedroom door had a malevolent yellow glow all around it, and black smoke was pouring in like some kind of evil fog that was trying to devour him.

He turned his attention back to the pouch and inside he saw something shiny. He prayed it was the brooch. He stuffed the bag into his pocket.

He coughed as he ran back to the dresser and grabbed the valise that Roman had used when he'd taken the train to visit Uncle Mikhail, then stuffed it full with as many jackets, shoes, and clothes that would fit. He was surrounded by the gray fog, but he still managed to see the open window. Kostya stumbled toward it and then went to throw the bag onto the bed so that he could climb out the window, but it wouldn't work with the mattress gone and he didn't have the time or the strength to pull it back on the bedframe.

Kostya had been trying to ignore the sound of the

crackling fire behind him, but he jumped when there was a loud pop. When he turned to look at the door he saw that flames were licking around the entire door frame. Kostya choked back a sob and pushed down his fear.

Turning back to the mattress on the floor he figured out what to do. He pulled back the flimsy bedframe and shoved it up against the wall so that he could climb onto its side. He lifted the valise then hefted it onto his shoulder and threw it through the open window. Kostya sucked in a deep breath of fresh air, then he shimmied out the window and dropped down into the melting snow. When he looked back at the house he saw where the fire was clawing toward the sky.

He turned back and saw the small footprints made by his brother and sister but he ignored them. He turned back to the house. Mama was dead, there was no hope for her. But maybe Papa?

He did everything he could to shut out the roar and heat of the fire as he crept around the side of his house, hoping against hope that his father might still be out front. When he got to the corner of the house, there was nothing.

No car.

No monsters.

Nothing.

In minutes that felt like a lifetime, he'd lost both his parents.

A searing pain jolted him as embers from the house hit his forearm. He hefted up the valise and ran to the church.

He still had his brother and sister to take care of. Now it was up to him to be strong and brave.

1

"Lexi, did you hear me?" Irina asked her daughter from across the dining room table. Kostya heard the frustration in his sister's voice, and he couldn't blame her. What had happened to his little Lexi? It was like a switch had been flipped. It had only been a year ago that his niece would come running to the door to give him a hug when he came to visit. Now when he came over for dinner, she wandered down to the table, usually late, with her nose stuck to her phone. Could turning thirteen really change a girl this much?

"Lexi," Irina said louder. "Put down your phone and participate with the people who are at the table. Am I making myself clear?"

His niece immediately shoved her phone into her back pocket, recognizing the voice of doom when she heard it. Kostya turned to his sister and gave her a wink that neither of her two children could see.

"*Irinushka*, when is Tony coming back from Macau?" he asked.

His sister's eyes softened at his use of her childhood

nickname. "He should be home on Wednesday," she answered. "He said the quality levels coming from the new manufacturing plant looked great."

She shifted her eyes towards her daughter. "I have high hopes that Lexi will remember how to make conversation again by the time her father returns."

"Mom," Lexi whined. "You're always picking at me."

Lexi's older brother snorted. "She's picking on you because you deserve it," Roman said. Kostya looked at his fifteen-year-old nephew and marveled at the difference between him and his namesake. The only thing they shared was their soulful gray eyes. He wondered if his own brother had survived their escape from Russia if he would have ever turned into such an outgoing and confident young man.

Kostya picked up his water glass and took a long sip. Thirty-four years later and he could still be knocked back by a flashback of that treacherous winter and all that he'd lost as they'd crossed over into Poland.

"Don't be all sanctimonious, Roman. The only reason you're not on your phone is that Haley's just too busy with cheer and working at the ice cream shop to text you," Lexi teased. "Otherwise you'd be worse than me."

"I'm just smarter about how I play things. You need to watch and learn, little sister. Watch and learn." Roman picked up the bowl of beef stroganoff and served himself then passed the bowl to Kostya.

And just like that, Kostya was back in the present. He loved the way his niece and nephew interacted—when Lexi was off her phone, that is. Irina and Tony had done a wonderful job raising their two kids. He'd been worried when they'd gotten married so young, but they'd pulled it off.

"How about you, Uncle Kostya? Have you been anyplace interesting that you're allowed to talk about?" Roman asked him as he heaped green beans onto his plate.

"Does California count?" he asked. "I know it's not as exotic as China."

Roman snorted again. "So that means you can't tell us. Okay, so I'll bite; what was in California?" he asked.

Kostya thought about how to respond. "An Afghan friend of mine passed away not so long ago. I went back to California last month to check in on his widow and their two daughters to make sure they were settling in okay here in the States."

"That's so sad," Lexi said as she put down her fork. "How are they?"

Now *that* was the girl he remembered. "They're living with an Afghan American couple who are helping them navigate living here in the States. Right now their biggest hurdle is assimilating into school."

"Do they speak English?" Roman asked. "You and Mom didn't when you got here, and Mom said that was the toughest thing about coming to America."

"They don't," Kostya answered.

Irina caught his eye and grimaced. Pain lanced through Kostya like a knife. It hadn't been learning English that had been so damn hard. Hell, the schools and dealing with the foster care system were a comparative breeze, even losing Mama and Papa eventually faded, but losing Roman was an open wound to this very day.

"Are you going to see them again?" Lexi asked.

"Soon."

"How old are they?" she asked again. Before he could

answer, she turned to her mother. "Don't I have some old clothes that I could give them? I know that some of them are really cute and we were saving them for when your friend Melanie's daughter gets a little older, but can't we give them to these girls instead?"

Looking at this beautiful girl that his sister had created helped take the pain away. "Taja is eight years old and Nazy is five. A friend of mine's mother has probably bought out Nordstrom to kit them out, but if you can think of something special for either of them, I'll tell them it came from you and they'll treasure it."

"Nordstrom?" Lexi asked.

"A *friend*?" Irina raised her eyebrow.

Kostya focused on his niece. "The lady has the big bucks," Kostya laughed. "Lexi, besides shopping at Nordstrom for the clothes, she probably bought them both a pony."

"I want to hear more about your friend, Konstantin," Irina ordered.

Kostya winced and Roman snorted. It was always serious shit when his sister used his formal name.

"There's nothing to tell," he assured her.

"Is your friend a male or a female?" Irina persisted.

He grunted. "Female."

"Ahhhhhh." His sister smirked.

"What's that supposed to mean?"

"Just that you don't have any female friends, so this is significant."

"You're right, Mom. Uncle Kostya has never mentioned a woman." Lexi turned to look at him with too-old eyes. "Is she your girlfriend?"

"Yeah, is she?" Irina asked, her eyes twinkling.

I'm so screwed. How do I explain Lark Sorensen? Still, she isn't a girlfriend...

Kostya opened his mouth, and Irina raised her eyebrow.

"This stroganoff is delicious," he finally said before he took a big bite.

"Seriously, Uncle, you need to get with the program," Roman told him. "Girlfriends rock. And I'm talking about girls as friends. You need to get some women in your posse."

Kostya shook his head.

Really? I'm getting schooled by a fifteen-year-old?

"He's kind of right, Uncle Kostya. Maybe in the olden days, people didn't have friends of different sexes, but nowadays they do. It's more...more..." Lexi turned to her brother. "You say it."

"Healthy. Seriously, Uncle Kostya, you spend too much time with the guys from your team. They're great guys and all, but you need to get out more. Mom is always saying you need a social life and all. Mom has guy-friends and dad has girl-friends. You met them last Christmas, remember? It's all cool. It's not like they're having sex or anything. But you could probably use some sex."

"Okay, enough!" Irina put up her hands. "Roman, really, you have seriously crossed a line, and I've raised you better than that, haven't I? I need you to apologize to your uncle right now."

Kostya snuck a peek over at Lexi and damned if she wasn't nodding.

Holy fucking hell. What has this world come to?

His lips twitched.

"Uhm, kids, I really appreciate your concern, but I

gotta tell you that my sex life, or lack thereof, wouldn't be something I would clue you in on."

"Thank God," Irina muttered. "Roman?" she growled as she gave her son the stink-eye.

"I'm sorry, Uncle Kostya." Then he turned to his sister. "But we worry about you."

"Yeah," Lexi nodded. "You're the best. We just want you to be happy. Some woman would be lucky to have you." Then her eyes sparkled. "I wouldn't mind spoiling one of your babies."

Kostya gave his sister an incredulous look. "I blame this on you," he pointed his fork at his baby sister.

"This is not my fault. This is all Tony. We Russians are stoic, you know this. But the Italian side of the family just can't help themselves." She shrugged.

Kostya still had a hard time wrapping his head around his little sister marrying into the big Romano clan. He was always invited over to Tony's parents' house for the holidays, but more often than not he found excuses not to attend; it was just too overwhelming. Irina, God bless her, always let it slide.

"Okay, time to serve dessert," Irina announced. The kids perked up.

"You made dessert?" Lexi asked.

"No, your uncle brought it."

"Cool. Where'd you get it from?" Roman wanted to know. The boy had one hell of a sweet tooth.

"I got apple and berry strudel from Kolache." He saw his sister's eyes go soft. Their mother had always made it for them. Even though Irina had only been three years old when they had to flee, the strudel was one of the few things he knew that Irina remembered from their time in Russia.

"Sweet!" Roman crowed as he jumped up and headed to the kitchen.

Lexi followed. "You better not snag all the berry strudel before it gets to the table," she admonished.

"You're a good big brother," Irina said in Russian.

"You make it easy," Kostya replied in kind. "You're raising good kids. They scare the hell out of me, but they're good kids."

Irina laughed. "You'd raise good kids too. I agree with Lexi, I wouldn't mind spoiling some of your babies."

Babies? I barely saved you, Irina, how could I ever have babies?

2

PULLING INTO THE PARKING LOT AT LITTLE CREEK, KOSTYA
rolled his neck, working out the kinks from the weekend.
It was funny, but the weekends were always the stressor,
never the time at work. He wondered if his nephew was
right, maybe he did have a problem with his priorities.

Stop with the worthless thinking, Baronakov!

Kostya snorted. Shit, he had to be tired and stressed if
he was referring to himself by his actual last name instead
of the one that had been given to him when he arrived in
the States. He stepped down from his forest-green Land
Rover Defender and locked her up. He took a deep breath,
forced himself to focus on something calming, and smiled
at the shine on his baby's chrome. It had taken him almost
a year to get the 1981 vehicle restored to mint condition
when he'd found her in that Tennessee barn.

That goddamned Drake Avery had conned him and
some of his team members into going hunting down in
the scenic Smoky Mountains. Turned out that he wanted
free labor from them first—fixing up the local youth

activity center that had been decimated by a tornado —*then* they were going bow-hunting.

Kostya's lip quirked up. At least he'd conned members of the Night Storm and Black Dawn teams as well. It hadn't been too bad; with the fourteen of them working they'd made short work of the construction. To tell the truth, Kostya wasn't much into hunting, he'd just wanted a chance to spend time with the other teams, and it turned out that the other lieutenants had as well. Drake acted like it had been his plan all along. Truly, Kostya didn't know how Lieutenant Mason Gault handled such an ego on the Midnight Delta team. But, there must be something to the guy, because the three of his team members who had gone to Jasper Creek still kept in touch with the man. However, he was pretty sure Jase was staying in touch with one of Drake's sisters more than he was with Drake Avery.

Enough with the trip down memory lane, time to get shit done.

Kostya gave a chin lift to the Command Master Chief who was herding four newbies for the construction battalion maintenance unit. Ned had his hands full—one of the kids' boots was untied, and another one looked like he was Roman's age.

At least they're not my problem.

His cell started ringing the exact moment he opened the door to his tiny office.

"Barona here," he answered.

"I've got five of the six you wanted," Gideon said.

Kostya frowned.

Not good.

"Let me guess, it's Kelly who's a no-show."

Gideon sighed. "Yeah."

Kostya shut his office door and put his phone on

speaker so he could multitask. This was the third time in the last six months that some kind of bullshit had occurred that kept Landon Kelly away from base when he was supposed to be here.

"What is it this time?" Kostya asked as he shuffled through the files on his desk while waiting for his second-in-command's answer. "And it better not be fucking Angelique."

He pulled out the file he needed—of course, it was at the bottom. He opened it and shook his head. It was going to take at least an hour to fill out these forms. The Navy was supposed to be paperless, so why in the hell was there still so much paper?

Kostya looked down at his phone on his desk, which was eerily silent. "I take it by your non-answer, that the problem *is* Angelique."

"Yeah," Gideon bit out the answer. "I don't know what it is about Landon, but this is the third crazy girlfriend he's had in the three years he's been on the team. We should have known better than to use him for this training exercise, but knowing you, that's exactly why you're using him. This was a test, wasn't it?"

Kostya raised an eyebrow. "Go with your instincts, Gideon," he purred.

"Shit, it *was* a test."

"If Petty Officer Kelly can't make it to a simple training assignment or meetings on time, who's to say that he won't let us down when it comes to an actual mission?"

"I hear you, boss."

"You handle the others and explain they've been chosen to take part in the joint mission readiness exercise with Marine Capt. Julie Lockhart and her squadron. Grab Jase to take Landon's place. He'll be available."

"What about Kelly?" Gideon asked.

"Don't ask such a stupid question," Kostya snorted. His lip tipped upwards; he could see Gideon wincing in his mind's eye.

"I take it you're going to be calling Landon?" Gideon surmised.

"Not necessarily calling him. Did he give you an ETA?"

"He said no later than ten hundred hours."

Kostya looked at his phone. It was eight hundred hours now, and Landon lived twenty minutes away from base.

"Gideon, you handle the initial briefing with our selected men."

"And our meeting after lunch with the Marine squadron?" Gideon asked.

"I'll be there for that." Kostya set down the file and picked up his keys.

KOSTYA HAD all of his men's info on his phone, so it took just fifteen minutes to navigate to Landon's small duplex. When he pulled up, it didn't take a genius to figure out which side of the old house belonged to his man. It would be the one with the front window completely shattered, and clothes, furniture, and a mattress strewn across the front lawn.

Classy.

As soon as he opened the door to his SUV, he could hear shrieks coming out of the window.

"You don't love me! You promised me forever! How could you go back on your word like this? I've given you everything. Everything! I've wasted the best four months of my life, and I'll never, ever get them back."

Kostya winced. He felt a headache coming on. He wasn't sure if it was due to the high-pitched shrills that were surely aggravating every dog within a mile radius, or if it was due to the pointless idiocy that Angelique was spewing.

He was midway up the walkway when he heard some kind of God-awful noise coming toward him. It wasn't artillery, it was a cacophony of music. It was like The Allman Brothers were having a live concert at the same time some Hip Hop group that one of the guys on Max's team always listened to were on stage.

My head is going to explode!

Two trucks crested the ridge, coming in hot. One blue, one red.

"Aw, hell." Kostya dug his fingers into the bridge of his nose. "Seriously?" Whoever these yay-hoos were, they were driving two of the largest personal trucks on the market.

The red truck swung out and shuddered to a stop. The driver jumped out, slammed his door, and hot-footed it up to Kostya. The other driver stayed in his truck and cranked up "Midnight Rider" then leaned on his horn.

"You Kelly?" The kid in front of Kostya demanded. He probably wasn't even old enough to drink, but he was a big kid. He pushed his chest out so that it touched Kostya's.

Yep, it's a shit day.

"No, I'm not Landon Kelly. Who are you?"

"Angelique is my sister. Kelly's screwed her over, and me and my brother are here to teach him a lesson."

A crash had them both looking to the left, and they

saw a rather small flatscreen TV break into pieces on top of a pile of books.

"I don't know, it seems like Angelique is holding her own," Kostya observed.

"You never even gave me a key." Her whine stretched into a howl that made her sound like she was part coyote.

Now that Kostya was close enough to the duplex he could hear Landon's response. "And that should have told you we weren't serious. For God's sake, Angelique, every time we were together, we did it at your apartment and I went home. Last night was the first time I invited you here, that should have told you something."

"Exactly. I brought a suitcase and everything. You betrayed me!"

Kostya grimaced when the dumbass in front of him poked him in the chest. "Do you hear that? That bastard strung her along like she was nothing."

Poke.

Poke.

Poke.

"Back off," Kostya said mildly.

He really didn't need this to escalate.

Poke.

I'm too old for this shit.

"Seriously, knock it off." Kostya's voice was serious.

"Whatchya going to do, old man?" The kid poked him again.

Aw, hell.

Kostya grabbed the young man's wrist and wrenched it down, spun him around, then shoved his arm high behind his back until he squealed in the same high pitch as his sister.

It must run in the family.

"I warned you to back off." Kostya shoved him to the ground. "Are we clear now?"

Dumbass cradled his wrist to his chest. "You broke my arm."

Kostya gave him a cold stare, not even flinching as something else thudded behind him. The Gregg Allman music stopped and he turned to see another beefy young man running toward him. His head was down as if Kostya were a tackling dummy.

For fuck's sake.

A half-second before the next idiot was going to slam into him, Kostya stepped out of his way. He watched dispassionately as the kid sprawled onto the cement sidewalk, his head bouncing once off a concrete step.

"Petty Officer Kelly," Kostya yelled up towards the house. "Get this situation under control. Now!"

"Lieutenant?" Landon shouted down.

"Yes," Kostya yelled back up. "You have one minute. If you fail to do so, I'm coming up."

"Yes, Sir."

"Don't touch me," Angelique shrieked.

Kostya walked over to the man who had tried to tackle him. He'd hit his head hard. Kostya gently turned him over and examined his skull. It wasn't cracked. The kid pushed up from the ground and glared at him.

"You fucker." He tried to take a swipe at Kostya, then fell back onto the cement.

"Give it up," Kostya said as he grabbed his arm and pulled him up into a sitting position. "You and your brother need to take your sister home."

He looked up as the door to the duplex opened, only to gift him with more screaming as Landon carried his illustrious girlfriend over his shoulder. Angelique kicked and beat him on his back with her fists. She had the vocabulary of a Marine drill sergeant.

"Who are *they*?" Landon asked as he stood on his porch.

"Her brothers."

"Great, they can have her," Landon said with a relieved sigh. Then he eyed both of the injured men. "Shit, boss, can either of them drive?"

Even though he'd been busy with the offensive lineman, he'd kept an eye on the kid nursing his arm.

Kostya nodded toward the brother who was standing. "He can drive one-handed. Dump her into the red pick-up."

"I'm not going anywhere with Earl!" Angelique shrieked. Landon ignored her ear-piercing howls and walked toward the red truck.

"If you keep my stuff, I'm calling the copsssssss!"

Kostya winced. It was like she was practicing for a contest to shatter glass.

"Angie! Enough!" The lineman pushed himself off the sidewalk and stumbled over to Landon and his sister. "If you don't put a sock in it, I'm going to tell Ma that you missed church last Sunday because you were hungover, and not because you were serving food down at the mission like you told Daddy."

"You wouldn't dare." Finally, she uttered something in a reasonable decibel.

"Try me," her brother said as he pulled her out of Landon's arms. "I've got her from here."

"I want my stuff." She pouted as her brother set her on the ground.

"She's not allowed back in my house." Landon peered at the three siblings. "I'll be right back. Don't move."

"Aren't you going to hit him? He disrespected me," Angelique whined. But this time she sounded like a young woman and not a hyena on meth.

Kostya watched as the brothers gave each other a look. "Angie," the one named Earl started. "You need to stop doing this. The last time you called the cops, they sent the sheriff, and you know Rayleen; she said she'd put your ass in jail. Remember?"

"But he's a SEAL. Sheriff Rayleen would report him, and he'd get into trouble."

"Anyway, Rayleen used to babysit you, there's no way she'd believe any of your bullshit."

"But I *love* him," she wailed. "I want him in jail."

Aw, fuck. How messed up was she?

"You really are stupid." Earl gripped her arm and opened up the truck door to hoist her inside. "The last thing you need is the Navy pissed off at you."

"What about my car?"

"We'll come and get it later," her other brother said.

"What about my stuff?"

Landon jogged down the sidewalk with a pink zebra-striped overnight bag and a purse covered in rhinestones. He thrust it at Earl.

"Here."

"Sorry about your stuff," Earl murmured to Landon as he got into his truck.

Landon shrugged. He watched as the two brothers drove off, then turned and looked at Kostya and sighed. He was shaking his head when he walked back to Kostya, but he looked him in the eye when he stood in front of him, which Kostya appreciated. Kostya waited for Landon to start, and the kid didn't disappoint him.

"Lieutenant, I don't want to be kicked off your team, but I know you have every right to do so."

Kostya nodded and waited for his man to continue.

Landon looked over his shoulder at the catastrophe in his yard. "I don't know what happened. I really don't. One minute Angelique was calm as a cucumber then she turned into a woman I'd never seen before...she was...she was...hell, I can't even explain it."

"I was here, no explanations are necessary."

Kostya waited for Landon to continue. When he didn't say anything, Kostya shook his head and started speaking.

"Kelly, I don't care how good you are, if you aren't available when I need you, you're useless to me, and what's worse, you're no good to the rest of your teammates."

Landon nodded. He didn't offer any excuses, which Kostya appreciated.

"You've been a member of Omega Sky for four years now. In the last six months, you've let me down three times. This is your last shot. You got it?"

Landon nodded.

"Do what you have to do and get your ass to base, pronto." Kostya didn't wait to see how his man responded. Instead, he turned to his vehicle and left.

3

LARK SORENSON ROLLED HER SHOULDERS AS SHE SLOWLY drove her rental car along Ohio Drive Southwest to Hains Point. Even in the cold weather, with the trees bereft of leaves, the place settled her. Here on the Point she could watch a gorgeous sunset and let her mind drift. It was a different world here in Washington D.C. than where she grew up in California.

"You're not even listening to me, are you?" Amy sighed from the car's speaker.

Lark shook her head to clear it and then looked down at the dash. "I am too. I even parked the car and everything, just so I could concentrate on you," Lark protested.

Her best friend laughed. "I call bull-pucky, your mind was wandering. Where are you?"

"Hains Point." Amy grew up in a not-so-nice part of Baltimore and as soon as she'd been old enough she'd gotten a crap apartment near the Capitol and started waiting tables; Amy knew D.C. like the back of her hand.

"What's got you down?" Amy asked. "If you needed to

watch the sunset, something must really be bothering you."

"Hey, wait a minute, girly. Don't even try it, we were talking about you."

She heard Amy sigh. It was the second sigh in five minutes, things must be serious. Lark tried to cajole her friend to talk. "Come on, dish. Is it a guy? I hope it's a man. You haven't been laid in so long, I think certain parts of your anatomy might be developing cobwebs."

Amy snorted. "That's not how it works, Lark, haven't you been keeping up? Actually, your hymen grows back."

Lark shouted with laughter. When she finally got herself back under control, she focused on the dashboard again. "Nope, hadn't heard that one," she admitted.

"That's because you've gotten some in the last eighteen months. However, I don't think Jerry really counts."

Lark sat up straighter in the Chevy Malibu rental car. "Jerry counted. I was with him for the whole summer."

"I'm not talking about the fact that you boinked him for three months, I'm talking about the fact that you managed to pick yet another teeny-tiny little dweeb. When are you going to date someone with a little backbone? Hell, all the guys you choose, you could squish with your pinky finger."

"That is *so* not true. Think about Claus back in college, he was six foot five."

"He weighed one hundred and fifty pounds if he weighed an ounce!" Amy exclaimed.

"He did triathlons, he was fit," Lark defended the poor guy.

"His collarbones were sexier than yours, and his elbows were so pointy that I almost lost an eye that time we went to the movies."

It was a lost cause. Amy was right. There was not one guy she'd dated that she couldn't have fought off in a dark alley. Now it was her turn to sigh.

"I heard that. You sighed. Don't tell me it just registered that you've been choosing men who aren't just pathetic, they're pathepic!"

"Huh? Are you hanging out with teenagers again?"

"I'm hanging out with people in their early twenties, and if you weren't so career-minded and dating such weak-assed-boring men, you'd know that pathepic means pathetic to the epic degree!"

"Amy, I'm putting a gun to my head if I start dating some hipster who knows that word. And anyway, I'm surrounded by manly men. Think about it, I know some of the toughest men on the planet. There's the Brits I was just hanging out with last month. You can't call them pathepic or dweebs. Hell, I don't want to think about what they could destroy with their pinkies."

Lark was met by silence.

"Amy are you still there?"

"Sorry, I was fantasizing about those commandos and their fingers, and how I could make use of them."

Lark flushed. Suddenly she wasn't thinking of British special operatives, nope, now she was thinking about a certain big, blond Navy SEAL.

She sighed again.

At least those thoughts took her mind off her informant for a moment. For the first time in five months, Lark had caught Candy in a lie and now she couldn't get ahold of her. Something was wrong.

"I heard that sigh. Come on, 'fess up. Tell me what's bothering you." Amy pestered her again.

"Oh hell no, we're not talking about me again, nor am

I going to let you take us down some weird conversational bunny trail. You called for a reason, so tell me what it is. I have a reception I need to get to. So tell me what's going on, girlfriend."

"It's my mom," Amy said quietly.

Dammit.

Lark could hear the dejection in her friend's voice. Patty Linden had a hell of a lot to answer for. It took years for Amy to develop any kind of self-esteem after living with her mother's emotional and sometimes physical abuse, but for the most part, Amy was past that.

"Please tell me it was only a phone call," Lark pleaded.

When Amy didn't answer, Lark knew it was a visit.

"Why'd you go over there? What's wrong?"

"I got suckered. She said she was babysitting my cousin's kids and she needed help. I should have known there wasn't a chance in hell that Carla would have left Jim and John with her. When I got to Mom's place she was higher than a kite and wanting money, of course."

"Of course she was. You didn't give her any, did you?"

"It was awful, Lark. She had a knife and used it on me." Lark could hear the anguish in her friend's voice.

"I had to call the cops. She totally took me by surprise."

"What do you mean she used it on you? How bad are you hurt? What hospital are you at? I'll be there in five minutes."

Lark started her car, trying to think how long it would take to get to Baltimore from Washington D.C.

Amy gave a wet laugh. "And that's why you're my best friend. That was three days ago. She nicked me on my outer thigh. They stitched me up."

"How many stitches?" Lark demanded to know.

Amy took a while to answer. Finally, she said, "Twenty-seven."

"Goddammit!" Lark yelled. "You should have called me before you even called the cops!" "Chill, Lark. It's okay, Carla's been babysitting me, I got kiddy cuddle time, and now I'm home. I was hoping I could see you tomorrow, cause I knew you were in town."

"You're seeing me tonight." Lark glanced down at the cocktail dress she was wearing. Fuck it, Riya would understand if she didn't make it to see her acceptance speech.

"No, I'm not. I know you want to spend time with Riya and her husband. I already took a pain pill and I'm going to be tired in about sixty seconds, and asleep ten minutes from now. So tomorrow, girly. I'll see you tomorrow."

"So, in other words, you played me."

"Yeppers. But I *do* want to see you tomorrow. I could use a hug."

"I'm bringing breakfast."

"I'm counting on it," Amy yawned.

Lark tapped her steering wheel after Amy hung up. She picked up her phone and called Candy again. She didn't answer. What in the hell was going on? She and Candy had a pact; they both wanted to see those men at Sanofi taken down. Why wasn't she answering?

"Candy, it's me, Lark. Call me when you get this message. We need to talk about what you told me last week—it doesn't check out. I know something's wrong. You know you can trust me. I won't let anything happen to you. I'm on your side in this thing. Call me."

Lark hung up the phone. She really hoped the woman would get back to her soon.

LARK WALKED into the bar of the Kimpton Hotel Monaco before the festivities were due to start. She knew exactly where she wanted to sit since she'd been there before; far back corner, in the shadows, where she could watch people coming in.

She almost missed a step in her glittery high silver heels when she saw Kostya Barona in her spot. What were the chances that she'd just been thinking about him two hours ago, and there he was? She should go say hello, but she couldn't. If it had been one of the other SEALs she'd worked with in Afghanistan, she would have, but not Kostya. She changed course and headed to the one high chair that was open at the bar.

"What can I get you?" the bartender asked as he placed a napkin in front of her.

"Single malt scotch, Jameson."

"Reserve?" he asked.

Lark smiled and shook her head. "I want to still be able to make my mortgage."

The bartender laughed. "Got it. I've got you covered, and it will still go down smooth. Straight or on the rocks?"

Lark lifted one pale blonde eyebrow and the bartender chuckled.

"Straight it is."

He turned back to the shelf and didn't have to reach up onto his toes to grab a bottle, so Lark knew her drink wouldn't break the bank. When the short glass was in front of her she slid her credit card over.

"Do you want to start a tab?"

"Sure, why not?" She smiled and did a quick shimmy in her seat to make herself comfortable.

Shit.

Lark leaned back slightly and felt the back of the bar seat.

Good, nobody should have seen me wiggling my damn ass.

She took a sip of the liquid gold and the burn felt good.

Damn good.

She took a minute to take a surreptitious look in the mirror behind the bar. Kostya looked comfortable in *her* booth. His arm was resting along the back, his ankle propped over his knee in that pose that men always took when they were relaxed. He looked like some kind of sultan surveying his kingdom. But he wasn't really. He was an operative, through and through. It gave her a punch of excitement to realize that she was the only person in the bar who knew that. She watched him some more.

Kostya was very careful to look like a man who was just sitting back and enjoying his drink. His eyelids were at half-mast, but she would bet all the money in her checking account that his eyes were moving and he was aware of every single twitch that every person made in this place.

Shit, which would have included me wiggling my damn ass!

Kostya's eyes caught hers in the mirror and his lip twitched. He raised his glass slightly as if in salute before taking a swallow.

Fuck!

His drink was in the same highball glass that hers was. God help her if he was drinking Jameson too.

Keep it together, Sorensen. Remember, this is a man who has provided you with help in the past. You need to keep on his good side.

She lifted her glass in return and gave one of her own smiles.

"Hi. I don't remember seeing you around here before."

Lark stifled a sigh as she glanced at the man in the thousand-dollar suit to her left.

"Hello," she answered politely.

"My name is Langley Redford, I'm Senator Wentworth's Chief of Staff." He held out his right hand to shake. She spotted his wedding ring on his left hand.

What a sleaze.

"Hello Mr. Redford, I'm Lark Sorensen."

She wasn't surprised when he held her hand for seconds too long. "I think I've heard your name before. Which member of congress do you work for?" he asked.

"I work freelance, but usually my articles get picked up by either Vanity Fair or The New Yorker."

He dropped her hand like she'd told him she had leprosy. "You're a reporter?"

"An investigative journalist. Traditionally my articles take months to research," Lark paused. "But I did start out working as a reporter for a newspaper in Idaho. It was in the sports section. Consequently, I'm a big basketball fan."

"But you *are* a reporter." The capped white tooth smile had disappeared.

"And you *are* a Chief of Staff."

His smile was back in full force. "I am. So Vanity Fair huh? Do you do fashion?"

God save me from idiots.

"No, I investigate things. You know, things like the fact that your senator only voted sixty-seven percent of the time last year. All-in-all I don't think you're doing all that great of a job scheduling his time...Langley."

She would've liked to call him out on being married,

but he hadn't had time to make a pass yet, instead, he'd only asked her about her work.

She watched as his face flushed. It wasn't a good look for him. "How did you know that?" he sputtered. "Are you doing an article on my senator?"

"Maybe," she said slowly.

"We haven't authorized that."

Lark wanted to laugh at his affronted expression, but she didn't. "You *have* heard of the First Amendment, right? *Congress shall make no law respecting or prohibiting the free exercise of the press*? Sound familiar?"

He sputtered again.

"But no, I can't say that writing about politics interests me, so you're safe. However, there is a lot of gossip about Wentworth's abysmal record. If I were his chief of staff, that might concern me."

"Are you giving civics lessons again, Lark?" A deep voice rumbled behind her, close enough to cause her hair to shift.

"I didn't know she was with you, my apologies," Redford said, holding up his hands in surrender.

Once again, the gold wedding band stood out.

"Lark, you must not have seen me when you came in. Let's go to our table." Lark didn't turn around, but Kostya must have done something because the bartender handed her back her credit card.

"I've transferred everything to your tab, Lieutenant," the bartender said.

Kostya's fingers drifted along her neck, then down her shoulder until he tangled his fingers with hers and tugged. "Grab your clutch, I've got your drink," he whispered into her ear.

Lark remembered another place, another time when

they'd held hands like this. It had been months ago. How did this man keep getting under her skin? Why did he keep creeping into her thoughts?

Get it together!

She forced herself to concentrate on the present.

"It was nice meeting you," Lark said to the bartender because it was. As for Langley, she didn't say a word as she slid out of the seat and turned to look up at Kostya.

He was so big. She'd forgotten.

How did I forget?

As if he could read her mind Kostya gave her a warm and encouraging smile, tugged her hand again, then picked up her drink and guided her to his table. He kept his stride small so that she could easily keep up in her heels. When they arrived at the table, he motioned her toward the booth so she could sit next to him.

"Maybe I want the chair," she said with an arch look, determined to keep things in the moment.

"Do you?"

"No," she admitted.

"Admit it, you're like me, you don't like your back to the room," he said as she slid into the booth. "The only reason the seat at the bar didn't make your flesh crawl was that you could observe everyone in the mirror."

He slid in beside her and put her drink down next to his.

"You're right." The liquids in the glass matched. "What are you drinking?" she asked.

"Jameson. Same as you, right?"

She nodded as she took a small sip of her drink.

"So, have you always liked to observe everyone around you, or was it after our time in Afghanistan?"

"You mean when you, me, Cullen, and Nic got to

spend twenty-four hours suffocating in a dark cage together?" she asked sweetly as she took another sip of her drink.

Kostya laughed. "Yeah, that would be what I'm talking about."

Lark set her drink down and continued to rest her arm on the table as she looked up at Kostya. "I've been an investigative journalist for eight years, so being aware of my environment is almost like breathing." Her lips twitched. "Sound familiar?"

Kostya nodded. "It's definitely a skill that's been drilled in for me and mine. But what about since Afghanistan? That drive over the border in the back of the truck was pretty hairy. Any nightmares?"

Lark bit her lip. She hated owning up to any kind of weakness, especially to a big man like Kostya Barona. Life had taught her that strong men like him could take advantage.

"Lark?" he prompted gently.

What the hell, he and all the others had been so kind and caring, not just to me, but to Samira and her two little girls. Maybe I have it all wrong.

"Yeah, I'd be lying if I said that the Afghan trip didn't mess with me a little. I have to leave the bathroom light on now, isn't that sad?"

Kostya put his hand on top of hers, brushing his thumb over her knuckles. "No, it's not sad at all. I'd say it's pretty normal. Anything else?"

She gave a sheepish grin. "I've kept up with Nic and Cullen. Did you know Cullen is a dad now? He and Carys had a baby girl."

"I knew she was pregnant, but I didn't know they had a little girl. Gideon hasn't been keeping me up to speed."

Lark chuckled. "Bad Gideon." She pulled her hand out from underneath his and took another small sip of her whiskey. "Has he been keeping you up-to-date on the Nuri family?"

"No, smartass," he smiled. "I've been keeping up on Samira, Taja, and little Nazy all on my own. I'm not sure that your mother has bought them enough stuff. Do you really think that Nazy needed a pink mini-Bugatti that actually drives? She's only five."

"Holy shit." Lark slapped her hand over her mouth. "She didn't. Please tell me she didn't, I'm begging you."

"She did. And for Taja, she got her a globe of the world that's bigger than she is." Lark waited, she knew there was more to come. "It lights up," he continued.

"And?"

"I looked it up online. It's the world's most detailed globe. It costs over fourteen thousand dollars."

Lark folded her arms onto the table and dropped her head into them. "Sometimes my mother is a little over the top," she mumbled.

"Hmmm, I hadn't noticed." She heard the muted laughter in his voice.

Lark looked up at him from underneath her lashes. His smile was kind.

"Please tell me you have relatives who embarrass you, so we can compare notes," she begged.

"Nah, my sister is pretty great. Anyway, your mom means well, it's not her fault she has more money than God. She earned it, fair and square. I admire that."

Lark lifted her head to really look at him. Kostya seemed to mean it. That was such a breath of fresh air.

"What about you? Are you checking in on Samira and her daughters?" Kostya asked.

Lark nodded. "I might not have heard about Mom's over-the-top gifts, probably because Samira knew I would get in a twist about them, but yeah, I've been keeping in touch," Lark told him. "A lot of the time we talk about Ebrahem. She doesn't have anybody who remembers him, and I do."

"He was a good man. A damn good man." Kostya said, his teeth gritted. "Did I ever thank you for what you did for his family?"

Lark gave him a surprised look. "You must have."

He shifted so that he was looking directly at her. "No, I don't think I ever did. You sacrificed your safety in Afghanistan and told everyone that you would not be rescued unless we took his wife and daughters. Nobody does that kind of thing."

She gave him a confused smile. "Sure they do."

He tugged on a strand of her hair, ensuring he had her attention. "No. No, they don't. So thank you. Thank you for Ebrahem, and thank you for me. Yeah, it's great that your mom took them under her wing and is spoiling them rotten, but you're the one who kept them alive."

"I'm pretty sure it was you and the others who figured a way to get them over the border to safety," she grimaced. "Anyway, can we stop talking about this? It's getting kind of mushy."

Kostya laughed. "God forbid we get mushy. Okay, okay. Are you here to watch Riya get her award?" Kostya asked.

Lark nodded.

"What's your connection?" he asked.

"I've known Riya since my university days. She was my T.A. in freshman biology. She's three years younger than me, but it didn't matter, she's crazy smart."

"UCLA?"

"Close, it was the University of San Diego. I really thought I wanted to write fiction, and their creative writing department is a bitch to get into. Only fifteen undergrads are selected each year, and I was one of them. For once, my mom's influence had nothing to do with my success and I grabbed it with both hands."

"Do you still want to write fiction?" Kostya asked as his arm went back up over the back of the booth and he sipped from his drink.

"Absolutely not. I like reality too much, it's more interesting. I'm keeping all of my notes and I might take one of my articles and turn it into a book. I've been approached by several publishers. But that would take at least a year out of my investigative reporting time, and usually, something pops up that grabs my attention and I just don't have the time."

Lark was crazy aware of Kostya's strong arm resting behind her. It was as if his heat were surrounding her. It was the second time in her life where she didn't have to force herself to remain calm and relaxed in the presence of a big man in her personal space. Inside, she would normally panic, but she was always able to put on a good front. But back when she was with Kostya and the other Navy SEALs in Afghanistan, she might have been irritated as hell, but she hadn't been overwhelmed or panicked by those big, strong men when they were forced into such a small space together.

"What about you? Any urge to ever write your memoirs; after all, more and more SEALs are doing it."

Kostya snorted. "Even if I could string two words together, can't say that would ever be my thing."

"Uhm, excuse me, but you're a lieutenant in the Navy; isn't paperwork kind of like your life?"

Kostya picked up his drink and took a longer sip this time. "You've got that right. I had to sell a piece of my soul to the devil just to take tonight off from report writing to be here. But don't think that gets you off the hook. Tell me more about your relationship with Riya. Do you know Gray?"

"I went out to dinner and drinks with them and a few friends once in San Diego, so I met Gray. He seems like an upstanding guy, didn't say much. But..."

"But what?"

Lark carefully eyed Kostya. "Riya is a bit awkward in social situations, outside of the academic arena. There, she shines."

"Tell me about it," he encouraged.

"Well, the bigger the crowd, the more uncomfortable she gets. I was surprised to see that there were at least fifteen people at the table when I got there. The Riya I went to school with—hell the Riya from four years ago—wouldn't have put herself in a situation like that, but there she was. I could tell it was due to Gray."

"How?"

Lark's brow furled as she thought back. "Their seats were closer together than anybody else's. His arm rested on the back of her chair, and whenever the talk got too loud, or she paused too long to answer someone, he stroked her shoulder. Now I'm not sure, but there were times when I think that Riya had her hand on his thigh, not in a sexual way, but for comfort."

"What else?"

"There was one teammate who teased more than the others. His name was Dex. He said something about her I.Q. that clearly made her uncomfortable. Gray just murmured his name, and Dex immediately realized his mistake and apologized. Gray didn't make either Riya or Dex feel uncomfortable about it, he just smiled. He was really smooth. When I went back to my hotel that night, I remember thinking that Riya was in good hands."

Kostya shifted a little so that his gaze was focused solely on her, ignoring the rest of the room. "That's quite a lot of observation, Ms. Sorensen."

Lark shrugged. "What can I say? When a topic interests me, I pay attention."

"Have you noticed anything about me?" Kostya asked.

Lark tried to suppress a shiver, but she couldn't.

"I'm only asking because I've noticed quite a bit about you."

Damn, no matter how I answer, I'm screwed.

4

———

What am I doing? Lark is not anything like the women I want in my bed. Well, not normally...

He watched as she licked her bottom lip and thought about how to answer his provocative question. God, did she even realize what she was doing? Kostya didn't think so; he'd seen her in multiple situations, and she'd never come across as provocative. Alluring, sure, but not in a way that said she was trying to attract him or anyone of his teammates. Nope, she was always the consummate professional.

Except for Afghanistan, then she'd been a royal pain in my ass.

Kostya grinned.

"Are you going to answer my question?" Kostya asked.

"I haven't noticed as much about you as I did about Gray if that's what you're asking. At least not your mannerisms and such. Instead, I've focused more on your ability to take command and your intelligence."

She bent her head. Her shoulder-length blonde hair

shielded part of her face as she said the last part of the sentence.

Interesting.

"I've noticed things about you," Kostya murmured.

"Sure you have," Lark said with a grimace as she turned back toward him. "You noticed how much I bitched when we were in that god-awful cage in Afghanistan."

"Well sure," Kostya grinned. "That was hard to miss. But I also noticed the woman who refused to be saved unless we also brought Samira and her daughters to safety. I remember a woman whose commitment to what she thinks is right is more important than her own life. That's what I remember."

Lark smirked. "Come on, Kostya, you're basically describing yourself and every other Navy SEAL. I'm not special." Once again she shielded her expression with her hair as she reached for her empty glass.

Kostya tucked her hair behind her ear, and Lark's head shot up in surprise.

"Lark, this is our job, we trained for this. But you doing it? That's something else entirely."

Her light blue eyes gleamed silver in the muted lights of the bar.

"Okay," she finally said. Then she pulled her phone out of her clutch and glanced down at it. "The reception is due to start in an hour and fifteen minutes. What do you think, should we go to the ballroom?"

"Are you bored with my company already?"

Her eyes widened just a bit. "No, of course not. I just don't want to have too many drinks before dinner since they're sure to serve wine."

"You know, we could sit here and not drink," Kostya pointed out. "There is something called conversation."

"Kostya, what are we doing here? I mean really? Yeah, I call you occasionally when some situation comes up that I think you could help with, but I do the same thing with Mason Gault and Kane McNamara."

"We're *talking*, Lark. If it takes us someplace else, well, who's to say."

Her eyes went wide, then changed to give him a considering look.

"Like where? Bed?"

"Is that where you want it to lead?" he asked quietly.

He watched as her eyes shifted and she took in his shoulders, his chest, then downward to his waist and further down to his crotch, then back up to his eyes. For just a second he could have sworn he saw trepidation. She bit her bottom lip, then cleared her throat and sat up straighter, and gave him a firm smile.

"Look, Kostya, you're a nice guy, but I really don't see a tangle of sheets in our future."

Well damn.

That was the first time a woman had so blatantly perused his body and he'd come up wanting. He didn't quite know how he felt about that. Kostya took more than a few seconds to think up a response.

"So, friends?" he asked slowly as he held out his hand.

She looked at his hand for just a moment, then smiled. He noticed this time her eyes were back to light blue. She shook his hand.

"Friends."

"I'M BORED," Gideon said for the fourth time as they finished up another lap around the obstacle course.

Kostya looked over at his second-in-command from where he was he was leaning over. The bastard was sweating, sure, but was he breathing like a three-pack-a-day smoker? No! Not like Kostya was. Shit, at forty-one, he was feeling every damn one of those years after having gone a third time around the obstacle course. He should have stopped after the second time—and he would have if Gideon hadn't dared him.

Asshole.

"How come Night Storm got a mission and we didn't?" Gideon whined.

Kostya pushed up into a standing position and laughed. He couldn't help it; Gideon had sounded exactly like a petulant four-year-old.

"You've been babysitting your brother's kids again, haven't you?"

"Yep. I think I've got Kyle's voice running on a loop in my head, like some kind of earworm. It's killing me."

Kostya laughed again. "So why do it?"

"Michael's ex is giving him a hard time. When it's his time with the kids and he has to go to work, he has to leave them with a babysitter, then his ex has a shit-fit. But if he leaves the boys with family, she can't kick up as much of a fuss with the judge."

"That is reason one hundred and ninety-seven I'm thankful Debra and I never had kids," was Kostya's heartfelt response as they started to walk away from the obstacle course.

"Plus the fact that she had no spine and you would have been stuck raising them by yourself, as well as continuing to raise her," Gideon uttered sarcastically.

"What are you talking about?" Kostya's tone was mild. The divorce was nine years in the past, so hearing something negative about Debra no longer stung.

"Just that she's the normal type of woman you like. Like Landon, you definitely have a type."

Kostya gave his friend a look out of the corner of his eye. "I know for a fact I don't like strippers. So what are you talking about? I've dated women who have been everything from waitresses to vice presidents of banks—I'd say I don't have a type, my man."

Gideon snorted. "I'd say you're wrong. Every single woman wanted you to rescue them from some sort of situation."

"I call bullshit. Think about Mary, she didn't have anything going on in her life that she needed rescuing from."

"*Sure* she didn't." Gideon's voice was mildly sarcastic. "Think about it Kostya, she'd been sexually assaulted years ago, and you were the first man she reached out to help her overcome that trauma. See? Rescue."

"How do you explain her dumping me?"

"*After* you fixed her."

"And Susan?" Kostya asked curiously.

"The hedge fund manager?" Gideon clarified.

Kostya nodded.

"She was a ballbuster at work, but as soon as she got home, she wanted you to make every goddamn decision for her. Hell, was there a time she ever decided what to have for dinner?"

Kostya thought about it and realized there hadn't been.

"See, that's the type of woman you like. You want to be

the hero, over and over again. You want to go back in time and rescue your mom."

Kostya stopped in his tracks. Gideon had gone two steps forward before realizing that Kostya wasn't with him. He looked backward.

"Aw, hell. I didn't mean it," Gideon said as he rubbed the top of his closely shaved head.

Red swirled in front of Kostya's eyes as he tried to focus in on Gideon, but it was difficult because he was watching his mother's stomach bursting open, her blood spraying across the walls and ceiling and finally landing across his father's stunned face.

"Kostya?"

Kostya shook his head, trying to clear the blood from his vision.

"Kostya, are you with me?"

"I'm..." Kostya cleared his throat. "I'm with you."

"You sure didn't seem like you were with me." Gideon's voice was dubious.

"I just didn't expect to be put on a psychiatrist's couch by my best friend, so I got a little shook, what can I say?" Kostya forced a chuckle. Gideon still gave him the stink eye. "Come on Gideon, we need to get a report from Captain Lockhart and see how our guys are doing."

Gideon gave him a knowing grin.

"Damn. I take it from the way you're smiling that you've already hacked into their systems?" Kostya lifted his brow.

"Hacked is such an ugly word," Gideon said as he opened the door to the locker room. "I might have peeked into a few places to see if there were any problems so I could address them with members of our team. That's what you pay me for, isn't it?" Gideon asked innocently.

Kostya couldn't disagree with that. He went to his locker and grabbed clean clothes and a towel before heading to a bench to untie his boots. God, he needed a shower.

"So, what is the Captain going to tell us?" Kostya asked.

"Should be nothing but thumbs up. As a matter of fact, she plans to stay out a little longer and have Jase do some training with her men."

"Not surprised," Kostya said as he headed for the shower. "So I shouldn't expect to see my guys back this week?"

Gideon shrugged as he turned on the water.

Kostya went through the roster of men who were still with him in case they were pulled in for a mission. He'd selected the men carefully for the training exercise so he wouldn't be left hanging. The only change was having to send Jase Drakos in Landon Kelly's place.

If Landon failed to show again, he'd have him doing paperwork for the next six months!

KOSTYA'S SISTER called that night and invited him over for dinner. Normally he'd be all-in, but his conversation with Gideon had gotten under his skin and he couldn't settle.

"Sorry, *Irinushka*, I have too much paperwork I've got to get done," he lied.

"Okay, but I expect to see you next week. Tony will be back then and he's going to try to grill and you have to be here to make sure he doesn't turn the steaks to charcoal."

Kostya laughed. "I promise, I promise."

On that note, he hung up and then walked over to the

back of his house and looked out the large window to gaze at the back bay. The water normally soothed him, but not this afternoon. All he could think about was a feisty, sexy blonde.

"Dammit," he muttered, then strode back to the kitchen and scooped up his cell phone. He punched in Lark's number.

"Kostya?" she answered on the second ring. "Is something wrong?"

"Are you still in D.C.?" he asked.

"No, I'm in Baltimore."

Kostya headed to the formal dining room that he'd made into his home office and opened up his laptop. "Why are you in Baltimore?" he asked.

"Sick friend," Lark answered succinctly. "Kostya, why are you calling?"

He could see her reporter antennae sticking up even over the phone. He called up his favorite airline and checked out flights to Baltimore. In seconds he saw he could be on a plane in less than an hour, but he winced. In good conscience, he couldn't do it. He just couldn't, not when he and his team were on stand-by. He switched the flights around. He could be picking her up at the Norfolk airport by eight o'clock tonight.

"How is your friend doing?" Kostya asked.

"She's actually doing pretty good. I'm thinking I can fly home to Manhattan tomorrow."

"That's good, that's really good."

"Why?"

He made another couple of keystrokes. "Can I take you to a late dinner tonight?"

There was a long pause.

"Are you asking as a friend?"

Kostya rubbed the back of his neck as he pictured Lark in the slinky dress she'd been wearing at the Kimpton bar. "No. I'm not asking as a friend," he admitted.

It was an eternity before she answered. "I thought we agreed this wasn't a good idea. I specifically told you that you weren't my type." Lark's voice was breathy.

Breathy was good.

"Lark, I have no idea what in the hell is going on either. I'm on standby, and I can't get my ass to Baltimore, otherwise I would be there in a heartbeat to entertain a hypothesis I have."

"And what's that?"

"That friends make a great foundation for something more than just friends."

"Kostya," Lark sighed.

That was definitely not a 'No.'

"Look, Lark, I just want to take you on a date, is that such a big deal? You already said that you intend to fly home tomorrow. You can just as easily catch a flight from Virginia Beach tomorrow."

He glanced down at his computer. "I already figured out that there's a plane leaving from Baltimore in an hour. I can be picking you up in less than three hours."

Kostya winced at Lark's laughter. "You're kidding, right?"

This time he kept quiet.

"You're not kidding," she finally said. Again, her voice was breathy.

"I'll get you a hotel, no pressure, Honey. I just want to take you out to dinner."

"This is insane. You're crazy, you know that, don't you Barona?"

"Yep."

More silence.

"Kostya, I'm not going to sleep with you. Scratch that. I'm not going to have sex with you. You understand that, right?"

"I got that, Lark. I'm not going to ask you to...but."

"But what?"

He loved that suspicious reporter voice. It turned him on.

"I'm going to be working to tempt you into a goodnight kiss before I leave you at your hotel room door. The hotel room that I'm paying for."

Lark snorted. "You're not paying for my damned hotel room. I pay my own way."

Kostya's smile was fast in coming. She'd agreed.

"Lark, normally I'd be coming to you and I'd be paying for everything, but I can't right now, I'm on standby, so I'm paying for your hotel room."

"Look, you big oaf. You can pay for the damned plane ticket, you can pay for dinner, but I'm paying for my own hotel room, you got it?"

"Text me your details so I can make your plane reservations, and I'll send you the confirmation. I'll pick you up from the airport."

She took so long to reply he had to look down at his phone to make sure she hadn't hung up.

"You know this is a bad idea, right?"

"You're wrong; this is the best idea I've had in ages. Now don't forget to text me." Kostya hung up before she could change her mind.

Why had she let Amy convince her this was a good idea? She knew Kostya thought he'd done the convincing, but it was really Amy. She knew Lark's background, she knew about the overgrown step-grandfather Lark had had to live with for the majority of her early childhood. Amy knew all the ugly stories, yet went right on ahead and just shoved her out of the nest.

"You're the one who said you were over it, but based on dweebs one through thirty-nine, you're not. You also don't believe in counseling, so off you go into the deep end. I've got just the dress."

Lark knew she was stuck.

Stuck. Stuck. Stuck.

"You do realize this isn't the deep end, it's the middle of the ocean?"

"He's a SEAL, he can save you." Amy pulled a blue body-con dress out of her closet and shoved it at Lark. "Now, quit with the whining, you're giving me a headache."

"This is too small," Lark whined.

"What did I just say about whining?" Amy demanded to know as she shoved Lark into the bathroom.

That was three hours ago.

Lark hefted her backpack up higher on her shoulder as she pulled her carry-on behind her. She looked down to make sure all of the buttons on her overcoat were buttoned. They were. She looked up and saw Kostya's blond head high above the crowd. He was easy to spot because he was taller and broader than everybody else waiting at the bottom of the escalator.

She felt a shiver run down her spine—his expression was positively hungry. This was *so* not a good idea.

Then why the hell am I here?

Lark squared her shoulders as she stepped off the end of the escalator, making sure that the heel of her thigh-high boot didn't get caught.

Goddamn, Amy!

"Let me take that," Kostya said as he gently pulled her backpack off her shoulder.

He smells good.

"Thanks," she muttered as she kept her eyes on his chin. "You could have just texted and picked me up outside at the curb, you didn't have to park."

Somehow Kostya was carrying her suitcase along with her backpack and still had one hand at the small of her back while the crowd parted for them as they headed to the exit. "It's easy enough to park." At the sound of a smile in his voice, she risked looking into his eyes. She saw the raw heat emanating from his gaze.

She missed a step, but he was there and he caught her around the waist, steadying her.

"Thanks for coming, Lark." His voice, his accent, the power and fire almost had her stumbling again.

What the hell?

She gripped her handbag until her knuckles turned white. Kostya stopped steering them toward the parking garage. Instead, she found herself pressed into a corner, his heat surrounding her.

Kostya gently traced his fingers over her tight knuckles, then tilted her chin up so that their eyes met. "It's just dinner, I promise."

She swallowed.

Okay. Okay. Dinner, I can do dinner.

She sucked in air, forcing herself to breathe. She caught his scent. Hints of the sea, leather, and something indefinably Kostya.

"Talk to me, Lark," Kostya whispered. She heard nothing else, just his voice. She remembered listening to him in the dark in Afghanistan; back then she could forget how big he was, how powerful, how he could snap her like a twig. But this was Kostya. The man who made her feel safe.

He took a step backward, but two of his fingers traced down from the pulse point at her temple, along her cheek, until they rested at the corner of her mouth.

"Please, Honey, say something. Anything."

This time when she looked into his eyes, she didn't see hunger, she saw tenderness and comfort, the same expression that had been on his face when he'd crouched down in front of little Taja and Nazy back in Afghanistan. Another small piece of ice cracked, letting in a glimmer of light. She smiled.

"Of course, dinner." She stood up straight. "Stop looking at me like that. I'm here, aren't I? I'm hungry and you promised food," she said briskly.

His eyes glanced down to her relaxed hands, then back up to her face and a slow smile started. Her toes curled and she grinned back at him as she pushed by him. "Get a move on, big guy, I'm going to bankrupt you at the restaurant. You better not cheap out on me."

Lark heard a crack of laughter behind her right before Kostya put his hand around her waist and continued on to the parking garage.

"Ms. Sorensen, I'll have you know, the taco truck is not cheap."

Aw, hell, he's funny.

DAMN, I like this woman.

Kostya watched her scoop up another bite of her marionberry ice cream and he practically groaned. How long had it been since he'd bedded a woman? He thought back and realized it had been too damned long. Lark's bee-stung lips wrapped around her spoon as she sucked off the ice cream and it took everything he had not to groan. His glance swooped up to her eyes to see if she was pleased that she had his balls in a vice and he got a surprise. Her eyes were closed. Instead of studying him, she was lost in her own personal heaven.

Fuck, she wasn't teasing him, she was just that blissed out.

How the hell am I going to end this night with just a kiss?

Kostya glared at the waiter as he placed the check on the table and ogled Lark. The man made himself scarce, fast. Kostya pulled out his credit card and continued to watch the show.

"You're going to give me a complex," Lark said.

"Huh?"

"You're staring at me."

"Lark, I've been staring at you all night."

She gave him a cheeky grin. "Okay, I admit there's been a little bit of staring going on between *both* of us, but that's only because we couldn't see each other for the thirty-six hours we were hidden in the back of that godawful truck."

Her entire body shuddered, then she smiled again.

Nope, this woman was not a victim, no rescue needed here.

"Not many people could have handled that Afghanistan situation like you did," he said as the waiter took the bill.

"Don't you mean women?"

"English is my second language, which means I use my words precisely. I say exactly what I mean, and I meant people, man or woman. You're impressive, and I'm not the only one who thinks so." A blush crawled up her neck to stain her cheeks.

"I could never do what you and your team do on a regular basis. You are the ones who are impressive." She cleared her throat. "You realize that you're the definition of heroes, right?"

Kostya shook his head. "Lark, you're wrong. We have a job to do and we do it—it's just that simple. I came to this country as a political refugee. America took me and my sister in after we lost our parents."

He paused as he saw the soles of his father's shoes when the monsters dragged him out of the house. There had been a hole near the big toe, his blue sock poking out.

"Kostya?" Lark's voice was soft.

"America is my home. I love my country; I could think of no higher purpose than serving her. I'm not a hero, I'm a soldier."

Lark reached over and put her dainty hand on top of his. "We'll just have to agree to disagree."

Kostya wasn't a stupid man, he wasn't going to let an opportunity slip by. He turned his hand over so that their fingers could tangle. "You ready to leave?"

Her eyes searched his. "A kiss, nothing more."

"I keep my promises."

"I know that, Kostya, that's why I'm here."

He ushered her out of the restaurant and tipped the valet when he brought his Bronco to the front. Kostya tilted his chin to the kid who nodded, then Kostya opened the passenger door and assisted Lark in. He headed back to the Hilton where Lark had made her reservation. He waited for her to start a conversation and when she didn't, he didn't bother to try either.

He pulled up to the front and gave his keys to yet another valet, then grabbed Lark's luggage before quickly joining Lark at the front entrance.

"Aren't you going to check in?" he queried when she bypassed the reception desk.

"I already did online. They arranged for my phone to be my key card."

"Slick," he said as he pressed the button for the elevator. "Gideon would love to know about this technology."

Lark grinned up at him. "I'll bet you a steak and lobster dinner at the Kimpton in D.C. that Gideon knew about this technology *before* it was put into use," Lark teased. She unbuttoned her coat and took it off.

"I'll take that bet."

"You really think that Gideon didn't know about that?" Lark sounded surprised.

"No. Now that you mentioned it, you're absolutely right; of course, he did. I just liked the sound of us having another dinner at a hotel."

Her laughter rushed over him like an Atlantic wave during a summer heatwave, welcoming and refreshing. The elevator door swooshed open. He walked a little bit behind her, admiring how the blue-colored dress molded to her thighs and ass.

She stopped in front of a room and waved her phone in front of the lock. He watched as the green light showed and she opened the door.

"We're going to go into your room so I can set your things down," he told her.

Lark nodded.

He turned on the lights, ensuring everything was in order, before setting her suitcase on the provided rack. "I assume you want your backpack on the desk?" he asked.

She nodded again.

"Am I allowed to see you again tomorrow?" he asked as he positioned himself in front of her.

Lark nodded a third time.

"Are you going to ever talk again?" he teased.

She started to nod again, then cleared her throat. "Yes."

He smiled slowly and reached up to cup her cheek. Her pulse was beating wildly in her neck and he stroked over it with his thumb. Her skin was so soft, that the fall of her hair felt like silk as it drifted over the back of his hand.

"What time should I be over?" he asked quietly.

"Um, don't you have to work?"

"Tomorrow is Saturday."

"Oh yeah." He moved his thumb so it feathered over her bottom lip.

"Lark?"

"Hmmm?"

"What time?"

She licked her bottom lip and he groaned. He'd known Lark Sorenson for three years now, and he knew damn good and well that she wasn't teasing him, which only made it worse.

"Do that again." He traced his thumb over her now wet bottom lip, and his cock pressed against the zipper of his slacks.

She shook her head, and her eyes focused.

Damn. Dazed had been a good look for her.

"Until I sample the kiss, Barona, there's no need to make plans for tomorrow."

"Point taken."

She reached up and pushed the fingers of her right hand into his hair, her short nails scraping against his scalp. After one more stroke of his thumb, he lowered his head and brushed his lips against hers.

Electric. Her nails dug in deeper and it felt good.

He pulled her other hand up so it could rest on his chest, then he gently cupped her jaw, turning her head slightly so the angle was right, and pressed another whisper-soft kiss against her lips.

"Two," she moaned.

"Those weren't kisses. I was just testing the waters, Honey."

She opened her mouth again, probably to say something, but he wasn't having any of it, so he covered her mouth with his. He slid his lips against hers. The texture was warm, wet velvet, and when he ran his tongue along her inner lip he tasted her berry-flavored sigh.

Lark started to pet him, her left hand kneading his dress shirt.

He wanted nothing more than to feel her fingers, her hands, touching his bare skin. For just a moment he was tempted to unbutton his shirt, but he stopped himself. That wasn't part of this, so instead, he wrapped his arm around her waist and pulled her closer, then deepened the kiss.

Lark slid her hand upwards and twined it around his neck. Even in her high-heeled boots, she was a tiny little thing and had to really reach. Kostya bent further, his tongue coaxing her mouth open even more.

Lark let out a little mewl, and he stroked his hand up

her back even though he really wanted to grab the firm globe of her ass.

Just a kiss, Barona.

He traced long, languid strokes up and down her spine as he explored her mouth, glorying in her taste and passion. She scraped her nails down along the back of his skull until she reached the sensitive nape of his neck. He thought he would explode. He pulled away from her.

"Lark," he groaned. "What you do to me."

"Don't stop," she pleaded.

He moved his hands and slowly cupped her cheeks. They were hot, he figured his were too. "You don't really mean that."

She breathed deeply. Once. Twice. Then she nodded. Her smile was shaky.

"You're right, just a kiss."

She sounds as regretful as I feel.

She took a step back and looked around her hotel room.

"So did you figure out what time I should pick you up for breakfast?" he asked.

"I already made plans to go over to Cullen and Carys' house to see their baby girl." He liked that again she sounded regretful. "It will be a quick visit because Carys is taking a little bit of a road trip to see her friend Sarah since Cullen's out of town, so this is my chance to see the little cutie."

"Why don't I go with you?"

Lark's expression brightened. "That'd be great."

"So eight o'clock, we can have breakfast, then head on over. How does that sound?"

"Good."

5

THE CALL CAME JUST AS KOSTYA WAS PULLING UP TO THE Hilton the next morning.

"Kostya, where are you?" Simon Clark said by way of greeting. That was not good.

"Atlantic Avenue," Kostya said, not wanting to tell him the Hilton. It would bring up too many questions.

"Get to base as fast as you can. You've got half your team in that fucking training thing with the Marines, right?"

Kostya drove past the valet and whipped his Bronco back out the driveway to Atlantic Avenue.

"Not half, only six. Gideon's with me."

"Thank fuck." Kostya heard the relief in Simon's voice. "We've got a problem. Get everyone to the ready room, STAT."

Before he could even say yes, Kostya was met with a dial tone.

He took one more longing look at the Hilton in his rearview mirror and stepped on the gas. He figured nine miles over the speed limit shouldn't get him pulled over.

He depressed the call button on his phone and called out Lark's name.

"If you're running late, that's good. I am too," Lark said as she answered the phone.

"I wish it were that simple, Honey. I'm not going to be able to visit with you and Carys. As a matter of fact, it's wheels up for me and the team and I don't know when I'll be back in town."

"That's an immediate thing, right?"

"Yes, it is."

"Well, I'm not going to ask any questions, even though that goes against the journalist code." Her laugh was half-hearted.

"I appreciate that."

"Can I tell you to stay safe?"

"I would appreciate that too."

"Stay safe, Kostya, I mean it. I've decided I want another kiss."

He stopped at the red light and smiled.

"You do realize I didn't promise to stop at just a kiss next time."

He saw the crosswalk light counting down; he needed to text his team.

"I get the feeling you know how to play things by the seat of your pants. We'll figure it out as we go along."

"Yeah, I guess we will," he agreed.

"I mean it, Kostya, you and all of your team—you get back here with every single hair in place, you got it?"

She was a fierce little thing.

"I hear you. I've got to go, Honey."

"Okay, goodbye."

She hung-up.

He scrolled through his phone and went to the group

text for his team and typed in three short words before the light changed.

READY ROOM, STAT.

HE HAD DRILLED into every one of his men to have their go bags with them at all times. It was the reason why they all insisted on always being the ones to drive.

His phone rang. It was Gideon's ringtone.

Fuck! This is not going to be good news.

"Talk to me," Kostya answered.

"Got Mike's kids. Gotta do a pass-off. It's gonna take me an extra thirty to get them over to the precinct," Gideon said calmly.

"Okay. As soon as the kids aren't with you and you're safe, call me, I'll conference you into the ready room so you can listen in." Kostya knew that his paranoid computer geek friend had a satellite phone, so security wouldn't be an issue.

"You got it."

Kostya hoped to hell that was the only call he was going to receive. He had six of his men that were mission-ready—they were the best of the best, and if Commander Clark was saying now, he meant *now*.

He made it to base without attracting the attention of any member of the sheriff's department, which was a blessing. When he hot-footed it to their building he saw Ryker's Harley parked in close. There was not a man or woman on Earth who would touch that thing while they were gone if they valued their life, but Kostya was going to see if there was a place to stow it inside. The last thing he wanted was that beauty to be murdered if a hurricane hit while they were off God knew where.

When he got to the ready room, Commander Clark, Ryker McQueen, Lincoln Hart, Sebastian Durand, and Landon Kelly were present. Landon gave Kostya a grin as he went over to the podium where his boss was shuffling through some papers. The man was radiating energy, which again, concerned Kostya because Simon Clark was known for being cool as a cucumber. It wasn't that he was nervous or upset, just that Kostya could tell that something was up.

"Do you have six or seven men?" Simon asked.

"Seven," Kostya immediately answered. "Gideon's the only one who won't be here immediately. He has to drop off his brother's children."

Simon nodded, looking down at a report, before thrusting it at Kostya. "We can go over some of the basics before Gideon arrives. You're going to be dealing with damn near arctic conditions."

Kostya winced. They'd trained up near Prudhoe Bay, Alaska twenty-five months ago, in January. Five days of diving, then they'd spent two weeks in the Denali Park and Preserve. Mateo and Lincoln hadn't been with the team then and Jase was one of their best trackers in the snow and he was on the training mission. He knew Mateo Aranda was good, because his team—

"What?" Simon interrupted him mid-thought. The man didn't miss a trick.

"Aranda came from Blue Cascade. I talked to Kelsey Hick's team when he transferred Mateo my way, and they'd just done a mission in the Andes, so he's good to go. From what I read in Lincoln Hart's file, he's supposedly checked out in arctic conditions, but I've got to ask him what he's done. I know he grew up in Minnesota, but that doesn't automatically make him prepared."

"One of the reasons you're going, even though you're not up on rotation, is the training you did up in Alaska two years ago," Commander Clark explained.

Kostya smiled at Mateo, who nodded to him as he came into the room and sat down. That just left Nolan and Gideon. As soon as he thought that, Nolan O'Rourke came in wearing a frown. Which was unusual; normally you could never read Nolan's expression.

"How do you want to work this?" Simon asked.

"Gideon has a sat phone. As soon as he's clear he's going to call in, are you good with that?" Kostya asked his boss.

Commander Clark nodded. "Let's get started. It'll take me a minute to access the briefing on the network. I was kind of depending on Gideon to take care of things."

"Don't we all?" Kostya sighed.

Despite his words, Simon Clark quickly set up his laptop and pulled up the presentation he needed. "Hit the lights."

Ryker McQueen was already at the wall and had them off before the commander finished his request. Five headshots appeared on the screen. Two women and three men.

"We've got five American biologists who have been missing for eight days. They were due to check-in at the Koivusuo Strict Nature Reserve in Finland six days ago."

"Then why are they saying they've been missing for eight days?" Nolan asked with his hand up in the air.

"They called in using one of their satellite phones eight days ago, so the European head of the Intercontinental Wolf Center thought everything was fine, even when they were so late showing up at the rendezvous point. He figured that the bad snowstorm was the problem."

"He didn't call them?" Kostya asked, managing to keep the outrage out of his voice.

"Not until yesterday," Simon sighed. "That was when he found out that not one of the team was picking up their satellite phones. What's worse, he finally had the bright idea to go back and check out the GPS tracking on the call he had received eight days ago. It turns out that the team was two kilometers over the border into Russia. They were in the Republic of Karelia."

"Wait a minute," Sebastian Durand interrupted. "How is that possible? I thought the border between Finland and Russia was littered with landmines?"

"Not on the Finnish side. They entered the Ottawa Agreement in 2012," Nolan explained. "But yeah, they sure would have them on the Russian side," he sighed. Then he turned to look at Simon. "But begging your pardon, Commander, how in the fuck did these yahoos manage to stumble their way into Russia?"

"All I can tell you is that without civilians doing dumbass things, we would probably be out of jobs," Simon sighed. "I'm willing to give them a little bit of leeway since the weather was so damned bad, but still...."

"So our job is to go into Russia, hunt them down, and bring them home, is that it?" Kostya asked.

"I wish it were that simple." Simon rubbed the back of his neck. "It gets worse."

"What were the wolf biologists doing over there in the first place?" Lincoln Hart asked.

"Currently, Finland is going ahead with culling the number of wolves and these biologists chose to go over and study that particular subspecies of gray wolf. Apparently, they want to talk the Finns out of their plan."

"During winter?" Lincoln asked. "Are they nuts?"

"Lately the weather has been turning on a dime," Nolan defended. "They probably didn't know it was going to get so bad."

"True," Lincoln admitted.

"Each member of the team has at minimum ten years of field experience," Clark went on to explain. "They're not neophytes, which is another reason that the guy wasn't all that worried when they didn't check in on time. The team leader of the expedition is Doctor Gwendolyn Lord. She's been doing this for twenty years. Last year she and her daughter did the Iditarod together."

"Well hell, then there isn't really an excuse for the team to have gotten lost like they did, no matter how bad the weather was. What the hell?" Ryker shook his head in amazement. Kostya had to agree with his assessment.

"The Republic of Karelia is huge, Commander. Can you narrow down exactly where the last sat call came in from?" Kostya asked.

Clark switched to the next slide.

"First, here is a weather map, showing the whole area. We have Finland and Western Russia. You can see the Republic of Karelia there. Before I zoom in, you need to see the storm bearing down on the Southern and Central parts of Finland on into the Western part of Russia, then on down to St. Petersburg. According to every weather agency, this blizzard is gearing up to be a once-in-a-century event. This is going to be a hell of a lot worse than the one that the biologists were caught up in. Some of the techs in the Pentagon think that even the satellite phones won't work, and the GPS will be really iffy. This might be a little tougher than normal. Are you up for it?"

"Hell yeah," Kostya's team all yelled out.

I love these guys.

"Okay, now to answer your next question." He switched to the next slide that showed the Koivusuo Strict Nature Reserve, and a dot over on the Russia side of the map. "This is where the call came in from. They were thirty kilometers away from the Reserve, about two kilometers over the Finnish/Russian border."

Kostya shook his head.

"What's that other place you have circled?" Lincoln asked.

Clark pointed to what looked like a small lake well over the border. "This is Lake Julia, or Kostya, feel like doing the honors?"

Kostya pronounced, *"Ozero Yulya-Viyeks"Yarvi"* with a Russian accent, "but Lake Julia will suffice," he said with a hard smile.

"When Captain Hale and I were briefed over at the Pentagon this morning, we were let in on a little secret, and it dovetails nicely with a very plausible scenario of what could have happened to our biologists."

Kostya felt his lips twist into a warped smile.

Here comes the kicker.

"Now, what has everybody's panties in a twist is that all of them had satellite phones. All of them have at least seven years of fieldwork, and the idea that all five of them aren't answering doesn't seem possible."

"Unless they're all dead," Kostya said.

"Now, there's our optimistic Russian lieutenant," Ryker grinned.

"Can it," Clark quickly spit out. He wasn't used to the

way that the men of Omega Sky teased one another. Kostya gave Ryker the side-eye and Ryker shrugged, but he shut up.

"Now, before I was so rudely interrupted, I had more to say," Kostya said drily to deflect Clark's attention off of his man. "I find it hard to believe that not one of them would have called in if they were in a dire situation, not if they were such seasoned field workers. Isn't that how you see it?" he turned to Clark.

Clark nodded. "What's more, the Pentagon had eyes on activity going on in the Russian side of Karelia near Lake Julia. That's about one hundred and forty kilometers over the border. There was activity being monitored last fall, before the snow."

"What were they seeing?" Kostya asked.

"A lot of supplies were being sent in, things like cement trucks, supply trucks, and personnel. It looked like they were gearing up to build something. The area they chose was in the Karelia Forest, so there is no way that a finished installation would have been captured by a satellite with all of that old forest growth."

"But no matter how much of a snowstorm they were in, they couldn't have gone another eighty kilometers in the wrong direction and stumbled on this installation," Sebastian spoke up.

"No," Kostya said slowly. "You're right, Seb. But there would have been surveillance cameras along the Russian side of the border. If the cameras didn't see them, there probably would have been guard towers that very well could have picked up the satellite phone signal."

Commander Clark nodded. "That's the theory."

"Well, the good news is, we have a place to start. We get to play in the forest, in the snow," Ryker grinned.

Oh, joy.

"The US Division of the Intercontinental Wolf Center is bringing us in six days too late. But, I have to tell you, men, I have a bad feeling about this one. Not bad like they're all dead, but bad like this is going to be a goatfuck."

Kostya's head jerked from the satellite image on the screen to look over at his boss. In all the time he'd worked for Simon Clark, he didn't think he'd ever heard his boss say something like that.

Simon gave him a wry smile and shrugged.

"When Gideon gets here, all of you kit up. There's a plane that will get you immediately out to Ramstein Air Base in Germany. The closest Finnish airport to the Nature Reserve is Joensuu. It's not closed at the moment, so come hell or high water, that's where you'll be flying into. None of that bullshit that you end up flying into Helsinki. I'll make sure the Prime Minister is called."

Simon flashed another map on the screen, showing where Joensuu was. Kostya looked across the ready room and took a moment to look at each of his team members. Every one of them knew the truth—if this was the blizzard of the century, there wasn't a chance in hell they'd be flying into any damn Finnish airport but the big one...if that. But nobody was going to burst Clark's little bubble of sunshine.

Kostya watched as his men nodded, then his phone rang. It was Gideon.

"You missed it," he answered. "How far out are you?"

"Fifteen minutes, I'm coming from downtown."

"I'll get everything you need, then we'll meet at the airfield. I'll fill you in there."

"Got it."

Kostya watched his commander pull together his files and close up his laptop. Something was up. Simon Clark was a realist; he'd been Kostya and Max's lieutenant for a million years back when they were both young and before Simon's hair was the color of steel. Kostya had never known the man to spew bullshit like he just had, saying that the Joensuu airport would be open. He needed to talk to Max and see if he'd noticed anything.

6

Kostya looked out the window of the truck as they passed yet another mind-numbing kilometer. All he could see was a canvass of white. He hated snow with a passion. Thirty-five years later he could still remember what it felt like when that bastard Fedor had forced him and his brother and sister to go on even when it was obvious that Roman was burning up with fever.

Kostya shoved that memory aside and concentrated on the here and now because it was his job to deal with it, so he did. It was something he learned how to do when he was seven years old and he'd had no other choice but to focus on putting one foot in front of the other and carry Irina so they had a chance at living. Even when it seemed like his world had come to an end.

Stop being morbid! It's just snow!

His lip curled up as he took joy in the fact that he wasn't driving, Lincoln was. The weather was absolute shit, but Linc was doing an amazing job. There was only one fly in the ointment.

Landon Kelly.

"If I shove him out the door, we can make it look like an accident," Nolan murmured to Kostya. He was the SEAL closest in age to Kostya, and on certain things, he could often read Kostya's mind. Like, for instance, the fact that Landon hadn't shut up for the last two and a half hours and was sorely in need of a muzzle.

"Linc asked the kid to talk, remember? He said listening to somebody helped him drive since he can't get a radio signal, which makes no sense considering the fact that the SISU truck is the pride of the Finnish military."

"You gotta admit, the seats aren't that bad," Gideon said from his left. Kostya grimaced like he gave a shit at this point.

"I can pull up songs on my phone, for God's sake," Nolan practically groaned under his breath. "I'd even listen to whatever god-awful music Landon has on *his* phone if I didn't have to hear his inane chatter anymore. Does anybody in their right mind actually watch the Headless Singer?"

"It's the Masked Singer," Kostya corrected quietly. "Unfortunately my niece does, so I hear about that shit from her too. It makes my ears bleed."

"But Landon knows who has been screeching in it each season. How? How? Next, he's going to tell Linc he plays with Barbies."

Ryker snickered from across the aisle.

"Who wants to bet that he starts spouting his Call of Duty scores?" Mateo asked, careful to keep his voice down.

"Nah, that's a total given," Sebastian sighed. His Cajun accent was strong which meant that he was at his wit's end too.

"Agreed," Kostya nodded. He squinted at Mateo as he

assessed him. The man might not have been with his team as long as the others, but he had Landon's number, that was for damn sure. "Man who guesses closest to his C.o.D. scores wins the pot. What do you say, fifty each?" Kostya proposed quietly.

Gideon outright chuckled. "Oh, I'm in." He rubbed his thick winter gloves together in glee.

Kostya's head jerked around to look at his second-in-command. "Keep your voice down. Also, I don't like the sound of that at all, Smith. Have you been checking his stats? You creep around online far too much. You need to get laid more often."

All the men in the back laughed.

"Whatchya laughing about back there?" Landon called from the front.

"I call foul. Sebastian's laughing too fucking hard. Apparently married life with Giana is agreeing with him," Ryker said as he nudged the man with his shoulder.

"I can't help it if my life is perfect," Sebastian smiled.

Kostya liked hearing that. After all the shit Sebastian had gone through with his grandfather and uncle he deserved some happiness.

"Ryker tried to tell a joke, then couldn't remember how it ended. So pathetic," Nolan called out to Landon.

"Oh," Landon responded. Then he started talking to Linc again.

"I have not checked out Landon's or anyone else's Call of Duty statistics for that matter," Gideon whispered. "That's a little too juvenile for me. But I do like the idea of making educated guesses on statistics—that's right up my alley, so count me in."

"Ah, he just thinks he's some kind of logical Mr. Spock, therefore he's going to blow it," Ryker grinned. "I vote for upping it to a hundred. This is going to be one long drive."

Every man nodded, then Gideon shoved his elbow into Kostya's ribs.

"You okay?" he whispered really low, making sure that Nolan, who was on Kostya's other side, couldn't hear him.

Kostya appreciated, yet didn't appreciate Gideon's question. It sucked having friends who knew so much of your history.

"Fine," Kostya muttered.

Gideon gave him the side-eye. Kostya shook his head a minuscule amount, and Gideon got the message.

Or he damn well better have!

"I say Gideon has to put in two hundred since he can come up with educated guesses on stats," Ryker chuckled as he put quote marks around the words educated guesses. At least Kostya assumed that's what he was trying to do with his heavy gloves.

"McQueen, that's a damn fine idea." Sebastian smiled broadly as he turned to Gideon. Gideon didn't even frown. The man was just too damned sure of himself.

Kostya looked over at Nolan. "You keeping tabs?"

"Yep. The pot's at seven hundred." Nolan bit the glove off his right hand and pulled out a notepad.

Kostya liked it. After two hundred kilometers of Landon's incessant chatter, they needed something to keep them from scooping out their eardrums with spoons.

"How lame, you have to actually write this shit down? You can't remember?" Gideon scoffed.

Nolan pulled out a notepad and pencil from his backpack. "Give me your guesses, gentlemen. And for being a sarcastic asshole, you go first, Gideon."

Mateo snickered; that was the worst position to be guessing.

"We're not falling for that, O'Rourke. You'd end up being last, because you're holding the paper. We're on to you," Gideon mocked quietly. "Tear up the paper into pieces, pass the pencil, we'll all write our guesses with our names, and you'll hold them."

"You know, at this rate, you might have to put three hundred dollars into the pot for being an annoying prick," Kostya said evenly. The laughter started up again.

"What's so funny back there?" Landon asked again from the front seat.

They all laughed harder.

"Just reliving your story about the Masked Singer," Nolan prevaricated.

Landon turned farther in his seat so he could see everyone. "I know, right? Wait until I start telling Linc about that one episode of the Bachelor. I bet some of you remember it, it was epic!"

"You should save some for when Ryker's driving," Nolan responded.

"Good idea," Landon said as he turned around to look out the windshield.

"I will get you back," Ryker growled at Nolan through gritted teeth.

"It's going to be hard to top that," Kostya noted.

Nolan collected everyone's guesses.

"Okay, we're still not even close to where we need to cross into Russia, so let's see if we can get some shut-eye," Kostya suggested. "We're still fourteen hours out before we're going to get to the Joensuu airport, and that's only if we can actually stay on the road and continue on at a reasonable rate of speed."

"I say we bet on that," Ryker piped up.

"Shut the hell up, McQueen. We never bet on parts of the mission, don't be an asshole."

KOSTYA DECIDED to get some sleep when Ryker took over driving, which was possible since the man didn't need his co-pilot to talk to him. Instead, he and Sebastian sat up front in companionable silence.

Kostya glanced around the back of the SUSI. Almost all of his men were in some stage of relaxation, but most importantly Landon was asleep, so all in all, he should be able to finally get some shut-eye. With that pleasant thought, he let his mind drift and found himself with Lark Sorenson in his arms. This was odd; in the many years of his career, he could count on one hand the times when a woman occupied his thoughts like this.

He shook his head to clear his mind. He needed sleep and thinking about Lark was not the way to get any.

Kostya employed a technique that he'd learned very early in his career, even before BUD/S to get to sleep fast, a technique he'd taught Lexi and Roman when he'd babysat them as hyperactive children.

He relaxed his entire face, forehead, jaw, and tongue. He dropped his shoulders, letting them relax, then began slowly inhaling and exhaling to relax his chest. He continued to relax his body, ever downward—pelvis, thighs, knees, calves—all the way to his toes. He pictured lake Coeur d'Alene in Idaho at sunrise the week he'd camped alone after his divorce. It took three renditions before he could sleep because a beautiful blonde reporter with silver-blue eyes kept roaming around in his thoughts. Finally, she departed and he slept.

He even managed to stay mostly relaxed when Mateo and Nolan took their turn, even though it was boring as hell. After six hours of their driving, Kostya drifted off to sleep again.

When the all-terrain vehicle slowed, Kostya opened his eyes, immediately knowing it was his turn to drive. He glanced around the back and noted that Landon's eyes were open. Gideon was supposed to be with Kostya during his turn up front, but he was still asleep, so Kostya decided to forego a navigator for the first bit of his drive. When the truck actually stopped, everyone's eyes opened.

"You ready?" Gideon immediately asked Kostya.

I should have known.

Kostya shook his head. "Rest. I'll call you up when I need you." He'd seen Gideon working on his computer during Ryker's turn at the wheel and when Mateo was driving.

When Kostya and Mateo met outside of the truck to do the switch, Mateo shook his head and yelled over the wind.

"It's a bitch," Mateo told Kostya. "The visibility is next to nothing, we were doing about ten klicks an hour." Nolan nodded disgustedly in agreement.

"We're finally close to Joensuu here in Finland," Mateo explained. "According to the GPS, when it decides to work, it shows we're about another five klicks from the outskirts of the city."

"How are you staying on the road?" Kostya asked.

"Carefully," Mateo answered. "That's the reason we're going so slowly."

"Good call," Kostya praised his men. "Now get back there

and relax. At the rate we're going we'll be trading off driving a few more times before we get to Koivusuo Reserve."

"You got that right," Nolan yawned as he headed to the back of the truck.

Kostya planted his ass in the driver's seat and checked out the fuel situation. Mateo and Nolan had filled the tank before they'd started out, and he still had almost a full tank of fuel left. This SISU that the Finnish colonel had loaned them was a Godsend.

He looked out the windshield at the shards of snow pelting the window.

I hate snow.

Kostya took off the brake and started forward. His men were right; ten klicks was the fastest he could go, and it took all of his concentration to keep it on the road.

"Jesus," Gideon breathed as he pushed himself into the front passenger seat of the truck. "No wonder the Joensuu airport is closed. Is there even a town somewhere past our windshield?" he muttered.

Kostya glanced at the truck's clock and realized he'd been driving for almost a half-hour. Out of the corner of his eye, he saw his second-in-command fiddle with the navigation system that every driver had been relying on. It was the best GPS system the military had, they'd been upgrading it and using it for years. Not that it was doing any of them much good in this once-in-a-lifetime blizzard.

"It's time to break out the new toy." Kostya could hear the glee in Gideon's voice.

"What are you talking about?"

"I've got something that is going to get you and the rest of the team harder than two bottles of Viagra."

"I'll bite. Whatchya got?"

"A GPS system that will actually work."

"You mean something that will show me that Lake Pyhäselkä is actually there to the south of us, that this GPS isn't managing to show on the screen?" Kostya asked sarcastically.

"How'd you know about the lake?"

"I'm old school. While you were reading some technical journal or figuring out how to take over the world, I was studying the regional maps of Finland on the plane."

"Damn right you're old. You've been driving for thirty minutes, isn't it time for your nap?" Gideon grinned.

Asshole.

Gideon was only four years younger than Kostya, but he sure liked rubbing it in.

"Toy. Now," Kostya grumbled.

Gideon pulled his backpack onto his lap, then took out a block of plastic and aluminum, with two rubber stubs coming out of its sides. He flipped a switch on the side and the obligatory green glowing screen appeared.

"So that brick is actually going to help us? How in the hell is it going to do that?"

"Cosmic rays, my man."

Kostya rolled his eyes, then something triggered in his brain. Shit, he'd been briefed about this at least a year ago. It was after all the goatfucks in the Kandahar mountains in the middle of Afghanistan when they couldn't get any GPS signals.

"This is the one that means we're not dependent on radio signals from satellites. Instead, it uses whatever the fuck a muon is that is made from cosmic rays."

"That's the basics," Gideon nodded. "But it gets better.

Muons are a natural source of radiation that can pass through rock and be used at high altitudes."

Kostya felt his spine tingle. "Water too?"

"Yep, they're testing it now in submarines. Kostya, this is going to be a game-changer. This blizzard, it's nothing." Gideon pointed to the screen. "There's your lake. Let's see if it can find the Loch Ness Monster."

Kostya slowed to less than seven kilometers an hour and glanced over at the screen. "Dumbass, that's in Scotland, not Finland."

What Gideon was holding in his hand was downright magical. "Zoom in, I want to see the road."

Gideon did, and Kostya finally had a clear idea of where he was going despite the fact he was almost at zero visibility with the snow coming directly at them.

"Is that a semi I see damn near crossways on the highway coming up?" Kostya slowly took his foot off the accelerator and lightly tapped the brake.

"Dammit, looks like it to me," Gideon answered.

The truck came into view, but they stopped meters before they would have hit it. "Magical," Kostya breathed.

"You and your maps suck ass," Gideon grinned.

"The day's going to come when you and your computers just don't cut it. You're going to have to depend on your gut, and you are going to be so fucking screwed."

"Not going to happen," Gideon assured his friend. He turned to the back of the truck. "Up and at 'em. We've got work to do."

Kostya glanced back and saw that all of his men were already awake and ready to rumble. Of course they were, that's how they operated. All of them knew that when their truck stopped, they were needed.

"Throw on your headgear and turn on your comm systems, we've got trouble outside," Kostya said.

They immediately put on their helmets, facemasks, and goggles, and if Kostya hadn't taken note of where they'd been seated, he wouldn't have been able to tell them apart.

"What's up?" Nolan asked through their comm system.

"Trouble," Ryker answered with a laugh. "The question is, how bad. So how bad, Lieutenant?"

"Nothing that should require a gun," Kostya answered as he climbed in the back and grabbed his goggles and face mask. He'd already been wearing his comm device around his neck, he just hadn't activated it.

Kostya heard Lincoln mutter, "Should." That was Lincoln Hart; his man was as pessimistic as he was. He liked that about the man. He and all of his men would be locked and loaded as they vacated the truck, because *should* didn't mean jackshit.

"We've got a semi blocking a good part of the road. The good news is it isn't tipped, the bad news is, we can't tell if other cars or trucks are involved, or if there are injuries. Don't see any emergency vehicles," Gideon explained.

It didn't matter how fucking sweet their arctic gear was —the second the doors to the SUSI opened, it was fucking cold. Kostya jumped out and led the way to the semi. They spread out, Gideon took the right followed by half the team and Kostya took the left. It took just moments to assess the situation and realize there was nothing they could do for the driver of the truck, or for the family of three in the car that had been partially crushed underneath the backend of the full trailer.

Kostya insisted on handling the body of the little boy

who couldn't be more than ten years old. As he held the fragile figure surrounded by the swirling snow, it was as if he was back in time, seeing the snowflakes crystallize on Roman's eyelashes, the only color on his face the blue of his lips.

Sebastian broke open the lock of the trailer and his men pulled out boxes of appliances to make room for the bodies.

"I got ahold of the authorities in Joensuu," Gideon told them over the comm system. "Come daylight they'll send someone to pick up the bodies and notify next-of-kin."

The men were all subdued as they climbed back into the SUSI. Kostya drove around the wreck and continued down Route 74. The snow had tapered off, just a little. Now Kostya was able to increase his speed to eighteen kilometers an hour. Who knew, he might get to the Koivusuo Strict Nature Reserve within the week.

Okay, fine, we'll be there by tomorrow evening, it'll just feel like a week.

LINCOLN WAS DRIVING AGAIN WHEN THEY MADE IT TO THE west side of *Ozero Yulya-Viyeks"Yarvi,* in Russia. It had taken five days from the time they'd left Helsinki. They could have made it there faster if they hadn't needed to take a day and scout out where the cameras, guard towers, and landmines were and ensure that they circumvented them.

Right now there was a break in the storm and the sun was shining, but according to the International Weather Bureau, it wasn't going to last for long. Besides it not snowing, Kostya was also thankful that the howling wind was silent for a change, too. It made it easier to think.

They were all taking a break from being cooped up in the all-terrain vehicle, God knew they needed a chance to stretch their legs.

"It's beautiful," Ryker said in a hushed tone. He'd grown up in Southern California. Kostya managed not to roll his eyes. He took a deep breath. He could swear that the air smelled different; it was as if he could taste Russia.

Gideon looked over at Kostya. Even behind his

polarized goggles, Kostya could feel his piercing gaze. His friend didn't know his *entire* story. He knew that his parents died in Russia and that he and his sister were Russian refugees, but he didn't know about Kostya's brother, Roman. It was a story he couldn't bring himself to tell.

"Do you have a lock on where Commander Clark said the Russians were building?" Kostya asked Gideon as he came closer.

Gideon pushed up his goggles and peered down at the device in his hands and nodded. "It's fifteen kilometers southeast of the lake." Kostya held out his hand and Gideon gave him the device.

Before examining the GPS, Kostya took another look around and studied his men. They all looked in good shape, some even had the good sense to be putting on sunscreen. Gideon looked around and smirked.

"There's one thing I won't be needing."

Kostya looked at his friend's mahogany skin. "Still isn't going to make up for the burning sensation you suffered from losing the pool to Ryker. Wasn't that two hundred dollars?" Kostya grinned.

Gideon shrugged. "I forgot to factor in that Ryker more than likely plays Call of Duty *with* Landon regularly."

Kostya snorted. "Seems to me that was a pretty major oversight."

"Yeah, well, I noticed you lost out on the pool, too." Gideon smirked.

Kostya sighed. What could he say, Ryker had snookered them all. He looked down at the upgraded navigation device and hit the toggle button.

"So, fifteen kilometers southeast of the lake?" he asked

Gideon again.

"That's what the satellite images showed two months ago." Gideon nodded. "They saw the trucks going in, but never coming out."

"What the hell kind of trucks made it into the forest? Are you telling me there are roads in there?"

Gideon unbuckled his arctic backpack and fished out his tablet. They went back to the SUSI and bent over the hood. After spending days in it, neither of them was eager to get back into the vehicle. Gideon pulled up a map of Western Russia and zoomed in on their location. "This road encircles the lake and will eventually get to a highway that leads into St. Petersburg. The trucks went into the forest here." Gideon pointed to a spot where there was no discernable road breaking off into the forest.

"Do you have the sat images on your tablet?" Kostya asked.

They immediately flashed on the screen. Apparently, Gideon had once again anticipated his request.

"Can you zoom in?" Kostya asked.

"Nope, this was as good as it got. I already asked the techs to get clearer images and they couldn't."

"So we have no idea what they were hauling or what they were driving," Kostya said in disgust.

"Nope."

"And when the satellite passed again?"

"Nothing."

"What are you thinking we can do with your magic box?" Kostya asked Gideon.

"Go to where they drove in, then do a grid search and see if anything solid pings. Not trees or rocks, but more like a building." Gideon grinned at him. "But you already knew that."

"Seemed like the logical thing to do," Kostya agreed.

Gideon sobered up. "Do you think they're alive?"

"I really don't know. But I think somebody in there," Kostya said pointing to the screen, "knows. I intend to go in there and shake things up and get some answers."

"How far are you willing to go to get answers?" Gideon asked quietly.

Kostya gave Gideon a penetrating stare. "Things in Russia have supposedly changed since I was a child. The Soviet Empire collapsed and now we're all friends and on the same side, right?"

Gideon nodded. "Sure, we share a space station."

Kostya's jaw tightened. "Don't you fucking believe it. Leopards don't change their spots. Sure, some of Russia embraces the West, but there is a part of Russia that will always be a power-hungry autocracy. It might smile to the world, but deep down there will always be a small dark underbelly that can't be trusted."

Gideon frowned. "Kostya, that's cold."

"No, that's real. I'll know who we're dealing with when we get there. It'll be on me to decide how I play things. You will all be out of it."

Gideon snorted. "So sorry, Boss. That is so not how things work. I believe we are called a team. I know English isn't your first language and all, so you might want to go look that up, but in a team, we work together."

"Oh, I'm so sorry, Chief Petty Officer, didn't you hear? I'm what is called a lieutenant. That's an officer, which means I outrank you. That's a word *you* might want to look up. You and all of the other enlisted men might want to remember that when I give orders tomorrow. You got that?"

Gideon rolled his eyes. "Sure I do."

Asshole.

THE GOOD WEATHER lasted exactly two seconds as far as Kostya was concerned. How in the hell had that happened he wanted to know as he glared up at the dark sky that was spitting a blanket of snow down on him.

"Got anything yet?"

"You asked that thirty seconds ago, Lieutenant," Gideon muttered into his mic. Kostya didn't bother to respond. His second-in-command knew damn good and well that Kostya had not asked thirty seconds ago—it had been precisely ten minutes since he'd asked for an update. Kostya and his men were in the forest following a grid pattern search and rescue protocol, being directed by Gideon. They'd been at this since sunset and it was nearing midnight. Seriously, Gideon should be in a better mood since his happy ass was planted back in the SUSI coordinating things while the rest of them were balls-deep in slush.

Kostya tramped past the clearing and was once again under the deep, aged forest growth where he was protected from the snow. It was eerily quiet and sent his mind spinning backward in time to when he had been a shivering seven-year-old carrying his baby sister and cajoling his older brother to keep up, glaring at the big man who had greedily taken their diamonds to get them over the Russian border but unwilling to do more than lead them.

Gideon's voice jerked him to the present. "Got something. It's big and it's square, underneath the trees." He gave out the coordinates. Kostya calculated where his men were and realized that Sebastian was the closest. Hell, he was almost on top of whatever the Russians had built.

"Sebastian, halt," Kostya commanded. "Linc, Landon, you're closest to him. When you're together, reconnoiter and report. Gideon, can you pinpoint any smaller items, like the number of vehicles?"

"Give me a few and I'll have a diagram flushed out of what's there and I'll send it to all of you via your handhelds."

"Sebastian, did you see any sign of a path that led to the facility?" Kostya asked.

"Negative."

"I've got something, Lieutenant," Landon answered. He must be crossing over tracks to get to Sebastian.

"What?" Kostya asked.

"No discernable path, what with all the snow, but you can see the cut trees."

"We'll stay far away from that entry point, Boss, as we enter," Linc said.

While Kostya waited for another report from that trio, he turned his attention to his other men.

"Mateo and Nolan, you head northwest one kilometer around the back of the coordinates. Ryker, I'll meet you a kilometer southwest from the coordinates. Gideon, get us that map, STAT."

"On it," Gideon replied.

"Linc and Landon are with me," Sebastian reported.

Kostya breathed a sigh of relief as he started jogging to where he was going to meet Ryker. He was happy the team went back to radio silence. He knew that their new communication frequency was supposed to be tighter than a gnat's ass, but it was his job to worry. Of course, the new magic box—

Kostya shook his head, he needed to start referring to it by its proper name; Muometric Positioning System, aka muPS, which only made him think of the frickin' Muppets.

He felt his handheld vibrate against his thermals and stopped so he could fish it out from under his parka. He looked over the map that Gideon had sent, which looked pretty damn good, and spoke into his mic. "How accurate are the dimensions?" he shot out to Gideon.

"Spot on. You've got two T-90s."

Kostya winced; that was exactly what he'd deduced.

"Shit," Ryker muttered. "They have tanks."

"Who cares, we have Semtex!" Landon said with glee.

"What's this *we* shit? Lincoln, tell me you haven't given the kid any of the Play-Doh, I don't trust him." Sebastian's Cajun accent came over the receiver loud and clear.

Kostya heard Linc snort. "Not bloody well likely."

"Ah, come on, be cool. I'm dating this new woman. She's a sculptor and she works with clay all the time. I'd rock it with Semtex."

"Shut up, all of you," Mateo snarled. "We have tanks. It looks like one main building and three outbuildings. Do you hear dogs?"

"Negative," Linc answered.

"Well, that's something, at least," Mateo muttered.

Mateo needs to learn how to ease up just a little. I'll have to talk to him when we get home.

Kostya watched as Ryker jogged up close to him. Ryker pulled down part of his face covering. "He's dating a sculptor?" Ryker mouthed.

Kostya shrugged. His head hurt just thinking about it.

He twirled his finger, then pulled out his binoculars and Ryker followed suit. First, he looked to see if he could spot Mateo and Nolan, but he couldn't. He grunted in satisfaction; it meant that the arctic camouflage gear was working. He then turned his attention to the buildings. There wasn't even a fence around the perimeter.

Hmm, so they're that sure of their security out in the middle of nowhere.

"You'd think we would be seeing some kind of smokestack for heating," Sebastian said over the comm.

"It's got to be an underground geothermal system," Gideon explained. "The whole thing sounds pretty damned sophisticated for being in the middle of nowhere."

That's what Kostya was thinking too. This wasn't just some station set up to spy on Finland, this was a major operation that Russia wanted to protect. He wasn't so sure it had anything to do with being close to their Scandinavian neighbors.

This is not good, not good at all.

"Can you report this to Commander Clark?" Kostya asked Gideon. With the shitstorm snowstorm, he had no idea how good the satellite phones to the US were going to be. Hell, the only reason the commlinks between the eight of them were working was because of proximity.

"It's a no-go," Gideon said.

Kostya had figured as much. He just wanted command to know they were onto something big, not that he was going to let either the brass or the suits get in the way of his mission. He knew in his gut that this place knew something about the scientists' disappearance and he was going to get to the bottom of it, no matter what he had to do.

8

"No sign of tracks," Linc reported.

Ryker swept his glove over his goggles so he could peer at Kostya.

"That's because they're not dumb enough to be out playing in the snow at the butt-crack of dawn," Ryker said.

Kostya nodded in agreement. "Go in slow, men, we have time. I want to take this nice and easy, no mistakes. Give reports as soon as you get to a building or one of the vehicles."

He listened for everyone's agreement before he and Ryker started forward.

Kostya held back and let Ryker take point. His man's lean-muscled body ate up the distance and they were soon at the first outbuilding.

"Team, hold up."

"What is it?" Gideon asked.

"This outbuilding is made out of cement blocks. Does anyone else have eyes on any of the buildings? Are you close enough to see what kind of building material was used?"

"We're not close enough," Linc reported. "But besides the tanks, I've got one humongous two-sectioned tracked truck. And when I say humongous, I'm talking Hulk-sized. Lieutenant, if you're saying the buildings were made out of cement blocks, trucks like this sure as hell could have hauled them in."

"Do you think this could be a Vityaz?" Gideon asked. Kostya could hear the excitement in his second-in-command's voice. Shit, his man was geeking out again.

"Gideon, I don't know what the fuck a Vityaz is," Lincoln answered. "But if it is an all-terrain vehicle that looks like it might even have amphibious capabilities, this might be your guy."

"Shhieeeyt!"

Yep, new tech did it for Gideon Smith every damn time.

"Kostya, what's the significance of the cement blocks?" Gideon asked.

"It would be a pain in the ass to haul in. Normally in this part of the world, everything is built with wood. This is some heavy-duty protection."

"You would have thought that being in the middle of butt-fuck-nowhere would have been protection enough," Linc said. "And hell, building an electric fence would have been far easier."

"Or maybe it's more about keeping something in," Kostya said slowly. He didn't like this. What were they hiding?

"Way to shit all over a sunny day, Boss." Gideon sighed into his microphone. Kostya heard the others laugh.

"We're at an outbuilding," Nolan reported. "Mateo and I will check out all sides and report what we find."

"We're here at the vehicles," Seb reported. "We're going to check them all out and report back."

"Take pictures and send them to me," Gideon told them. "I want to know what we're up against."

"Why not just disable them now?" Nolan asked.

"Boss?" Sebastian queried.

"I would love to, but there's no way to do it quietly. Set the charge so we're set up to take them out at a moment's notice. As for the new love in Gideon's life, the Vityaz set something up that you can easily take off. My gut's telling me we might need it later."

"Roger that."

Kostya tilted his head toward the outbuilding he and Ryker were coming up to and his man immediately moved to the left to scout out the north side of the building. They'd meet up on the east side.

As Kostya went around the south side it was easy to see that whoever built the place wasn't much for aesthetics. All the windows were close to the roofline. They were only to let in some light, not for the occupants to enjoy the view. Normally, it would be tough for somebody from the outside to peek into, but they didn't take into consideration that someone would be standing on days and days of snow accumulation, which made it easy for Kostya to peer inside.

With his arctic camouflage and the snow pouring down behind him, he wasn't too worried about taking a peek in the window, but he was still very careful when he did lift his head to peek in. It was all in shadows inside the building. Still, he was able to make out some things, and from what he could see it looked like one of those cleanroom laboratories. He looked closer, trying to determine if they were creating pharmaceuticals or computer chips. Kostya found his answer in the corner; there were a bunch of vials beneath what looked like eyedroppers. Yep, this was definitely *not* computer chips.

He did another comprehensive scan, checking to see if there was anything else of interest, but he didn't come up with anything, and there were definitely no heat signatures. On the west wall, there were three doors. It looked like the whole back wall was nothing but offices. He had to hope that Ryker would be able to tell him what was in there. He reported his findings, knowing that Gideon was keeping track of everything.

"Ryker, are you able to see into the rooms behind the closed doors on the west side?" Kostya asked.

"I have two windows with offices, but for your third door, there isn't a window. Maybe it's a bathroom or closet."

"Could be. I didn't get any heat signatures." Kostya said.

"Me neither," Ryker concurred.

Kostya headed toward the east side of the building where he would meet up with Ryker.

"Mateo, Nolan, what did you find?" Kostya asked.

"I see nothing but cubicles from where I'm standing, no people," Mateo reported.

"Matt, it's different on this side," Nolan explained. "I've got two people in the cubicles. They're hunched over clicking away. From the way they're concentrating, I'd say we could waltz right in and do a tap dance and they wouldn't notice."

"Techno-geeks like Gideon, huh?" Ryker chuckled.

"Sure, try to sneak up on me sometime, I dare you," Gideon responded.

"Ryker, did you see anything else?" Kostya asked as

Ryker stomped through the high snow up to him. "Besides what I told you, there was also a door on the northeast side of the building. It was locked."

"Are you getting all of this, Gideon?"

"Yep, I'm plugging it all into the diagram," his second-in-command assured him.

"Okay. Mateo and Nolan, head on over to the big building and meet up with the others. Ryker and I will check out the third outbuilding."

Kostya knew it was southeast, but visibility was still not worth a damn so he pulled out the muPS device and pinged where the third outbuilding was, just to double-check. As soon as he did, he motioned for Ryker to follow him. It was now three in the morning in the middle of the blizzard—all in all, they *should* be safe from any Russians patrolling the area, but Kostya never counted on *shoulds*.

"Any sign of life?" he queried his team.

Everybody responded in the negative, but Nolan had more to say. "But that doesn't mean anything, Boss. I can barely see Mateo and he's a meter away from me."

"And today's pessimist award goes to Nolan O'Rourke," Ryker quipped.

"That is a highly coveted award since it normally goes to our lieutenant." Kostya could hear the smile in Gideon's voice.

"Can it, all of you. What's the word on those tanks? Do you have them ready to blow?" Kostya wanted to know.

"Finished those, now working on Gideon's toy. Needed to make sure that the placement was just right," Linc answered.

Lincoln was good, but Kostya would have felt better if Nolan was setting the charges. It was like Nolan O'Rourke had been born to do demolitions. He had a gift.

"Sebastian and I have checked things out while Linc's been playing with Play-Doh. There's no sign of people," Landon said.

"Of course, any tracks would have been snowed under in five minutes," Sebastian said dryly.

"I'm done. Let's get a move on and check out the big building. If everyone else is coming up empty-handed, we're going to have all the fun." Kostya smiled when he heard Linc's easygoing chatter; it meant he was confident in what he'd done with the Semtex.

"Gideon, are you positive that the big building is nothing but a square?" Kostya asked as he looked once again at the sketch that Gideon had sent to each of them.

"Yeah, I've triple-checked it since I sent it. They weren't trying to win any architectural awards, that's for sure."

"Hold on, Lincoln. Let Ryker and I check out the last outbuilding before you get all excited about tackling the main building. For all we know this last one is the barracks and armory and it will take you all out."

"And our leader takes back the pessimism award away from Nolan O'Rourke," Lincoln chuckled.

As soon as they got to the third building, Ryker and Kostya worked like a well-oiled machine. Ryker went clockwise and Kostya went counterclockwise. That would have them meeting at the front close to the tanks.

It was the same damn set-up as what he'd seen in the last building, basically a clean-room to manufacture pharmaceuticals. What kind of biological terror were they creating that they had to do it in the middle of nowhere behind concrete walls?

"I've got no signs of life. What about you, Ryker?"

"Nope, just the lab equipment, but at least it's only set up as a Biosafety Level two."

Shit. Kostya had forgotten that Ryker had been part of the team that was in Sierra Leone during the Ebola outbreak, which had been so horrific. No wonder he could recognize the difference between biosafety lab levels.

"You heard the man," Kostya said into his mic. "The third building is clear, now it's time to focus on the main building."

His men knew what to do and where to go. He met up with Ryker at the front of the third outbuilding. Was this snow ever going to ease up? Now it was blowing straight at him and it was like he was in a wind tunnel. Kostya glanced over at Ryker to make sure he was all right. Kostya had at least thirty pounds on him, so he wanted to make sure that he was keeping up. Ryker gave him a jaunty salute, so Kostya kept pushing ahead until he got to the back of the big building. It was the same as the outbuilding—the windows were up high, or they would have been if it hadn't been for all the snow. Not one of them had any kind of light showing from inside. Kostya jerked up on the sleeve of his jacket and saw that it was now a quarter to four in the morning, but still, he would have expected *some* light from inside.

"Hey, do any of you see light coming from inside?" he asked his team.

He received nothing but negative answers.

Was it possible that the people inside had lost power?

"Who's found doors?" Kostya asked.

"You know about the two here in the front," Landon answered. "The doors are steel, could be reinforced. Can't get too close, there are cameras out front."

"On the northwest corner, there's a door. Another

metal awning. Two wet cigarette butts. But I would bet my last dollar there are dozens more under the snow," Nolan reported. "No cameras."

"How about windows?" Kostya asked. "We've got five on the south side, three too small to get in, two large enough to crawl into. The three on the west side were all too small. What about the rest of you?"

"Sounds like we have the same window configuration here on the north side as you do on the south. Three small, and two large enough that everybody but you and Mateo and Gideon could squeeze through." Nolan reported.

"Sebastian, what's the set-up on the east side?" Kostya asked.

"Just the two front doors with the camera. I haven't seen it move, but the red light on it tells me that it's active."

Well, there goes my theory that the power is off inside.

"You guys stay away from the front doors. Go over to the north wall. Mateo and Nolan, go back to the west. Ryker and I will stay here on the south wall. I want every single window scoped out, I want to know exactly what we're dealing with. Give your counts to Gideon."

This is where Ryker shone. He was fast and accurate in these types of situations, and he scoped out three of the windows to Kostya's two. At his second window, Kostya stopped and considered what he was seeing. It was a small room, with three bodies lying down, all of them with heat signatures. From what he could tell, they were all lying on the floor.

If this was some kind of complex they had built out here in the middle of nowhere, they would surely have set up suitable housing facilities for the people who were running things. Nope, these people lying on the floor weren't expected. Kostya would bet his bottom dollar that they were three of the five missing biologists. He just hoped to God that the other two were somewhere else in the building.

He reported in what he was seeing.

"Okay, this is what we've got," Gideon announced.

"Sebastian and his team reported a big ole goose egg when it came to people. Their windows lead out to what looked like offices and a conference room. Mateo and Nolan turned up twelve people in total, all in bed along the west wall. Our erstwhile leader probably found three of our targets on the south wall while Ryker came up with two people spooning in a bed, also on the south wall."

"Lieutenant, I don't suppose you saw your targets through the larger window, so somebody could get through?" Gideon asked hopefully.

Kostya snorted. "Hell no, only people in the movies get that lucky."

"How should we play this?" Ryker asked. "The large window close to you are your snugglers, but you can't fit through."

"Mateo and Nolan, what's the configuration of your people? Can you tell if they're behind closed doors?"

"Yes," they answered in unison.

"There's no real way to be quiet about this if we go through the window," Ryker said.

"Wait a minute," Gideon interrupted. "I didn't hear any one of you mention someone manning some kind of desk. So I'm thinking the camera at the front door is not being monitored, unless it's being monitored by those two geeks in the outbuilding, which is kind of useless." Kostya heard the disdain in Gideon's voice. "Those front doors are the farthest from all of the sleeping quarters you've pinpointed."

I really like having him on my team.

"He's right," Kostya said into his mic.

"So now we get to close in, right?" Linc asked.

"I'll come around and meet you. Seb, Landon, and I will go in. Linc, I want you to stay outside in case we need to blow the tanks. Ryker, you continue to watch from outside to see if we need help; you'll be the backup who can come through the window. Mateo and Nolan, you keep your eyes on everyone on the west side."

Kostya listened to everyone's affirmatives as he made his way through the heavy snow to the front of the building.

Jesus, that Vityaz is fucking huge! It makes the two tanks beside it look like children's toys.

When he got to the doors he saw that Linc was just setting a charge to blow the door open.

"Don't worry, Boss, it's going to be a baby blast," he assured Kostya with a grin. At least Kostya assumed he was grinning behind all of his arctic face gear.

"Did you hear that?" Kostya said into his mic. "There's going to be a small blast in the front to get us through the doors. Hopefully, the sound of wild banshees screaming out here will cover up the noise."

The four men stood back as the door was blown, then ran inside.

"Nobody even rolled over," Mateo assured him.

"The lovebirds are fine," Ryker said.

Kostya took point and had Sebastian and Landon following him along the southern hallway. The sounds of the blizzard were even kind of loud in the building; it was amazing anyone was getting any sleep, but that didn't stop him and his men from being quiet.

Kostya was pretty sure that it was the third door that housed the three people sleeping on the floor, and he tried the doorknob. It was locked. He lifted his foot and kicked it open.

"What the hell?" a man said in English.

"Now what?" another man asked in Russian. His accent was British.

Yep, these were his biologists.

"The snugglers are awake," Ryker warned them over the comm system.

"All quiet on this side," Mateo reported.

"Same," Nolan said.

"Sebastian and Landon, handle the two next door. Don't use deadly force, I don't know what we're dealing with yet."

Sebastian nodded.

Kostya walked into the room, found the light on the wall, and hit it. Three pairs of eyes peered up at him, one woman and two men, all looking the worse for wear. He recognized them from his report. They'd found the scientists, but two were missing.

9

"You're Rice, Harper, and Iris Robinson, right?"
Kostya asked the scientists.

"Who are you?" Harold Rice asked. His voice was
hoarse, and when Kostya got a good look at him, he could
see that he'd been beaten.

"United States military, Sir. I've come to take you
home."

"Really?" The woman asked. Her voice was weak.

Kostya managed not to wince when he looked at her.
She was wrapped in three thin blankets—obviously, the
men had given up theirs to give to her. But even with those
coverings, it was clear that she too had been badly abused.
What was worse, she was trembling, and if Kostya had to
guess, she was suffering from a fever.

Getting her back to the SUSI in this weather will be a
bitch. Good thing we didn't blow up the Vityaz.

"There are two more people in your group, aren't
there?" Kostya asked. "Doctor Lord and Benjamin Leeds.
Do you know where they are?"

"Ben's dead," the woman choked out. "They killed

him. They kept saying we were spying on them and wanted to know what we were looking for."

"We haven't seen Gwen for two days," the third man in the room said. Kostya recognized him as Ted Harper. He looked to be in his early sixties and he didn't seem to have suffered as much, which was a blessing. Hopefully, he could make it out of this mess without much trauma.

"She was asking too many questions. I told her to keep her mouth shut," Harold Rice spoke up again. "She just couldn't help herself. She's been the wrong person to lead this expedition from the start."

"Harold, stop." Iris couldn't say anymore, she went into an agonizing coughing fit. Kostya winced again. She sounded bad. They needed to get her out of here as soon as possible.

"Nolan, you seeing anything on your side?" Kostya asked into his mic.

"No. Why? Whatchya got?"

"Need a medic. Get in here." Kostya stepped out of the room and went over to where Sebastian and Landon were with the couple, who were naked and huddled up against a wall. "Landon, you got this?" Kostya asked.

Landon nodded.

"Seb, go trade out with Nolan."

Sebastian left the room about the same time Nolan was coming in. He peered at the naked couple.

"Not here," Kostya said to Nolan. "I need you next door. One of the biologists doesn't look too good, see what you can do to help her."

Nolan nodded. Kostya turned his head to the couple huddled on the bed.

"Where is Doctor Gwendolyn Lord?" Kostya snapped out the question in Russian.

"Who?" the woman asked.

"The other woman. The other scientist."

"I don't know," she answered.

Kostya pointed his assault rifle at the man. "And you? What don't *you* know?" Kostya asked in a deadly sarcastic tone.

"You have to believe me," he begged. "I work with computers. Both of us do. We're not part of what goes on in the labs. That's where they took her."

Kostya frowned. The lab hadn't shown any sign of life. Dr. Lord was a biologist, did they mean they had her working there?

"When was the last time you saw her?" Kostya asked them both.

Neither of them answered.

Kostya walked further into the room and pushed down the man's blanket with the muzzle of his rifle until it was pointed at his flaccid penis. "I'll ask again," Kostya enunciated each word in slow Russian. "When was the last time you saw Doctor Lord, and where was she?"

"She was being dragged out of the conference room..." His voice trailed off.

"Finish it," Kostya demanded.

"I don't know any more. I swear."

Kostya pressed harder with his rifle's muzzle and piss began to dribble down the man's leg.

The woman leaped off the bed, not caring that she dropped her blanket and she was naked.

"How disgusting! You're pathetic."

"Dasha, you know what happened, tell him. Please." The man turned his tear-filled eyes to the woman.

"You're lying, I know nothing," she spat.

Kostya pointed his rifle at her. "Get back on the bed

and sit down," he commanded. Dasha looked behind her and sat as far away from the urine-soaked bedding as she could.

"No, sit next to lover-boy."

Dasha gave Kostya a horrified look. "No," she protested.

"Then tell me about the American woman. Otherwise, I'll have you lie down face first in the piss."

"Fine," Dasha said as she threw back her long black hair over her shoulder. "She thought she knew so much," the woman said with derision. "She works with wild animals, what could she know?"

"Where did they take her?"

Dasha smirked but didn't say anything.

Kostya moved with lightning speed and grabbed her by the scruff of her neck. He shoved her face so that it hovered an inch above the urine stain. "Tell me where she is, Dasha."

"All right. All right," she screeched.

Kostya pulled her up and shoved her back against the wall.

Dasha's eyes darkened as she stared up at Kostya. "You know what, I don't think I will tell you anything. You speak Russian, but you're American. I can see it in your eyes. You won't hurt me. Americans don't have the stomach."

Fuck this shit.

"Try me," he said as he pulled out his Ka-Bar knife.

Her eyes widened.

"I'll ask you just one more time, Dasha," Kostya purred as he stepped forward and traced the tip of the knife along her collarbone. "Where is Doctor Lord?"

"They have her outside," she stuttered. "Grigor was

sick of her whining about our project. Always she says that our formulas are off. But she knows nothing."

"Did he kill her?"

"Nyet," Dasha sighed. "Anfisa would not allow, so she had one of her men throw her in the all-terrain. He gave her enough to live through the storm. Anfisa thinks we need to listen to this woman, that she might have something to contribute to our program, but she's wrong. Grigor is the greatest scientist in all of Russia, he knows what is needed and what isn't. Dr. Lord is not needed." Dasha pushed at Kostya's hand and he pulled back the knife. "I have told you everything." Her eyes were defiant.

"Linc," Kostya called into his mic.

"Already on it," his man responded. Kostya knew he'd be checking inside the Vityaz.

Kostya shot a look over to Landon. "You've got them both?" he asked. Landon nodded. "I don't want them setting off an alarm when we leave."

"I'll take care of it."

Kostya gave a chin tilt, then strode past him to the next room where Nolan had his med-kit out and was giving Iris Robinson a shot. Nolan looked up at him and by his expression, Kostya could tell that they had a problem on their hands. "I want her and the other two ready for transport in three minutes, you got it?"

"I'm going to need help," Nolan told Kostya, but before he could answer, a harsh thud came over the commlink.

"Goddammit!" It was Lincoln's voice. Kostya started running to the front of the building as he heard a loud crash and then a sharp scream in his ear. It was a man, but it didn't sound like Linc.

"Watch out!" A woman shrieked.

A muffled grunt.

"*Sooksin!*" a man cursed in Russian.

Then there was silence.

"Are you all right, Ma'am?" Lincoln sounded out of breath.

Bitter cold hit Kostya's face as he ran toward the all-terrain vehicle. The passenger side door wasn't open, so he ran around to the driver's side. It wasn't open either. He kept going until he found the rear open, and he jumped aboard. He didn't pay attention to the dead man; instead, he focused on Lincoln and the figure he was crouched over. She was huddled in a heavy winter coat.

Linc looked up at him. "She's good."

Kostya squatted down next to her head. "Doctor Lord, we need to get you and the others out of here." Her bare hands reached up and gripped the front of his jacket.

"Can't leave. They have to be stopped," she panted.

He didn't care about anything she might have to say, they needed to leave. *Now.*

"Gideon," he growled into his mic as he scanned the vehicle. It would house his entire team as well as the biologists. "Tell me how to drive this thing."

"The Vityaz?"

"Yep. I need a crash course." He got up and Doctor Lord hooked her arm around his leg.

"Stop. Are you in charge?"

"Yes. Lady, we've got to get out of here before everybody wakes up. We have an advantage at the moment, but it won't last long." Kostya ripped his leg away from her grasp.

"We can't go. Tens of thousands of Americans will die. Maybe hundreds of thousands."

Kostya turned around and saw Linc's expression. He looked concerned, like he was buying into what she was saying. Kostya hadn't been worried from the moment Ryker said that they were only dealing with a Bio Safety Level Two. Kostya knew they couldn't be dealing with any really dangerous biological agents.

"Doctor Lord, what are you talking about?" Kostya asked.

"They think they're just going to kill our cattle and it won't harm humans but they're wrong, the formula is wrong. The aerosol that they intend to use to disperse the chemical, changes it. We won't know until it's too late. So many will be poisoned and die."

Kostya looked at Linc.

The doctor continued. "But it doesn't matter. Even if they just did what they were intending, it would be catastrophic to America's food supply. We have to stop them no matter what."

"So they are working on biological warfare," Kostya muttered. No wonder this team was in the middle of nowhere. Did the scientists even think about the fact that they were put here because the Russian government thought things might go wrong—and if they did, they were expendable?

"Who's in charge?"

"Two people are heading up the project. His name is Grigor Petrov, he's the head biologist. And then there is Anfisa Nikitin. I don't know exactly what she does, but Grigor is scared of her. Hell, everybody is."

"Got it." Kostya turned away from the doctor. "Did everyone hear that?" He was met with a chorus of affirmatives.

"We need to shut this shit down. Gideon, have you been able to get anybody in the States?" he asked.

"Negative, there's still no satellite signal."

He looked down at Gwendolyn. Linc now had her covered in a Mylar blanket. "Nolan, I want the other American biologists out here, stat."

"Got it," he said as he left the vehicle.

The sooner he could get all of the scientists out of the firing line, the better.

"You need me to show you what needs to be destroyed." There was fire in the doctor's eyes.

"Who will know how to replicate what has been done here?" Kostya demanded to know.

"Grigor is hoarding the information. I really think he's scared of Anfisa. I think he knows that his usefulness will be over the day he finishes the project."

"Get her to explain exactly what's going on." Gideon's voice was tense. "I find it hard to believe that Moscow wasn't monitoring every move that Grigor made, even if he thought he was hiding it."

"I agree," Kostya said.

Nolan stepped into the back of the vehicle carrying Iris Robinson. Behind him came Harold Rice, then Sebastian helped Ted Harper up into the back. He made his way over to the doctor as fast as he could.

"Thank God, I thought you were dead," he cried out.

Kostya left them to their reunion. "Nolan, stay with all of them. Sebastian and Linc, come with me." He slammed the door shut behind them.

How could the wind and snow be even worse than it was minutes ago?

He spoke into his mic even though the two men were huddled around him.

"We go in, we round up everybody, I want them all secured. I want to find Grigor and Anfisa. Got it?"

They nodded and said yes at the same time.

"Mateo, are they all still asleep?" Kostya asked.

"I've been going back and forth, and yep, still no sign of movement."

"Linc, you're going to the north door. I want another baby blast. You enter there."

"Landon," Kostya started.

"Lovebirds are secured and silenced," he answered before Kostya could ask.

"Ryker?"

"Where do you want me?"

"You and I will take the south end along with Landon. Sebastian and Linc will take the north end of the hallway. Mateo, as soon as Linc and Sebastian enter, go to the computer outbuilding. I want everybody taken alive. Everybody have their orders?"

Again he received nothing but affirmatives, and they were off.

"Kostya," Gideon spoke in his ear. "If what the doctor said is true, I need to check the computers. We need to know what they were working on, and hell, maybe there was some stuff that wasn't transmitted to Russia."

Kostya would have bet against it, except you never bet on a mission.

"Is there any way you can talk one of us through finding out?" Kostya asked. It would take at least one hour for Gideon to get here, if not two. Then there was the off chance that someone would come across the SUSI and Gideon wouldn't be there to protect their vehicle.

"No," Gideon answered. "I need to be the one to do it."

"Then get here."

"Leaving now."

Kostya and Ryker met Landon at the first door along the west wall. Kostya tilted his chin, his meaning clear.

There were eight doors along the wall, one had to be a bathroom. Kostya silently moved in front of each, and when he found he found the door with the Cyrillic writing that said toilet—it was number four from the west —he quietly announced it in his comm.

"You two cover the first two doors, I've got number three." Kostya he said to Landon and Ryker.

"Blast coming," Linc said. "Three, two, one."

The blast hit.

Kostya hit the number three door with his foot, easily crashing through the door and the doorframe. Two shots above the bed stopped the man from reaching for his gun. "Don't move," Kostya yelled in Russian. The man dove for his gun anyway. Kostya killed him.

Before he could move to door number five, .45 caliber shots exploded through the door. Kostya plastered his back against the wall next to the door waiting for a pause in the shooting. When it came he went down low and fired round after round from his automatic rifle, blasting the room until he heard screams that were abruptly cut off. He looked over his shoulder, and both Landon and Ryker had their guns trained into rooms one and two, so they had their situations covered.

More shots were coming from the hallway in front of him. He looked up to see Sebastian shooting his gun into the room closest to the blown entry point. There was no sign of Linc. Ryker ran past Kostya to the final room that was unopened, door number six, and Kostya followed. Ryker slammed the door open with his boot.

"Don't shoot. Don't shoot." A woman screamed in English.

Anfisa.

Kostya would bet anything.

He was in the room in an instant. He jerked the gun that she was pulling from under her pillow out of her hand. She twisted, kicked, and fought before Kostya grabbed the blanket from her bed and wrapped it tight around her. He yanked the lamp cord out of the wall then ripped the cable from the base of the lamp and whirled it around her, tying it tight. That'd do for a minute or two, until Ryker scrounged up something that would work. He *always* managed to find something that would work.

"One dead," Sebastian reported.

"I killed two," Kostya said.

"Mine's secured and Landon's taking him to the supply cabinet," Ryker told him. Kostya knew that Landon couldn't speak Russian, but he had no doubt that somehow he would be taken to some kind of area where he would find something to tie everyone up.

"Everyone okay?" Kostya asked. "How about you, Mateo?" he asked into the comm system.

"Everything's under control, Lieutenant. They didn't put up any fight worth mentioning."

"I want them over here, STAT."

"You got it."

"What are you going to do with us?" Anfisa demanded to know. "I called out to St. Petersburg as soon as I heard you. You will be tracked down like dogs."

Kostya laughed.

"Lady, there is no way you could have gotten a signal, not in this blizzard," Kostya scoffed.

"Our technology is far superior to yours."

"Of course, I did." Even tied up, lying on the bed she managed to look like a haughty bitch.

Kostya bent down so his nose was almost touching hers. "Where is Grigor Petrov?"

"I heard the shots. You stupid Americans probably killed him."

That's what Kostya was afraid of.

He stood up. "Everyone question your prisoners, I want to know which man is Grigor Petrov. If they don't talk, search their rooms, there has to be some sort of ID."

"Already looking, Kostya, but everything's in the Russian alphabet. Cyrillic, right?" Sebastian said, pronouncing it correctly.

"Bring whatever ID you find to me, I'll read it," Kostya said.

"Gideon, how you holding up?" Kostya asked.

"This is not California weather! What the fuck! I'm in snow up to my nipples."

Linc laughed. "This is mild. I used to walk to school in snow worse than this."

"Uphill both ways, I suppose?" Landon guessed.

"Quit your bitching and get here," Kostya commanded.

Landon strolled into Anfisa's room with a roll of duct tape.

"Secure her," Kostya told the kid.

After a minute, Anfisa looked like a mummy.

"Are we gathering them up?" Linc asked over the comm.

"No, leave everyone where they are. I want them isolated," Kostya said. "Landon will bring everyone duct tape to secure them."

Anfisa's dark eyes were taking in everything he was saying. "You're going to die. You, your men, and those scientists. Not only did I make the call, but supplies are due in less than twenty-four hours. You'll be hunted down like dogs," she spat out.

Why didn't I let her take a shot so I could have killed the bitch?

He turned his back on her and shut the broken door and found Mateo and Ryker waiting outside the room holding different forms of ID, all in Cyrillic. "This one," Kostya said as he looked at a worn driver's license. "Is he dead?"

"No, just scared," Ryker replied. "This way."

Kostya followed him down the hallway.

Grigor didn't look like a scientist, he looked like a weight lifter. A scared weight lifter.

"Do you speak English?" Kostya asked in English.

Grigor stared at him, his face blank.

"Are you the lead scientist here?" Kostya asked in Russian.

"Da," Grigor nodded his head. "I am in charge of everything we do here." His voice was filled with pride.

"I thought Anfisa Nikitin was in charge. Are you saying that you are above her?" Kostya asked pleasantly.

Grigor trembled. "Nyet. Nyet. Of course Comrade Nikitin is in charge. I report everything to her. Everything."

"Well, that's too bad. If you had information that she was not aware of, then I would let you live." Kostya lifted his rifle and pointed it at the man.

He flung himself against the back wall of his room, covering his head with his arms. "Nyet. Don't kill me. I'm begging you."

"You are of no use. I only need her."

The man scrabbled backward, trying to worm his way behind the dresser as Ryker and Kostya exchanged glances.

"I know things. I know everything. Nothing will work without my knowledge. Nothing!"

He tried to push the dresser away from the wall so that he could slide behind it. Kostya heard Ryker's choked laugh.

"Where do you keep the information?"

"It's in my office, in the lab. Don't kill me. I have children."

"McQueen, grab him. We're taking him to the lab. Let him have a coat." Kostya went out to inspect the rest of the prisoners.

10

"Where did you learn to read and write Russian, doctor?" Kostya asked Dr. Lord in English.

"I grew up in Alaska. It was a small town and many of the original settlers were from Russia." She shrugged her shoulders as she continued to concentrate on the whiteboard in front of her.

"You're wrong!" Grigor shouted at her in Russian for the fifth time in as many minutes. "This chemical will only attach to a bovine liver. You have seen the different livers we have grown in the other lab, it only attaches to the bovine, not the human."

Kostya had seen the organs that were being grown in the other lab, and it had made his stomach curdle.

"I'm not talking about the liver. I agree with you, your pathogen only affects the bovine anatomy. It is when the pathogen combines with the aerosol that you end up with the problem. The particles attach to the mucus membranes in the sinuses and will mutate and travel to the cerebral cortex. Within a month every person who came into contact with this spray along with the cattle will be dead, and anyone they came into close contact with, or God forbid, was coughed or sneezed on, will have had this pathogen transmitted to them."

"Old Lady, you have no idea what you are talking about," Grigor scoffed. "We distributed this to our cattle-producing farmers in Kolomna in late October. They were ecstatic to have such a wonderous formula that would work for weeks to keep flies off their cattle, instead of the products that would only work for one day. I have not heard of one single problem. You see, you know nothing!"

Doctor Lord shook her head. "Great, were you using the infected pathogen or a placebo?" she demanded to know, but even Kostya knew that it was highly likely the Russians hadn't used something that would have poisoned their own cattle.

"A placebo, of course," Grigor said.

"Of course." Doctor Lord threw up her hands. "And that's where you made your big mistake. You haven't created something that will kill off part of America's food chain, you fool. You've created a biological agent that will kill hundreds of thousands of people."

Grigor gave her a pompous smile. "Woman, you continue to work with your wolves and let real scientists continue to work with things you can't possibly understand." He sucked in a breath to start talking again and Ryker stepped forward and grabbed him by the throat, throwing him up against the whiteboard.

He looked over to Doctor Lord, while Kostya looked on in satisfaction. "I don't know what this asshole is saying, but something tells me we're dealing with biological weapons, am I right?"

Doctor Lord nodded. "But this idiot doesn't even know he's created them." She looked at Kostya and Ryker. "I know you understood what he said," she said to Kostya. "He's right, a biologist who specialized in the study of wolves wouldn't understand what he was creating, but before I got into this, I worked at the University of Utah and got a Ph.D. as a bioengineer. Trust me, I get exactly what he's doing."

Ryker raised his eyebrow. "For real? I had trouble dissecting a frog in high school. What made you change to studying wolves?"

Her lips twitched and her eyes sparkled. "My late husband. What can I say, he was pretty enticing, and he convinced me to go home to Alaska and study wolves with him." Then she sobered. "But I don't know why I'm bothering to talk to this little man. He's probably already shared this with everybody in Moscow, so there's no stopping this train now that it's moving."

Kostya drew the doctor away from the whiteboard. He looked up when he saw Gideon walking into the lab and tilted his chin at him to go toward the desk at the back of the room. Maybe he had some good news, he sure as hell hoped so.

"Doctor Lord, you've been at this since yesterday. You need a break," Kostya said to the doctor as he looked down at her.

The woman in front of him gritted her teeth. "Lieutenant, I—"

"Kostya," he reminded her.

"Fine, Kostya. The pathogen combined with this aerosol is going to end up causing irreparable harm around the world. How are we going to stop this?"

"We'll find a way," he assured her.

She shook her head in defeat. "I don't think we can. Moscow won't realize what they have, and they'll mistakenly release something that they'll think will only compromise our food supply. They won't realize that they're releasing a bioagent."

Like some of them would even give a damn if they knew it was a bioagent. The motherfuckers. Still....

"Gwen, listen to me. What are the chances that someone with your skillset would have been the one who ended up here?"

She slowly looked up at him, her eyes bright with intelligence.

"There should be no way in the world that I should be here. It would be like someone winning the lottery three times in a row," she said quietly.

"That's my point," Kostya nodded at her. "And if you're here when everything says that you shouldn't be, then that says to me that you're meant to stop this thing."

"But I told you, it's in Moscow by now."

"Have faith," he said with a comforting smile. "Have faith."

Gwen's hand shot out and clutched at his sleeve. "Do you really think there's hope?" she asked desperately.

"I do. Remember, I might have spent most of my life in the States, but I lived in Russia during my formative years. We're a superstitious people," Kostya said with a small smile.

Gwen gave him one last lingering look, then nodded her head and turned back toward the whiteboard. Kostya went over to meet with Gideon.

"Give me some good news."

Gideon's smile was huge. "Grigor's computer is connected to the main server that is pouring all of its information to the database that goes to Moscow."

Kostya waited. He knew damn good and well that

there had to be more, otherwise Gideon wouldn't have a shit-eating grin on his face.

"Well?" Kostya asked.

"It's kind of interesting that there's a computer registered to someone who doesn't seem to be here, and when I dug deeper, that person was reassigned eight months ago to a project in Kazan, but they're still logging into this computer every day."

Kostya felt his own shit-eating grin coming on. "Let me guess. Because everybody in Moscow knows that this person no longer works here, they don't expect it to be connected to the server."

"You've got it."

Kostya turned around and saw that Ryker was still holding Grigor. "McQueen, let him down, Gideon has a few questions for him."

"She didn't lie, I found the communication that proves supplies were supposed to come in yesterday," Gideon said when he found Kostya in the lounge area. Kostya stepped away from Nolan and gave all of his attention to Gideon. "Is that all you've got for me? What about Grigor's information, it's been over twenty-four hours."

"I'm almost there, but this is more important. We've got a situation on our hands. It's bad. They planned to be trading out personnel; three security and two computer programmers along with food supplies. They're bringing it all in via another Vityaz and they'll be escorted by a tank."

"Were they coming out of St. Petersburg? If so, they must have been slowed down because of the weather."

"Agreed," Gideon nodded. "What has me most concerned is that the snow has slowed down a lot, and according to all the reports it will stop in twelve hours. People, including the supply vehicle, will be calling in. You or Doctor Lord will have to be available to take those calls."

Kostya took a look around the common area at all of the people who were restrained. He'd been worried about leaving them in the forest to die since some of them were just tiny little cogs in the wheel. Now they had a solution.

"No, Gideon, we need to have to be long gone by then. Start pulling everything relevant into the Vityaz, and I mean everything—computers, backups, any kinds of notebooks. I want you to confiscate phones, you got me?"

Gideon nodded.

"Then all of the other things that are connected to this project are to be gathered up and put into the other outbuildings."

Gideon started to slowly smile.

"Boss, are you thinking what I'm thinking?"

"Depends."

Ryker came up from behind him. "Please say that I can go play with Linc and use some Semtex. This shit is just evil. Growing organs in a lab just so they can come up with ways to starve people, starve Americans..." Ryker held up his hands and his voice trailed off. "I know we're not going to get to blow up anybody, not even that bitch Anfisa, but please tell me everything else is going up in smoke."

Kostya sighed. "Am I that easy to read?"

Gideon and Ryker shook their heads.

"No you're not," Gideon said. "It's the situation that's easy to read, it's what we all want."

"Gotcha," Kostya sighed. "Gideon, how much of this shit has made it to Moscow? We're not doing any good if they can replicate it again."

"I pulled up the data that was sent. According to Doctor Lord, it wasn't the vital formulas. As a matter of fact, it was early in the process and it was so far wrong that Moscow will be chasing their tails for quite some time."

Kostya rubbed the back of his neck. Grigor was the real problem; he needed to be neutralized.

"How soon can you get this done?" Kostya asked.

"Two hours, max," Gideon assured him. "Most of the sorting was already done as I parsed through everything to see what had been sent through to Moscow."

"Good."

Kostya looked across the room and spotted Nolan O'Rourke.

"Nolan, how's Iris doing?" he shouted out.

His man trotted over, and he was grimacing. "I don't care how we transport her, or what kind of gear she's wearing; this cold is going to be brutal on her. I haven't been able to get her fever down. The antibiotics just aren't doing the trick."

"There's supposed to be a break in the weather in twelve hours. I hate like hell to ask a helicopter to fly into Russian airspace, but if we can get something stealthy to fly in and out..."

It was a crap situation, but there wasn't anything else they could do if they wanted to give Iris Robinson a chance to live.

"Gideon, any luck getting a satellite signal?"

"Not since that four hours of clear skies. As soon as the snow started again I haven't gotten a signal. I've set the phone up so that it automatically tries every fifteen minutes. If it ever gets a signal, no matter how weak, it will ping me."

"Good. When you do, notify Commander Clark about our situation. If he's not available, get this to Captain Hale. We need a helicopter."

"Neither the Finns nor Swedes have a stealth helicopter. This is going to turn ugly."

"No, it's not. I have a plan," Kostya smiled.

"Aw, shit. We're in trouble now. Should I get the team together?" Nolan asked.

Kostya nodded.

11

KOSTYA COULD BARELY HEAR WHAT SEBASTIAN WAS SAYING in his ear. He pushed the helmet down harder on his head so that it would cover the receiver in his ear and drown out the sound of the tank they were in.

"Repeat what you just said," he ordered.

"The muPS is still only showing the SUSI up ahead. I haven't encountered anything else on the road, so I'm broadening my search."

Well, that was something, at least. Kostya figured it was two more klicks until they reached the SUSI, then they could add that vehicle to their convoy. It would be the most comfortable ride for Iris, and they'd need that if they didn't get the helicopter extraction.

"How are you holding up?" he asked Linc who was driving the second tank behind him with Sebastian manning the turret.

"It's all good," he assured him.

"Landon?" he asked as he looked over his shoulder for a brief moment. Landon slipped down from his perch up in the turret. "All I can see is white. What about you, Lieutenant?"

"Same. That's why I'm depending on Seb to tell us when we're close to the SUSI so we don't drive over the damn thing."

"Okay, now I'm telling you you're getting close. You need to head to the right and go past the SUSI," Sebastian instructed. "Linc, you go to the left; that will leave the Vityaz to get close so we can move Iris and the other scientists."

Kostya started slowing the Russian tank to the right, and off the road. Even with the infra-red viewer that came equipped with the tank, he could still hardly see.

Snow sucks!

Kostya had the tank clicked into lower gears as he gently applied the brakes. There it was! He could finally see the SUSI. "Linc, you okay?" he asked.

"Yep, coming to a stop now."

"Mateo, what about you?" Kostya asked the man who was driving the Vityaz.

"Holy God, it's a damn good thing I started braking a mile back. This thing doesn't understand the meaning of slowing down. There is something off with the hydraulics."

Kostya winced. That wasn't good.

"But you're stopped now, right?" Kostya confirmed.

"Yeah. Ryker jumped off before this monster was even stopped so he could get to the SUSI. He wants to get 'er warmed up."

Good. That was good. What wasn't good, was that Gideon hadn't reported anything, but then how in the hell could he when it was a winter wasteland?

They all had to wait much more than a minute. "It was

touch and go, but got this damn thing started," Ryker reported. "It's going to take a while to get it heated."

"I can't have Iris transferred into the cold," Nolan said. "Let me know when it's above freezing. He's going to get it warmed up before we transfer the scientists."

Again, Kostya wanted to ask a question that really didn't have an answer. It was going to take as long as it was going to take to get the SUSI warmed up. But it better not take longer than ten minutes!

He sighed. It was a waiting game.

"Lieutenant, I really want to thank you for helping me out of that pickle three weeks ago," Landon said from behind him. Kostya turned around in the driver's seat, trying to put an attentive look on his expression. What the hell, all they were doing was waiting around for the heater to warm up in the SUSI; listening to Landon talk could be entertaining, and for the men, too, since they were all linked up on the comm.

"Yeah, well, I'm glad it helped. Did you have any more problems?"

"None at all. I think her brothers drilled it home with her that she would get into trouble with her parents if she didn't behave. Not that she was underage or anything," Landon quickly explained. "I mean, I saw her driver's license when she gave it to the bartender. She's twenty-two, she just acts like a teenager."

"That's probably not the best choice in a girlfriend."

"Yeah, you're not the only one to tell me that," Landon admitted. "I got an earful when I made my weekly call home to Grandma Kathleen."

Kostya chuckled. "What did she have to say?"

"Well, I didn't tell her everything that happened. But she catches on about things." Landon rubbed the back of his neck. "She told me I was looking for love in all the wrong places."

Kostya heard Gideon snort and Ryker out and out laughed.

"I'm pretty sure that's a country song," Sebastian said, playing up his Cajun accent.

"Whatever," Landon smiled good-naturedly. "She made me promise to either go to church or to the local community center, so I did."

Kostya thought he might like Landon's grandmother. God knew the kid needed some direction.

"So did you go to church?" Mateo asked.

"No, I went to the community center. I tried to find something I could sign up for that had mostly women in the class. I hit the jackpot with the pottery class."

"Is that where you found your sculptor, the one who could help with the Semtex?" Linc asked.

"Yep, Ellen runs the class and she's amazing. We've gone out for coffee three times now. I finally took her out to dinner. She's a bit older than me, but I like that. Maturity is good, after Angelique."

"How much older?" Mateo asked.

"Eighteen years older," Landon answered.

"So you basically went from one end of the spectrum to the other in less than a month, is that what I'm hearing?" Gideon asked.

Jesus, Mary, and Joseph, this kid is going to be the death of me.

"Ryker, is the truck warm enough?" Kostya asked. He prayed it was.

"Yeah, it's good."

"Landon, get out there and help get the scientists settled into the SUSI."

The young man grinned. "You got it."

"I GOT 'EM," Gideon called out. "They're arranging an NH-90, as soon as the snow clears. They're expecting a lull in less than eight hours."

"So, they'll land in Russia?" Kostya asked the sixty-four million dollar question.

"They're going to let me know."

Kostya gritted his teeth. He didn't care if this needed to go up to the Admiral; he didn't want to see Iris die. Hell, he didn't want to see anyone die. Someone better damn well get them a helicopter here in Russia.

"Seb, where are we?" Kostya asked.

"We'll be hitting the southern tip of Lake Julia in ten more klicks."

If they could just get past that, then they could bypass the supplies coming in from St. Petersburg since that road would be coming from the south, and they'd be heading from the west.

"Who were the two up front in the SUSI when we were on this leg of the trip?" Kostya asked into his mic.

"Nolan and me," Mateo answered. "It was night, and the snowfall was brutal. I don't think either of us could tell you if there was any place big enough beside the road where we could pull off. I think we're screwed."

"I was in the passenger seat," Nolan said. "From what little I could see, there were drop-offs on my side."

"That's decided it then, we're going to pick up the pace. I want us to get past the southern tip of *Ozero Yulya-Viyek"Yarvi* before the backup transport from St. Petersburg shows up."

"I'll give it my best shot, but I'm not sure how much more this Vityaz has to give," Mateo warned. "I've even been rubbing her dashboard and singing to her."

"I don't care if you have to take off your shirt and French kiss the steering wheel, you do whatever you need to do to get her revved up," Gideon all but shouted. "Everything I've read about those machines is that they're the slickest things since a slip 'n slide. You should be able to work her without putting out," Gideon admonished.

"Yeah, well someone hasn't been taking care of her. The hydraulics are damn near shot," Mateo countered in a calm voice. Thank God he wasn't buying into Gideon's bullshit.

Gideon hardly ever popped off. Since he did it must mean that he wasn't getting good news from the brass. But he must still be fighting with them because he'd yet to report anything to the team.

Kostya increased their speed. "I want to hear from any of you if you're unable to keep up with the vehicle in front of you. In that case, we'll slow down. Sebastian, keep monitoring the roads with the muPS, I want to know the minute you find anything that looks like the supply vehicles from St. Petersburg."

"Understood," Sebastian answered. Kostya just hoped that Gideon's little gizmo was as good as he thought it was, especially since their convoy was moving and so were the supplies from St. Petersburg. God forbid they just ran into one another.

Kostya picked up more speed, and after two more kilometers, miracles of miracles he could actually begin to make out trees up ahead.

"Are you seeing what I'm seeing, Lieutenant?" Landon asked excitedly. "The snow is letting up."

"About damn time," Ryker muttered. "I know I said it was cool, but I've changed my mind. I miss the surf and sand."

"Pussy," Linc chuckled. "My mom goes ice fishing at least five times a winter. You wouldn't stand a chance in Minnesota, don'tcha know."

"I've got good news," Gideon said, interrupting the chatter. "As soon as the weather breaks, the Finns are arranging an NH-90 to meet us, and it can carry all of us. They don't care where we are."

Kostya's shoulders relaxed, just one tiny little bit. He was paid to think of all the ways that shit could go wrong, and God knew there were still a whole hell of a lot of ways it could.

"Sebastian, pass the muPS over to Gideon and you take over monitoring the satellite phone."

"Gladly," was Sebastian's heartfelt response. Every one of Omega Sky's team members felt pretty damn comfortable with technology, but they all bowed down to Gideon's expertise. He had the touch.

"I have a better shot of finding them if they're on the road coming south from St. Petersburg than once they're on this sorry-as-shit path," Gideon explained. "It's going to be harder to pinpoint them here because it's so narrow and it's so close to the trees."

Kostya grimaced. "Understood." He hit the accelerator even harder. There were no two ways around it, they needed to get past that this sorry-assed-road.

12

"THEY'RE ONE KLICK IN FRONT OF US," GIDEON YELLED.

"Oleg, ty kuda?" Kostya heard over the tank's radio. *"Pochemu ty ne v laboratorii?"*

Holy fuck, he'd been concentrating so hard on keeping the tank on the trail at the higher speed that he'd missed the fact that there was a pinpoint of a vehicle up ahead. He thought fast. He had to answer the man on the radio, but in case he knew everybody from the lab, Kostya had to disguise his voice.

Kostya started coughing, then he responded in a hoarse voice.

"There was an emergency," Kostya said in Russian. "We didn't have any way to contact somebody, and there was no time to wait for you." He coughed again.

"Who are you?" the other driver demanded to know.

"Who the fuck do you think I am? Are you so stupid you can't recognize my voice when I just have a little cold?"

The driver laughed. "Yep, you're Oleg all right. You're the mean bastard I know and love. But seriously, Oleg, it's against protocol to leave. Moscow will have your balls in a vice," the man chuckled.

"Like you've never done anything wrong before," Kostya scoffed. He prayed that he was playing the situation correctly.

"You'll owe me another bottle of that good vodka that the bitch Anfisa always gets. Then nobody will be the wiser."

Kostya let out a loud laugh, then let it go into another coughing fit. "I need you to pull to the side and let us pass. It's a matter of life and death."

"Quit being melodramatic. Tell me what's going on. Your orders are not to leave the compound, you know this. From where I'm sitting, it looks like that's a Vityaz behind you. What the hell, Oleg, do you want to spend the rest of your days shoved in some hellhole in Siberia?" The man started laughing. "Okay, okay, I know, I know, that damned cement box you're living in is a hellhole too, but for fuck's sake, I'm not sure I can cover for you."

Kostya laughed with him. "Old friend, I do not take risks, you know this. I have my orders. There was a bad accident at the labs, we did what we could but some of them didn't make it. The rest I need to get them to a hospital in St. Petersburg."

Kostya heard a distinctive click and knew that they were now just talking between the two of them. "I hope that bitch Anfisa was one of the ones that died."

"No such luck. She's still at the compound. It was her order to get these others to the hospital, but..." Kostya waited to see if the man would take the bait.

"But what?"

"Now that I think about it, it would be good for you to

know what was going on before you get there. She's in a foul mood, and she could take it out on you."

"Aw, fuck, that's just what I need. Fine, tell me when I get out to inspect the vehicles."

"Pull over to the side of the road," Kostya commanded. "That way when you see I'm telling you the truth, we can get past you and on our way to St. Petersburg."

"Fine," the man grumbled. "But you better have some vodka to give me for all the trouble you're causing."

"For the information I'm giving you, you should be giving *me* vodka," Kostya protested.

"Maybe so, but I know you. You always have bottles to spare, and I want one."

"Fine. Fine. Just pull over and I'll get you your damn vodka and fill you in on what's going on." Kostya said in his fake hoarse voice.

He shut off the radio. "Linc, need a couple of Semtex grenades stat."

"On it."

Kostya watched with bated breath as he saw the tank in front of him start to slow down and pull over to the side of the road. He saw the Vityaz behind him do the same thing.

"Mateo, how you doing?" Kostya asked.

"Gonna need to go off into the woods. No way I have enough space to brake without hitting Linc's tank."

"The woods?" Kostya grimaced. "How far?"

"As far as it takes for the trees and the brakes to finally stop this motherfucker," Mateo answered.

Not good.

Kostya had his tank stopped in the middle of the trail, doing his best to block the view of the vehicles behind him. "Landon, find something I can use that'll look like I'm carrying vodka," he shouted over his shoulder.

Kostya pulled off his rifle and tore off his outer arctic coat and gloves. They were too synonymous with American special forces, but he pulled down his goggles and tugged up the scarf so that it covered the lower part of his face. Hopefully, Oleg was a blonde.

He opened up the hatch and was hit with a blast of arctic air and biting snow crystals. He pulled himself out and reached down, hoping against hope that Landon had something to give him. Landon handed him a raggedy scarf that was wrapped around a fire extinguisher.

"Really? This is all you've got? This does *not* look like a bottle of vodka."

"Lieutenant, I've got you covered," Linc said over the comm system, "and I've got three Semtex grenades."

Kostya looked over and saw Linc pulling himself out of the second tank's hatch.

Where in the hell did he manage to get a red backpack?

Kostya dropped the shit that Landon had provided back into the tank and jumped onto the tank's track then down into the snow. He could see the other tank driver waiting beside his tank. He wasn't wearing nearly the amount of gear that Kostya was, despite the fact that he'd taken a lot of his shit off.

"Flip open your cargo pants pocket," Linc ordered him through the comm system as he jogged towards him.

Kostya turned slightly to look over his shoulder and flipped open two of his pockets, watching Linc as he approached him.

Kostya waited for a moment. Linc hustled over and gave him the backpack while surreptitiously shoving the three grenades into his two pockets.

"Hurry up, my balls are turning blue," the Russian yelled.

"This vodka will warm you up," Kostya yelled back in Russian. He turned to Linc. "Get in my tank. I need you to be ready for anything if things go south. You got it?"

Linc's eyes glinted steel. "I got it." He jumped onto the tank's track, then hoisted himself up so he could climb into the hatch and Kostya started walking toward the Russian.

"Thank God you're here, I really could use your help," Kostya started.

"Yeah, sure you can. My God, are you taking steroids? You look like you could break me in half," the Russian yelled out with a laugh.

This was his chance. Kostya took off like a shot, head down, and plowed his shoulder into the guy's stomach before he had an opportunity to react. As Kostya sat on his chest, the man went completely still and laughed up at Kostya.

"Who the fuck are you?"

"I told you there was a situation at the lab."

"Should have been paying closer attention. Even with all your coughing, your accent is off. you've lived in America too long." He gave the best laugh he could considering the fact Kostya was sitting on his chest. "You're a long way from home. What happened, did you miss Mother Russia?"

The tank driver showed no fear.

"There's not one thing about this Godforsaken country that I missed, especially all this fucking snow. Now tell me who else I'm dealing with in your tank and in the Vityaz. How many people?"

"Go fuck yourself." He smiled at Kostya.

"You tell me and you might live." Kostya grinned back.

"If you used to live here, then you know that if I live through this, my life isn't going to be worth living. Once Moscow realizes how badly I fucked up, I'm a dead man anyway." He shrugged his shoulders. "Do your worst."

"What about everyone else with you? Do you want them to die too?"

His eyes shifted.

"How many more are in the tank?"

Nothing.

Kostya punched him. The sound of his nose breaking was muffled by the wind. "Tell me, how many are with you in the tank?"

Still no answer.

"Are you right or left-handed?" Kostya asked.

No answer.

"I'm going to assume right-handed."

Kostya moved lower on the tank driver's body, keeping one knee on his left arm, then peeled his right arm up off the ground and lifted it high in the air.

He yanked back the man's pinky and ring fingers until they snapped. That time, his scream could be heard over the wind. He panted in pain.

"How many are still in the tank?" Kostya asked again.

When he started to form the word 'fuck' in Russian, Kostya squeezed his two broken fingers together, grinding his broken bones. The tank driver howled.

"No one," he yelled. "No one. Just me."

"And in the Vityaz?"

The tank driver glared up at him.

"You have three more fingers on this hand. But I'm going for your thumb. It's going to be pretty goddamn hard to jack off without your thumb working, now isn't it?"

"Seven people in the Vityaz," he bit out. "But only three are security."

"Dima! What's taking you so long?" a man shouted from the Vityaz. "What's going on?"

Kostya crunched Dima's broken fingers in even a tighter grip. "Tell them there's a problem with the tank and you had to pull over."

"What problem?"

"I don't give a shit, if you don't want both of your thumbs broken, think of something."

"Pavel, I have to refuel. I need ten more minutes," Dima yelled loudly.

"Wait a minute, what's that in front of you? Do I see other vehicles? I'm coming out."

"Great, I could use the help," Dima shouted back. "It's about goddamn time you did some actual work."

There was a long pause.

"Is that another vehicle?"

"There was an accident at the lab. They're rushing the wounded to a hospital in St. Petersburg. I've investigated. We need to let them by. Come out into the cold and see for yourself."

"No. No. There's no need."

Dima rolled his eyes back to Kostya. "See, nobody likes work. Are you going to kill me?" The man didn't seem scared, only curious.

"Linc, duct tape," Kostya said into the comm system. He knew damn good and well that there wasn't a chance in hell that he hadn't taken some with him when he left the labs.

Linc popped out of the tank hatch and came over to Kostya like a shot. "What's the plan?"

Kostya yanked Dima closer to him with his broken fingers, then pulled two of the Semtex grenades out of his hand. "Do you know what these are?"

Dima's eyes got wide. He nodded.

"You get to decide if your comrades live or die. If you can convince them to go on without you and go past our convoy as they head to the lab...they live. If they fail to do so. They die."

"They'll never go for it," Dima whispered.

"Then you will have killed your friends."

Dima looked at Kostya, then at Linc, then back again. "Why should I trust you? You've probably killed everybody at the lab already."

Kostya raised his eyebrow, allowing Dima time to think. The man was at least fifty years old; he hadn't survived in the Russian Army for so many years by being a fool. He realized that if he was still alive at this point, Kostya didn't want to kill him, especially after seeing that he could have easily taken out his tank and the Vityaz with the Semtex grenades.

Dima nodded. "Let me go talk to them."

Kostya snorted. "I'm not going to trust you that far. Let's go into your tank together and you can talk to them over the radio."

THEY DIDN'T HAVE much time.

As far as Kostya was concerned they'd used up all of their luck on this mission, and he wasn't counting on the NH-90 helicopter to actually be able to touch down and scoop all of their asses up, which was why he was driving as fast as he could. Still, they were at least twenty-four more hours with the way the roads were, and that didn't even account for all the reconnoitering they'd have to do at the border, in the fucking *good* weather.

They'd left Dima duct-taped in his tank and the Vityaz was on its way to the decimated compound. All communication devices there at the labs had been destroyed, but the bad part was that satellite communications would be up by the time the supply truck arrived so they could report into St. Petersburg and Moscow.

"Status." Kostya waited to hear what his team had to say. Landon, Mateo, and Ryker were with him, so they didn't say anything. They'd abandoned their Vityaz in the forest, and were now down to the two tanks and the SUSI.

"We're good," Linc reported from the tank.

"We're keeping up," Sebastian reported from the SUSI.

Nolan didn't report, which meant bad things for Iris.

"Gideon?" Kostya prompted.

"Talked to Commander Clark. He's still cutting through all the bullshit. According to the International Weather Bureau, a helicopter should be able to take flight in three to four hours."

"So it's just whether or not they'll fly into Russia," Kostya said.

"Yep."

At least the fuel situation was good since they stole Dima's extra supply.

"I'm going to call him," Kostya said.

Gideon chuckled. "He was expecting it."

As he hit the accelerator even harder, Kostya pulled

his glove off with his teeth and pulled out his satellite phone. He hit the number for his commander.

"Kostya," Simon Clark answered. "How do you see things?"

"One of the scientists will die for sure if we don't get that helicopter. If the snow lets up, that will allow for Moscow to send in their helicopters to intercept us. We'll have to abandon the vehicles and do evasive maneuvers in the forest as we make our way to Finland. Then we'll have to deal with all the shit at the border while we're handling the scientists, so that's going to be fun." He knew Simon would hear his sarcasm.

"And the injured woman?"

"She'll die."

There was silence as Clark assimilated the information.

"Understood. Expect a call in an hour." His commander hung up.

Kostya gritted his teeth. He respected the hell out of his commander, but this was one of the times he hated the fact that his old commander Liam McAllister had retired. Yeah, Simon was great, but Liam had more backdoor channels and was definitely willing to push the envelope and even break the rules when necessary.

"Gideon," Kostya called out.

"Yeah?"

"Find a spot that's three hours out where a helicopter can land, but also close to the Karelia Forest's interior so that we can head out."

"Got it."

"Nolan, I want you to work to get Iris ready for travel."

"Shit."

Kostya didn't say anything more, he knew his team

was on it. Every kilometer that he drove, the snow got lighter and lighter and the minutes ticked by like hours. At precisely sixteen hundred hours his satellite phone rang.

"Whatchya got?" Kostya answered.

"The Finns will land in Russia," his commander said. "Can you give me your coordinates?"

"I can do better than that. Gideon is figuring out a place for them to land that will be timed with a let-up on the snow."

"Good. I'll call him."

"Will it be the NH-90?"

"Affirmative." Clark hung up.

Kostya knew that it had defensive capabilities and would be able to pick up his team and all of the scientists, but the helicopter had no offensive capabilities. Would Moscow be on the lookout for a helicopter, or would they be looking for their convoy?

Kostya peered out of his periscope and noted how much more visibility he had. Gideon was right again; at the rate this was going, it would be clear enough for the helicopter to fly out of Finland and meet here in Russia. Maybe this *could* work after all.

It was another hour and a half, and the snow was down to just dusty flakes.

"Around this bend, then we stop," Gideon said into the comm system.

Kostya checked his watch. They were forty-five minutes early, but that was good. It gave them time to prep Iris and the other scientists if need be. He wanted the transfer onto the NH-90 to be as seamless as possible.

After the curve, Kostya saw what Gideon had been talking about. There on the left side of the road was some kind of rest stop. Nothing commercial, it just had a carve-out for vehicles to pull over, and there was some kind of tiny building that was a little bigger than a port-o-john.

All the comforts of home.

It wasn't much, but add that area with the road and it would be enough for a helicopter to land.

Another score for Gideon Smith.

"Everybody out of the tanks," Kostya said into his mic as he parked the tank underneath a cover of spruce and pine trees. As soon as the two tanks were parked the men got out and headed to the SUSI to see how they could be of help to the scientists.

Kostya heard Gwendolyn Lord before he saw her.

"There is nothing wrong with me. Of course, I'll be able to walk under my own steam." She sounded exasperated.

"What do you mean we might have to walk? I thought I heard someone mention a helicopter," Harold Rice whined.

"Dr. Rice, we'll know in an hour what is happening. In the meantime, we have to plan for all contingencies. Complaining about things won't help the situation," Kostya said.

"There you go, Harold. Maybe since a man is telling you this, you'll actually listen," Doctor Lord said. She was clearly sick of the man.

"How is Doctor Robinson?" Kostya asked as he turned his attention to Nolan. He saw that a makeshift stretcher had been created. No wonder Linc had grabbed two of the pool cues when they'd left the lab— they were perfect for handles. Linc was the world's best scrounger.

Nolan smiled. It was his fake one that only his team

would see through. He looked down at Iris, whose eyes were at half-mast. "We're doing good, aren't we, champ?"

She lifted her arm a couple of inches then stuck her thumb in the air. Nolan bent down to listen to what she said.

"Yep," he looked up at Kostya. "She's raring to go."

Kostya looked down at his watch again. Just twenty-five more minutes. He gave his medic a head tilt, and Nolan scrambled out of the SUSI. They both walked a few meters away to where they wouldn't be heard.

"How bad?"

"She told me that the same guy who beat and killed Benjamin Leeds also beat her. If it hadn't been for another Russian pulling him off her, she would have died too. She has internal bleeding, and it's causing the fever. All this time I thought I was just dealing with an infection that I could kill off with antibiotics, but those won't work. She needs surgery that I can't perform."

Kostya nodded and Nolan jumped into the back of the SUSI. Kostya spoke into the comm. "Everybody but Nolan, huddle up.

"I have good news, Finland has agreed to fly over the border and pick us up. Even better, the helicopter they're going to send is big enough for all of us."

"Hot damn!" Ryker grinned.

"Hold your horses," Gideon admonished. "You're dealing with Lieutenant Kostya Barona. He doesn't believe in good news. Please wait for the other shoe to drop if you don't mind."

Kostya's lip twitched. "As I was saying, we need a plan for when the helicopter doesn't show up. Now I actually do believe it will show up eventually, just somewhere else, and we'll have to hoof it to the next rendezvous point."

"Why walk it?" Sebastian asked.

"Because the supply truck will have made it to the lab by then, and they'll have probably sent helicopters of their own from St. Petersburg to look for two tanks and a Vityaz," Linc answered.

"Exactly," Kostya concurred. "We can't afford to just wait around like sitting ducks. We'll need to be as far away from the vehicles as possible."

Everyone nodded.

"Gideon, you're going to take point—"

The distinctive sound of a helicopter in the distance stopped Kostya's instructions. His heart jumped and he had to fight off a grin. His satellite phone rang. It was Clark.

"Do you see them?" Clark asked when he picked up.

"Affirmative."

"Hurry the hell up. Let's finish this thing. I want to see all this data you're bringing home."

Kostya could hear the anticipation in his boss' voice.

"Where are they coming from?"

"They sent it from their military base, but they're going to land back at Joensuu. It'll be a twenty-five-minute ride. The hospital there is expecting Doctor Robinson."

"Simon, tell them to prep for surgery. According to Nolan, she has internal bleeding."

"On it. Anything else?"

"Yeah. Thank you."

"Just doing my job."

The helicopter came into view and his men flew into action. By the time the helicopter landed, everyone was in position, with Iris Robinson being loaded in first. Kostya saw Nolan's look of relief when he was confronted with a makeshift bed and an IV hanger and a bag already set up with what Kostya had to assume was filled with antibiotics.

Kostya and Linc were the last ones in before they slammed the door shut. Kostya sent the pilot a thumbs up, then they were up in the air.

He looked down and gave the Russian snow the finger.

I'm going home!

He sat back in his seat and felt just a tiny bit of tension begin to fade.

Then Kostya was thrown up against the door and Linc fell against him.

What the fuck?!

The helicopter had just made a deep dive to the left.

Hell, have we lost power?

The pilot was yelling something in Finnish. Then he switched to English.

"Russians!"

Kostya turned and smashed his face against the window. He saw a gray helicopter coming up fast on their right. It zipped upwards. *Not good, so not good.* It would have the firing advantage. Their helicopter dipped again, then zoomed straight for the clouds. The NH-90 might only be defensive, but it had game.

"Mi-35M," Sebastian shouted out. "No missiles."

"It's our lucky day!" Ryker shouted.

"Boss, grenades!" Linc shouted at him as he twisted his grenade launcher onto his rifle. Kostya handed over a grenade that he fished out of his cargo pants pocket.

"Somebody tell the pilot we need to get in front and above and that we're shooting from this side. Three hundred meters."

"Four hundred," Linc corrected as he finished loading the grenade and slammed open the door.

Kostya looked up and saw Sebastian leaning over the pilot's seat.

Bullets hit their helicopter, and once again the pilot dipped and turned. He was doing the absolute wrong thing!

"Sebastian!" Kostya yelled. His man waved his arm at him without looking back. Kostya knew he was telling the pilot what he needed to do.

When their helicopter turned again, Linc and Kostya saw the Russian helicopter behind and above them, but Linc didn't take the shot. It was too close and the blast from the Russian helicopter above them would blow their copter all to hell. They needed to get above them.

"Sebastian!" Kostya shouted again. "Get us vertical now!"

He watched his man start climbing over the pilot's seat, then felt their helicopter zoom up, causing almost everyone to lose their footing. But Kostya was prepared. He'd had his hand braced against the doorway, and had his other hand holding Linc in place as he continued to aim the grenade launcher.

Kostya held his breath and watched Linc wait until they outpaced the Russian helicopter.

One hundred and fifty meters.

Two hundred meters.

Take the fucking shot!

Two hundred and fifty meters.

Take the fucking shot!

Three hundred and fifty meters.

Linc depressed the trigger.

Bullets ripped across the side of the NH-90, then Linc was flung backward.

The Russian helicopter didn't explode, but Linc had

hit the rotor mast! Kostya grinned as the propellers melted off the helicopter right before the machine began to plummet. He turned and saw that Nolan had dragged Linc to the center of the floor and had a tourniquet around his upper leg. From what Kostya could see, the high-powered bullet had not been a direct hit, thank God. Instead, it had grazed the outer part of Linc's lower thigh.

Kostya turned to look over the rest of the passengers. "Anyone else hit?"

Everyone shook their heads.

"Sebastian, ETA."

His man leaned over the pilot's seat, then yelled back to Kostya. "Thirty minutes."

Kostya knelt next to Linc. His color was good and he grinned at Kostya. "You thought I waited too long to pull the trigger."

"Yeah. But I knew I could trust you."

"That's why I like being on your team."

"If you like it so damn much, don't get yourself shot next time."

13

GODDAMMIT, WHY HADN'T SHE RESPONDED TO HIS TEXT?

Goddammit, he was acting like his niece!

I need to put my phone down and concentrate on the job. But why hasn't Lark texted back?

Kostya had his phone sitting on the table in front of him. The sound and vibration were both off, so there wouldn't be any interruptions during the briefing. Still, Linc caught him checking it and he saw his lip twitch upward. It made him want to nudge against his braced leg, just because.

Kostya grinned when Lincoln moved his chair so he could shift his injured leg farther away from him.

Kostya leaned into him. "I'd never actually hit you where you're injured," he assured his man under his breath

"I like being careful," Linc responded just as quietly. "Who is she?"

"Now let me tell you what our scientists have discovered in relation to the bioagent so far," Commander Clark said from the podium

Kostya and Linc sat up straighter from their seats in the back.

"Doctor Lord was immediately taken to Fort Detrick to work with the NBACC."

Landon's hand shot up.

"That's the National Biodefense Analysis and Countermeasures Center," Simon answered without waiting to hear Landon's question. Landon put down his arm and nodded.

"That was two days ago, and from what I'm hearing there's already good news." Simon looked up and gave a nod to Gideon. "From all the comps you and the team pulled, all of the computer analysts at Fort Detrick were able to confirm that Grigor's real data made it to Moscow. What they were actually given was a pathogen that was a placebo. The man was definitely paranoid."

"As he should be," Kostya muttered.

"And the actual pathogen?" Kostya asked from the back of the room.

"Well, that's not quite handled. Our scientists have definitely confirmed Doctor Lord's findings, but they have not found a way to counteract it. That's something they are working on. In the briefing I attended, I was told that..." Kostya watched with a small smile as his boss started reading from his notes. It was nice to see he wasn't the only one who struggled with all the scientific jargon. Simon began talking again. "I was told that they are working to determine exactly how the metabolic host cells are triggered by the pathogen so they can create effective countermeasures." The man looked back up at the team. "The scientist who was talking was confident they'd get this accomplished. I liked him, he said that he and his team had always completed their missions." Simon grinned.

Kostya looked around at his men, and they were all grinning as well. He looked down at his cell phone and pressed his thumb against it to unlock it. Still no response from Lark.

Dammit!

I LOVE MY JOB.

I love my job.

Lark held her breath as she walked past the pile of feces in the hallway. Damn, it didn't look like dog or cat poo, therefore it must be...

I love my job.

She thought back to the crack house that she had been invited to by Jeremy, a fourteen-year-old boy, three years ago. She tried to tell herself that this shitty tenement wasn't so bad. But it was bad. And it literally was shitty.

She pulled the sleeve of the raggedy hoody she'd bought at a thrift store over her hand before knocking on the door. She could hear the TV blasting inside, but nobody answered. This was where Jay Jensen lived, she knew this was a solid address. Lark balled her hand into a fist and pounded on the door.

"Nobody's home," a man yelled.

"It's about Candy," Lark yelled back. She knew that Jay had gotten Candy tangled up in a scheme that he was working at his old company, so she hoped that by mentioning her name he would open the door.

"Nobody's home, and I don't know anyone named Candy."

Lark rolled her eyes, then pounded again.

"Go away."

Lark continued to pound on the door.

After at least four solid minutes of pounding, the door was flung open, and she was confronted by a man who was her height, but just as wide. His shoulders were huge, and he looked mean.

Lark was blasted with the noxious scent of garlic and tequila as he shoved her and she fell back two steps.

I should have known.

"Get out of here."

"Your wife is in trouble."

He squinted at her, then his eyes shifted up and right.

Great, here come the lies.

"I haven't seen her in months."

"The last time she and I got together, which was three weeks ago, she told me that you'd been working together," Lark countered.

"She lies a lot. What's more, she's almost my ex-wife."

"Something's wrong. She's not at her apartment, and she hasn't shown up to work. I'm worried about her."

"And that's my problem why?"

Spittle hit her face and she wiped it off with her sleeve. "Don't you care that she might be in trouble?"

He propped his hand on the doorframe and leaned in, his belly almost touching her. "No, I really don't." He leered. "Why is it important to you?"

Because she's my friend, and because of you, I'm afraid she's got really bad people after her.

Lark stood her ground. "Because she's my friend, and I'm worried about her."

He pushed into her face so that they were almost nose

to nose. "Who the fuck are you? And what's in it for me if I help you?"

"I told you, I'm a friend of Candy's."

"If you're such a good friend of Candy's, shouldn't you know more than me? She and I haven't been together for over four months." He started to cough. He couldn't seem to stop. She could hear the phlegm rattling around in his lungs. He coughed some up, then Lark jumped back as he spit right next to where her left tennis shoe would have been. He gave her a brown-toothed grin.

"Look, Jay, Candy told me that she's still involved with you. She said that you and she have been working together on a project and that she meets with you at least twice a week, so that's why I thought you might know something."

"That's horseshit. The bitch is lying." He shoved her shoulder. "I haven't seen her in months, now get the fuck out of here." He backed up and started to close the door.

Damn, I'm losing him.

"Look, Jay, I don't care what you and Candy have been up to. It doesn't matter. She and I have our own situation that we're working on. I think something is really wrong. I was really hoping that you could think of something, somewhere or someone she might have gone to when she went on the run."

He frowned and gave her a slow, long look. "What kind of situation do you have going on?"

Gotcha.

"Nothing you need to know about."

His beady eyes shone. Not only was he sleazy, but he was also opportunistic and greedy.

"Don't be like that. If Candy is into something, then I should know about it. I can probably help. I taught her everything she knows. Especially if it has something to do with the bank she's working at."

Lark swallowed down a smile. Candy had told her what she'd been searching for at First United Commerce Bank, but Jay had always held some information back. Now was her opportunity to find out how Sanofi Manufacturing and Analytics was using the bank.

"I don't know, Jay, Candy has been helping me out a lot. I don't see how she could be doing even more for me. I just need to know where to find her," Lark said lightly.

"That's what I'm telling you, Candy always needs direction. She's a doer, not a leader. On the deal I'm running, I had to tell her exactly, and I mean *exactly* what to look for and where to look for it."

"Really?"

"Yep. Almost all of Sanofi's banking is done through Citibank, so that was why I was surprised to see these printouts with Candy's little shitty bank on them. I knew right then that they were lining their pockets, and I could get me a piece of the action as soon as I knew how much money was involved and how they were paying themselves. As soon as I knew that I could scare the shit out of them and they'd have to cut me in on some of the action or I'd blow their whole little scheme to the company president, then where would they be?"

"And," Lark rolled her eyes, "your plan worked so damn well, that Candy's on the run. Tell me, Jay, did you ever make any money, or did you realize you were up against the big boys and that's why you got rid of everything you had?"

Jay's eyes shifted, then he glared back at Lark. "It was a damn good plan, until Candy got scared. Pathetic bitch!"

"I take that to mean you got nothing."

"Well, I got something now," he growled at her. "I want in on your project."

"Why in the world would I give you a piece of my action? When you couldn't even see through the Sanofi op?" Lark asked incredulously. Again, she choked down a smile, knowing she was damned close to getting some names from Jay.

"If you tell me what you two are up to, and make it worth my while, that might help my memory," he wheedled.

Lark turned as if to walk away.

"Hey, where are you going?" He grabbed her shoulder and squeezed, then pulled her hard enough to bruise.

"I'm going home. You're right, you don't know anything, otherwise, you would have already tracked Candy down. I'm not going to waste my time." She tried to pull away from him, but he wouldn't loosen his grip.

"There was no need for me to track her down. I told you, I didn't need her anymore." He paused and gave her another once-over. "But you do, now, don't you?"

"I'll find her some other way."

"Really? How?" Jay sneered. "Candy don't have many friends. Coming to me was the best shot you had. Now you're stuck with me, and I want in. Don't try to kid me. You might not be dressed fancy right now, but you smell good and your hair's pretty. You have money. So, this situation you and my kind-of-ex have worked out is probably worth something."

Lark turned to look Jay in the eye. "What I have going on is easy money. I just need to know some information on my dying dad's accounts so I know which way to push." Lark paused and smiled. "I mean *guide* him, as he's divvying up everything between me and my sisters."

"Shit, my girl sure has her fingerprints all over that fucking bank," Jay cooed. He rubbed his hands together. "How much is dear old dad worth?"

"Well, I don't know, now do I?" Lark asked sarcastically. "I don't know what's in Daddy's accounts because Candy's running scared, and that's your fault. You need to call off the dogs."

He winced. "I don't think I can." Jay looked worried, then he dipped his hand underneath his t-shirt and proceeded to scratch his armpit. Lark managed not to cringe.

"When all of this started, I found out that those execs were up to something that they were trying to hide, and they were hiding, funneling, or laundering the money through First United Commerce, Candy's bank. Come on, it was a gift from God, or some such shit. I definitely was meant to deal myself in. I just had to find a way to leverage Candy and get her on board."

"How's that working out for you?" Lark asked sarcastically.

"Since Candy took a powder, not so good."

"So basically, it's in your best interest for me to track down Candy, too." Lark surmised.

"Not on this shit, it isn't. I got rid of all the papers I took from the office, and I deleted all the e-mails that Candy sent me on the guys. But I was counting on the cash that this operation was going to bring in. I promised my bookie I'd be able to pay him. You coming by here today is my *new* gift from God."

"Clarify your thinking for me, Jay."

"It's easy. You're rich. You might be holding out for *really* rich when daddy dies and you cheat your sisters, but you have money now."

"Maybe," Lark said slowly, reeling him in.

"You're like everyone else. Whether you're scared, rich, hungry, horny, mad, or afraid like those execs, I can always smell it on you. You're rich. I want my cut upfront."

"You mean your bookie wants his cut."

"Same thing."

Between Jay's garlic breath and body odor, and the smell of shit wafting its way from down the hall, Lark wanted out of the building...now!

"You're right, I can wrangle up some cash. I'll go to the ATM and meet you and give it to you. Would that be incentive enough for you to give me information?"

His lips compressed into a snarl. "It'd have to be more than some measly three hundred dollars in twenties from an ATM. I want at least two grand."

Lark laughed. "No way." She turned and took two steps down the hallway, breathing out of her mouth.

"Fifteen hundred," Jay yelled after her.

"A grand," she yelled over her shoulder.

"Fine. A grand."

She walked back to his door. "But I'm not bringing that kind of money here. Hopkins isn't the best part of Baltimore and isn't exactly known for its hospitality. You're going to have to meet me somewhere safe."

"Like where?"

"Meet me at the Starbucks on Ashland."

"That's too damned far."

"Suck it up. If you want a thousand dollars, I want a latte."

ARE YOU AVAILABLE FOR DINNER THIS WEEKEND?

Lark tingled just reading the text. It was as if she could hear Kostya's rough velvet voice and that slight sexy accent, right here, talking to her. It had been almost fifteen long nights since the kiss, and every night since then she had replayed being in his arms.

She itched to type back a YES, but she honestly didn't know. She was too damned worried about Candy. If she found out something, she *had* to follow up on the lead.

The door opened again, and Jay Jenson walked in.

It's a great day in the neighborhood, he's put on a collared shirt. Who knew that was possible?

He didn't bother with the line; instead, he scanned the store and headed for her table in the back. Lark found herself wincing at the man again as he adjusted his balls. What in the world had Candy ever seen in this man?

"You got my money?" he demanded as he loomed over her.

"Have a seat and stay awhile." Lark smiled sweetly.

"You got my money?"

"I said, have a seat." This time her tone wasn't so sweet. Her eyes were hard, and he sat down. "Jay, I've been thinking; ten Benjamins is a lot of money, and I want my money's worth. Not only do I want to know all the relatives and friends that Candy might be staying with, I want to know your associates."

His bushy eyebrows furled. "That's a no."

Lark laughed. "If you want your money, you better change that no to a yes."

He stood up and shoved his fists onto the table, pushing his foul-smelling face into her space. "If you don't want me following you home and taking that money, and taking whatever else I want, you'll just hand it over now, like the little scared prissy bitch you are."

Lark leaned back in her chair, crossed her arms, and laughed.

"You don't know my friends. My very *good* friends. One look at them and you would wet your pants. I didn't have them come inside with me because I said I could handle this alone, but if I press one button on my cell phone, they'll come in and rip you apart. I suggest you sit down, Jay."

He looked over his shoulder, then sat down.

"Wait a minute, I don't believe you." He started to stand up.

It took less than ten seconds for Lark to find the picture she wanted. She pulled it up and showed it to Jensen. "Unfortunately, only two of my friends could be here this afternoon. The youngest one, Nic, has a date." She tilted her phone so that both she and Jay could see the picture of Nic, Kostya, Cullen, and herself that Cullen had had Asher take of them when they'd finally gotten out of their cage after they crossed into Pakistan.

"Who are those guys?" Jay gulped.

"I told you, friends," Lark said easily. So now that we have that established, you understand how kind I've been with you. I could have just brought my friends to your apartment and demanded the information, but that's not my style. I leave that kind of crap to you and your cronies."

Lark reached into the front of her hoodie pocket and pulled out the bank envelope and put it on the table, along with a pen and notepad. "Now start talking."

"She has a sister, she lives—"

"I know about Rosie. I've already checked in with her. Try again."

He pushed back in his chair, tipping it so the front legs were in the air. "Do you know about her half-sister, Dawn?" he asked slyly.

Lark shook her head and picked up her pen. "Tell me about her."

"Dawn's a cocktail waitress over at the MGM National Harbor Casino. She's a looker. Bet she rakes in the tips." He licked his lips.

What a sleazeball.

"What's her last name?"

"Shit, I don't know. It started with a T. Taylor or Trevor or something. I only met her twice."

"I need more names than that," Lark pressed.

"There's that bastard of a boyfriend she had. She was always talking about how he arranged for a limo for their senior prom. She still had the hots for him twelve years later. Go talk to him." Jay looked over his shoulder. "I'm hungry."

"Too bad. What's the guy's name?"

"Wayne Foster. She talked about him so much, can't help but remember that bastard. Always comparing me to him. Did he ever take her out to Benny's for Ladies Night? Hell no!"

"Yeah, you sound like a real sweetheart."

"You got it." Jay gave her a smug smile.

Lark leaned in. "Now listen to me. I think Candy's running because she got really scared. I think you did something stupid, and these guys you've been working with targeted her."

Jay smirked. "I ain't done nothing."

"Yeah, you have. You got her involved with some shady shit over at Sanofi. You probably promised these guys the moon, then couldn't deliver, so you got Candy to do some searches on the men you were working with, in hopes that she could get you some leverage. And then when things got hairy for her, you threw her to the wolves. How close am I?"

"You've got quite the imagination."

"Hmmmm."

Jay dropped his chair down and it hit hard. He snatched the envelope up off the table. "If you see the bitch, tell her we're through. I'll sign the divorce papers."

He knocked the chair over as he left the coffee shop.

Lark looked down at her latte and crinkled her nose. She couldn't finish it after he'd breathed on it, she'd have to get a new one. She pulled her phone out of her pocket and looked at the picture and focused in on Kostya. She trailed her finger over his face.

I have it bad.

She flicked over to her messages and looked at Kostya's text for a long moment. It was Thursday. Chances were she'd have a better chance of finding Wayne and Dawn during the weekend, especially Dawn if she worked as a cocktail waitress. So dinner tomorrow, and work on Saturday.

Lark grinned.

I'm not rationalizing to see him sooner. I'm not.

Lark texted Kostya to arrange dinner.

14

"FEEL LIKE GAMBLING ON SATURDAY?" LARK ASKED WHEN Amy picked up her phone.

"Uhm, no."

Lark smiled. She knew that answer was coming. Amy was quite the little prude when it came to almost everything. It came down to growing up with a raging alcoholic drug-addicted, mother.

"Okay then, how about dressing up and letting me buy you an overpriced soda at an upscale nightclub where you might meet an attractive man?"

Amy snorted. "You already told me we're going to a casino, I'm not going to be meeting a man that I'm going to be interested in."

"Yeah, but you'll have fun looking them over and making up their backgrounds and why they're at the bar and if they're cheating on their wives. You love that kind of thing."

Amy didn't answer.

"Please?"

"Why are you going to a casino? Is this for one of your stories?"

"Kind of. One of my sources has gone missing. I'm tracking down her half-sister. I've managed to convince— i.e. bribe—the restaurant operations manager to find out if they had a Dawn T working at the casino. He explained that there was a Dawn Tanner who would be working on Saturday. I'm hoping that she'll know where Candy is."

"What in the hell did you bribe him with? A new car, or a spin around one of their luxury suites?"

"I admit that when I passed over the five hundred dollars that I might have flirted a bit, but I did not promise him sex. He was a little guy and I wasn't interested."

"Oh my God. Oh my God. Hell yes, I'll go with you. And do you know why? Because you are going to tell me every teeny tiny fucking detail about your date with the Navy SEAL. But my guess is, there was absolutely nothing teeny tiny about him."

"I was planning on telling you."

"Planning, shmanning. Not good enough. It's been over two weeks and I've heard nothing. It goes against the best friend code."

Lark looked down at her phone, then walked over to the mini-bar in her hotel room and grabbed a Toblerone from the basket. She needed chocolate before getting into this conversation. She tore it open and opted for the bed instead of the desk.

"Lark, are you still there?"

"Yeah, I'm here," she said with her mouth full.

Amy laughed. "What are you eating?"

"Toblerone."

"Toblerone? That means you're in a hotel. Where are you?" Amy asked.

Lark swallowed her bite of chocolate. "I'm at the Marriott here in Baltimore."

"Is that where your source lives?"

"Yeah. It's also where the defense contractor is headquartered. I just got in from New York yesterday, otherwise, I would have called you."

"You *could* have called before then and told me if you slept with a SEAL."

"And I *would* have called you if I slept with a SEAL."

"Dammit, Lark, I was counting on you." Amy sighed dramatically. "Do you realize how sad our lives are? Do you?"

Lark took another huge bite out of the candy bar. "Yes," she mumbled. "Yes, I do."

"Well, your life isn't that sad. Your life is exciting. You get to traipse all over the world and act like Nancy Drew checking out stories. I'm the one who manages a rundown little restaurant here in D.C.."

"Hey, you're living your dream."

"If I was living my dream, I would *own* this crappy little restaurant," Amy protested.

"When are you going to let me invest?" Lark asked for the umpteenth time.

"When pigs fly. Can we move on? I want to know how in the hell you could have put on my blue dress and not gotten laid."

Lark tossed the phone down on the bed and grabbed another pillow and put it behind her, then twisted until she was totally comfortable. "Amy, the man was amazing. He talked me into the whole thing saying there wouldn't be sex, but he would want a kiss goodnight. He was sooooo smooth."

"Tell me more," Amy sighed.

"The dinner was great. I learned so much more about him. You know those special forces guys are smart, right?"

"What do you mean?"

"Everybody thinks that they end up not making it as a SEAL because of BUD/S, and for the Deltas because of OTC, but it's so much more than that. These guys have to be *smart*. I mean really intelligent. Now some of them act like they're in junior high, but don't let it fool you."

"So does Kostya act like he's in junior high?"

"Nope, he's one hundred percent grown man." Lark's entire body tingled just thinking about him. "Amy, he's well-read, and the man could talk current events. We didn't have the same views on things, but when we disagreed about something it wasn't a big deal, we would just explain our different points of view and debate them and move on, no harm no foul. He actually *listened* to what I had to say."

"Okay, so the dinner was fabulous, then what?"

"The only real problem was the fact that he wanted to pay for the hotel room."

"Hah! He *did* want to have sex!"

"Nope. Well yeah, probably." Lark wiggled deeper into the pillows. "But the reason he wanted to pay for the hotel was that he said he couldn't come up to Baltimore for the date because he was on call. He was really over the top." Lark picked up the phone and whispered into it. "And you know what? I loved every minute of it."

"Of course you did!" Amy squealed. "Who wouldn't? Now tell me about the kiss!"

"So at the end of the night he walks me to my room, and we go inside. Amy, we know I've had this phobia about big men in my personal life, and we know why, but damn."

"Are you over it? Or did you have to fake it?"

"Apparently for him, I'm way the hell over it. There was just something about being cuddled against his broad chest, being held in his arms that was amazing. And Amy, he didn't just swoop in for a kiss. Uh-huh, he went all coaxy-like. Before he even really got started, I was pulling his head down and wanting a deeper kiss. His fingers were sifting through my hair, and when I touched his chest it was nothing but hard muscle and I wanted to rip his clothes off. I couldn't believe it was even me."

Lark waited for Amy to respond, but she got nothing.

"Say something!"

"I can't. I think I just spontaneously orgasmed."

Lark giggled.

"And you're telling me nothing more happened that night, it just ended with a kiss?"

"That's what I'm telling you. He was all noble and said that's what he promised and he was sticking to it. But, he asked me to go out for breakfast the following morning."

"Yay! Morning sex!"

"Not so much. His team got called away."

"Boo hiss, no morning sex."

"My thoughts exactly. Uh, Amy?"

"Yeah."

"Did I tell you I have a date with Kostya for tomorrow night?"

"*What*?" Amy screamed. "If you have a date with him on Friday, why in the hell are we talking about meeting up on Saturday?"

"I told you, I have to track down Dawn on Saturday. I don't have a choice."

"Go flirt with that guy again and see if she works on Sunday. Or better yet, see if she works on Monday; your hours are flexible. I have a job where I clock in. So don't give me this bullshit! I refuse to meet up with you back here in Baltimore on Saturday. Instead, I want to be hearing about a wild weekend of out-of-this-world sex with Kostya Barona. Do you get me?"

Lark laughed. Amy always made her laugh.

"I'm serious, Lark. My hymen has grown back, don't let it happen to you."

"I'm serious too. I've been having a bad feeling about Candy for over a week. There is no way I'm going to let her disappearance go on any longer than necessary."

"When you were doing all that flirting and giving away cash, why didn't you get her address?"

"I did. The address she had listed as her home was really a Chick-fil-A, and the phone number goes straight to voicemail. When I checked it out, I found out it's a burner phone. Hell, she's been working for the MGM for over a year, and she has a burner phone? Something's up. To begin with, you and I will be together, but once I place her, I'm going to send you away."

"Yeah, that's not happening. If she's all James Bondy, I want to make sure I have your back."

"What in the hell is going to happen to me in the middle of a casino?" Lark asked reasonably. "They have cameras everywhere. I just want to ask her a couple of questions."

"You promise not to go anywhere with her?"

"I promise."

"I still think you should be spending the weekend in bed with Mr. Muscles."

"You realize you're objectifying the man."

"Do you realize how long it's been since I've been close

enough to touch a man? Allow me a fantasy or two, I'm begging you."

Lark giggled at the way Amy whined. "Okay, we'll meet early before Dawn's eight o'clock start time. She works at the lounge called Blossom, so how about we arrive at seven, okay? And dress slutty, but nice."

"Do you want to define that?" Amy asked sarcastically.

"You're the one who taught me that, so don't even go there."

"Oh, you're right. Can do." Lark heard the smile in her friend's voice. "Do me a favor, take a picture of what you're wearing when you meet Kostya. I just want a visual. You get a triple-word score if you can get a picture of what he's wearing. And, you win double jeopardy if you sneak a pic of what he's *not* wearing."

"I'm hanging up now."

KOSTYA PUNCHED THE ELEVATOR BUTTON. This is not what he wanted to be doing. Well, it was, and it wasn't. He wanted to be taking Lark out to dinner in Virginia Beach, near his home, not here in Baltimore where she was staying in a hotel. It didn't matter how nice the hotel was, he was past this kind of bullshit in his life. When he zeroed in on a target, he knew what he wanted, and he wanted Lark in *his* home, in *his* arms, in *his* bed.

Get it together, Lieutenant.

By the time he got to her room and knocked on her door, he had his shit locked down tight. Lark opened the door and was holding up her phone with a wicked smile.

"Did you just take my picture?"

"Yep," she said with no compunction.

He watched as she sent a text.

"Would you care to explain?"

"I'm sending the pic to my friend Amy. I need her help tomorrow night and this is part of the incentive."

Kostya shook his head. "I don't want to know, do I?"

She looked up at him. "Nope, you don't." She took a step backward and he got a chance to take in what she was wearing.

Holy hell.

Red was definitely her color. As a matter of fact, she should never wear anything but red ever again.

"You look beautiful."

She bit her lip. Her lip which was coated with fire engine red lip gloss.

"Thanks," she beamed. "Hold on a second and I'll get my coat. Do you want to come in?"

"Yes. But I'll stay out here."

She gave him a confused frown, but said, "Okay."

He kept his foot in the door, keeping it open, and she quickly came back holding her clutch and coat. "This is a little bit of déjà vu."

"I was thinking the same thing."

"I probably should have suggested the restaurant. I wasn't thinking. I'm sorry."

Kostya kept his hand on her lower back as he ushered her down the hallway to the elevator. "It's okay, I somehow managed," he teased.

"Uhm, right." She shot him an apprehensive smile.

"Are you nervous?"

"Nervous no. Is my stomach a little fluttery? Yes."

Kostya pressed the button for the elevator and it slid open. There wasn't anyone inside, and they got in. He looked her over. The fact that such an accomplished and well-traveled woman, a woman who had stood up to an entire team of SEALs, was fluttery about a date with him was...interesting.

He smiled.

"Lark, you *do* know we're going to have a great time, and nothing's going to happen that you don't want to happen."

She turned to look him in the eye. "Well, that's what has me worked up. I'm not quite sure what I want to have happen."

He raised his eyebrow and she blushed.

"Okay, maybe a couple of possibilities have run through my head."

"Only a couple? Oh, Lark, I would have thought that somebody who studied creative writing at one point in time would have come up with hundreds of possibilities."

She took a deep breath. Her breasts pushed up against the top of her dress and Kostya did his best not to stare.

The elevator opened to the lobby. When they got to the revolving door, he helped her on with her coat. He tilted his head to the valet and the kid hustled to get a blue SUV that was parked up front.

"Kostya, did you rent that? Dammit, I wasn't thinking at all; you didn't need to do that. I rented a car when I took the train from Manhattan. I should have picked you up from the airport."

"Lark, take it easy. Everything's good." He slipped the tip to the valet and opened up the passenger seat for Lark and made sure her coat was tucked in before getting into the driver's seat.

"Seriously, Kostya, I'm usually more aware than this. I think it's the story I'm working on."

"Do you want to tell me about it?"

"Not right now. Right now I want to focus on you. I mean, our date."

When the light turned red he glanced over at her. "I'm looking forward to focusing on you too."

"Where are we going?" she asked.

"The Oceanaire. Rumor has it that I couldn't go wrong if I took you to a good seafood restaurant with an exceptional wine list."

"Rumor, huh?"

"Yep."

"And just where are you hearing rumors about me?"

He liked the sass in her voice.

"I'm not going to tell you. You're going to have to be a good investigative journalist and find out for yourself."

"Humph."

He chuckled. He could tell she hated not knowing what was going on.

"Can you give me a hint?" she wheedled.

"Where would be the fun in that? You're smart, you'll figure it out."

"Well, whoever told you is right. I love good seafood *and* good wine."

She crossed her legs and her dress rode up, offering him a better view of her thighs. Oh yeah, this was a good night.

"I take it I can't ask about that phone call you got the day we were going to see Cullen's baby?"

"'Fraid not."

"Has that ever been a problem for you in other relationships? The fact that you have to leave at the drop of the hat, and then can't tell your significant other where you've been or what you've been doing?"

Kostya gripped the steering wheel tighter and thought of Debra.

"It was for my ex-wife. I thought that I had made it clear before we got married, but she was sure that things would change after she put a ring on my finger. It was a mess."

Lark was quiet for so long that Kostya looked over at her. "What?"

"It's just that I hate that kind of thing. I hate it when someone thinks they can make someone change. It's a recipe for disaster."

"You've been there?"

"Oh, I lived it all right."

"Who was he?"

"No, I didn't explain that right. It was my grandmother. She had my mom when she was sixteen. Mom was literally a genius, so she was like Riya, got her Ph.D. crazy early, but she was into business. She married my dad, and he was in a car wreck before I was born. By then mom was left hanging onto the business they'd started and trying to handle a newborn."

"So she met someone new?"

"Nope, my grandmother did. Mom was working all the time, for years, and Nonnie was the one who raised me until I was nine. I don't remember a time when Grandpa Harris wasn't around, and—" She stopped herself.

"And?" Kostya prompted.

"And...and...it was a lot. Trust me, Nonnie and Harris were the poster children for dysfunctional."

"You know that now, but you didn't know that as a child," Kostya said as he pulled into the parking garage across the street from the restaurant.

"Oh no, you sure got that right, I didn't know that then.

Back then, I thought it was normal. I didn't realize I was just cannon fodder for Harris. No, that's not right, I was kind of like his hostage to keep Nonnie in line. Whenever she did something that he deemed unacceptable he'd take it out on me, and she'd immediately come back and heel like a good little doggie."

"And this was Beatrice Allen's mother?" Kostya asked incredulously. "I'm having a tough time picturing this."

"Yeah, well, believe it."

He noticed that her breath was coming faster. She was twisting the handle of her clutch.

"What kinds of things did he do?" Kostya bit out the question.

Lark cringed, then jerked backward, her shoulder hitting the car door.

Shit, this was not the time for any kind of aggression.

Kostya held out his hand, palm up. "I'm sorry, Honey," he said softly. "I didn't mean for that to come out so harsh. Do you want to talk about your time with your grandmother and Harris?"

Lark took a deep breath and then rolled her eyes. "Don't mind me," she said as she clasped his hand. "Just normal childhood trauma. No big deal."

She was good, her eyes were actually sparkling.

"I'm pretty sure you owe me a meal," she quipped.

"Honey, we can skip the restaurant. We can go back to your hotel room and order room service, or we can go back there and you can put on jeans and sneakers and we can eat at McDonald's and then go for a walk. And whatever we do, you can talk about your childhood or about all the other dresses you had to try on before you settled on this perfect red one. It's all up to you."

Lark started to giggle. "You're a goof."

"That's me, one goof at your service."

"Seriously, the moment you mentioned seafood and wine, my taste buds have been doing cartwheels. You can't deny me this."

"Honey, I don't intend to deny you anything," Kostya purred.

15

It had taken half the dinner for Kostya to start behaving normally around her. How could she have turned into Victim Number Two from a season of Law and Order? But she'd finally managed it. It was the Housewives of Simi Valley story that did it for him.

"How long did you work as a maid?"

"A little over three months," she answered. "You're right; I'm loving this lobster tail."

"I noticed." His blue eyes gleamed as she licked her fingers. He put another piece on her plate.

"Are you sure you don't want it?"

"Watching you savor my meal gives me more pleasure than me eating it," Kostya assured her. Heat hit her hard. Her stomach clenched as she processed his words and she pressed her thighs together...tight, trying to relieve the pulse of need roaring through her body.

"Now, tell me more about that story you wrote."

Lark blinked, trying to get her head together. "Uhm, yeah. Those women were a bunch of self-entitled bitches. They weren't just looking down their noses at the men and women they were taking advantage of, in some cases, they were abusing them. Blowing the lid off that scam was a highlight, let me tell you."

"I thought I'd read all of your articles, I missed this one."

"It was one of the first I ever wrote, so it didn't go national. It made it into the LA Times and that was it. But on the upside, I got to testify because three of the women didn't take their plea deals."

"You know, I'm having a hard time picturing you as a maid." Kostya leaned back in his chair and took a sip of his white wine. "Well, I take that back, I guess I could see you in a very specific French maid costume."

The way his eyes twinkled invited her to laugh at him, so she did. "You say some outrageous things, you know that don't you?"

"I like it when you smile, and I like it even better when you laugh."

Why does him saying that make me feel so good?

"You do realize, I was trying to do the same thing with you, don't you? That's why I started telling you this story."

"Well, it definitely caught my attention. Now I want to hear it all."

The waiter came and cleared their plates. "Would you like to see the dessert menu?" he asked.

"Yes," Kostya answered. "I'd like some coffee as well. What about you, Lark?"

"Coffee would be good," she nodded.

The waiter handed them each a dessert menu, and Kostya put his down on the table and looked at her expectantly. "So, how did you get hired?"

"I'd gotten wind of this story from the daughter of one of the women working for Esther Riggs. Her mother was born in America, but her parents were from Haiti. Her English wasn't good, and she wasn't quite sure what was happening. She lived at the Riggs' home, but she saw an envelope with her name on it, so she opened it. When she found a check from the government addressed to her, she took it to her daughter. That's when her daughter came to me. Leah and I knew each other when we had done a work-study course together."

"Why didn't you and Leah go to the police?"

"Her mother was scared to death. She knew that the Riggs family was well-known in the community and it would be her word against Esther Riggs when she went to the police. What's more, she knew she would be fired. Not only was she employed with the Riggs' but so was her sister, and then her husband was employed as a gardener with a friend of Esther's, and she knew that if she caused any problems, they'd all be fired."

"But wouldn't that be true if you investigated?"

The waiter came back with their coffee and they chose their desserts.

"Mirlande, Leah's mother, felt that if I investigated and found something, then the police couldn't cover it up and that justice would be served. So it was Leah's mom who got me the job at the Riggs' house."

"And you were a maid?"

"My backstory was that I aged out of the foster care system and I'd been living with a friend who wanted me to leave. Therefore I needed a place to stay. I didn't have a car, no education, and very little money. The only real problem with me is that I didn't have enough time paying into the system so that I could collect disability so I was worthless to her for her scams, but I think Esther really needed someone like me to be a gopher. I was put to work running all the errands. It was 'Stacy, go to the dry cleaners,' or 'Stacy, go back to Trader Joe's the avocados were too ripe,' or myriad other things."

"How come I'm betting you were always helpful getting the mail?" Kostya joked.

"Because you are a smart man." She grinned.

"After two months I was able to put a paper trail together that found fifteen women who were all members of the Simi Valley golf club participating in massive government disability fraud. Two of the women were married to doctors and were falsifying medical records for all of the staff to back up the disability claims. Hell, if they bothered to put just half the time, energy, and brainpower into something legitimate they could have made quite a tidy profit. But no, these greedy, self-serving shrews had to take advantage of innocent people who trusted them. People that they should have been protecting, not abusing."

Kostya was looking down at the table in front of her. She looked down to see what he was looking at.

"Ooops." Her peach tartlet had been smashed beyond all recognition.

"I think you were supposed to eat that."

She sighed. "Yeah, I think so too." She took a little bite and smiled. "It still tastes good."

"So what happened in the end?"

"Most all of these women ended up with time served and parole. But not good old Esther. She thought she was above all that, so she pleaded not guilty on all counts despite the advice of counsel. She ended up serving fourteen months. I got to testify. It was a beautiful thing."

"You're a bloodthirsty little thing, aren't you?"

"You can't have just noticed that."

Kostya laughed. "No. I got your number years ago, and in case I missed it, it was solidified when you were ready to rip all of our dicks off if we didn't help Samira and her two daughters."

Lark blushed. "I wasn't that bad."

"Actually, you were." He set down his empty coffee cup. "Are you done mangling your dessert?"

She nodded.

"Can I drive you back to your hotel and arrange to see you tomorrow for breakfast?"

"Let's discuss that when we get to my hotel room."

Lark enjoyed seeing his blue eyes darken.

"Did I tell you how much I liked this dress?" Kostya asked as he sat down in one of the two chairs that flanked the window in her hotel room. He watched her take off her earrings and put them on the dining room table in the living area of the suite, before walking toward him. She hesitated, looking at the empty chair, then back at him. He didn't want her to make the wrong decision.

He held out his hand. "Come here, Honey."

Her smile was pure temptress as she took his hand and allowed him to guide her onto his lap. "Like this?" she practically purred.

"Exactly like this," he praised her.

He eased his arm around her waist and pulled her closer to his chest. She didn't go easy, her body was a little stiff. He'd been replaying bits and pieces of what he'd come to know about Lark Sorensen over in his head, and adding tonight's tiny drama in the car. One day he wanted to hear the Harris stories, and he had no doubt there were many more than one. But right now, he concentrated on the fact that Lark was uneasy around big men, and God knew he fell into that category.

"I'm glad you agreed to go on a second date with me," he murmured. He waited for her to turn her head, he wanted to see what she was thinking.

"I am too."

"What do you think? Want to test to find out if that first kiss was a fluke?"

That got her head to turn. Her blue eyes were wide as she stared at him. "You don't think—?"

Kostya smiled warmly as he traced his fingers down the side of her jaw, letting them drop further, down to the rapid pulse in her neck. "No, I don't think it was a fluke. I can't tell you exactly where I was, but it was damned cold, and thinking about you warmed me the hell up, each and every time."

She began to relax against him, so talking was definitely the way to go. Kostya cupped her shoulder and coaxed her body to rest against his chest.

"Cold, huh?"

"Ice cold," he agreed. The way she melted into him warmed his heart.

My heart?

He suppressed a sigh. Of course his heart. Where else had this been heading?

"Lie back, *Sólnce.*"

"Solncè?" she repeated back to him, butchering the pronunciation. "What does that mean?"

"Little Sun." Lark gave him a quizzical look and he shrugged. "What can I say, I told you the thought of you keeps me warm."

She snuggled closer and Kostya tightened his hold.

"Sometimes the Russian in you really comes out. How old were you when you left?"

"Seven."

Lark leaned her head against his shoulder and looked up at him, her blue eyes cobalt. "So your parents got you out before the fall of the Soviet Union?"

She looked beautiful in his arms, her face lit by the moonlight coming in from the window. The idea of sharing the good and bad memories of his childhood with this woman didn't bring about the ache that he would have expected. Still, now wasn't the time, or the place.

Kostya reached up and brushed his thumb along her bottom lip. Her tongue peeked out and licked it. "My God, Lark, what you do to me."

She gave him a sultry smile. "I hope it's good, whatever it is."

"It is," he assured her. He adjusted her on his lap so that she straddled him. "I tell you what, let's save our childhood stories for some other time, all right?"

She looked down at where their lower bodies were connected, then looked back up at his face. She licked her lips and slowly smiled. "I can get on board with that."

Sifting his fingers through her silky hair, he cupped the back of her skull and guided her head down toward him, intently watching her lips as they parted right before they met his.

A pleasure unlike any he had ever felt before burst across his senses. The taste of Lark was sublime, honey and peaches and kindness and warmth slid across his tongue. Kostya closed his eyes, trying to bask in this moment of homecoming, because that is what it was. Every fiber of his being clamored for him to wrap his arms around her, tether her against him and never let her go.

She was it. He knew she was it. But she wasn't ready for this....for everything. He needed to take it slow.

As if she could feel his inner turmoil, she pulled away.

"Kostya?"

"I'm here, Baby."

She gave him a considering look and twined her arms around his neck. "You okay?" she asked.

"Oh yeah."

"Good," she drawled.

Lark tilted her head sideways and pressed her wet lips against his with a low hum. He felt her shudder and he thrust his tongue deep inside the recesses of her mouth. He plundered, needing to imprint her with everything he was, doing his best not to scare her. But his woman wasn't scared, no, not Lark Sorensen. She ground herself against his pulsing erection. He shot up off the chair, carrying her with him.

Lark sighed his name as she wrapped her legs around his waist and tightened her arms around his neck. He strode across her suite and shouldered opened the door to the bedroom, barely taking the time to admire the king-sized bed before easing her on top of the duvet. Lark whimpered when he began to unwind her limbs from his body.

"Don't go," she pleaded.

He pushed back the hair from her face and kissed her forehead.

"Not even the hounds of hell could force me away from you, sólnce."

His inclination was to kneel above her and begin the tantalizing journey of sliding up her dress, but he knew that big men made her uneasy. Lark wouldn't be comfortable having him loom over her, so Kostya slid down on the bed beside her and reached over to turn on the bedside lamp. She blinked twice, then smiled as her eyes adjusted.

"This time I'm definitely seeing a tangle of sheets in our future," she teased him, harking back to her words from their time in the Washington D.C. bar.

Kostya threw back his head and laughed.

Lark began loosening his tie. "Do you know how sexy it was when you showed up in a suit?"

"A tie does it for you, does it?"

"When *you're* wearing it, yeah." She slid it off his collar and threw it off the bed.

Pears and spice, that was what she smelled like.

I could get drunk on her scent.

She arched closer as he trailed kisses from her cheek to the back of her neck, surrounding himself in the silk of her fragrant hair. Lark jerked, her lips smashed against his, and once again he was lost in another one of her perfect kisses. One long, lush kiss merged into another, as Kostya pulled one clingy red sleeve down her arm, and then the other. Lifting his head, he hissed as he saw the barely-there lace bra enveloping Lark's breasts. Her nipples were hard buds that drew him like a moth to a flame.

"God, Lark," he groaned right before he drew one nub deep, laving it with his tongue.

"So good," she whined. Then she pushed him away and he felt her tearing at the buttons of his shirt. Kostya sat up and pulled his dress shirt from his pants and ripped it over his head. Lark shoved at his chest and he let her have her way as he fell onto his back.

Her fingers plowed through his chest hair as she slid upwards to place a trail of kisses up his neck until she reached his mouth. Again, Kostya tumbled into an onslaught of passion; Lark's taste and vitality were like a tsunami, but he needed more.

His hands reverently touched her smooth back, unhooking the clasp of her bra, then worked her dress down some more until he found that Lark was wearing a thong. He traced his fingers down her shadowed cleft until he reached her barely covered molten core. Need roared through him as he dipped his finger along the seam of her sex, glorying in the silky slide of her passion.

Lark ripped her mouth away from his and twisted her lower body. He couldn't understand her murmured words over the roaring rush of blood in his ears.

"What, Baby?" he asked looking into her eyes,

"More," she whispered. This time he heard her.

The sound of ripping lace permeated the room, and Kostya slowly pushed one big finger into the heart of Lark's body.

Her moans were like a song. Her shudders like a dance. Kostya watched her eyes, which were now navy, ensuring that his woman felt only pleasure by his touch. Before she could ask, he inserted another finger and he began a thrusting rhythm, mimicking what he soon intended to share with her.

Lark shoved her bra off and slid her breasts against his chest. Kostya wasn't sure who was being teased more, her with his chest hair, or him by the feeling of her tight little nipples. Lark opened her legs wider and he spread his fingers within her tight channel, preparing her for his penetration.

"Take off your pants."

He grinned at her order.

"It's cute that you think you're in charge."

Her head flew up and she glared down at him. "I *am* in charge. I'm the one who's on top."

Kostya chuckled as he pulled out his fingers and sucked on them. Lark drew in a deep breath. "You did not just do that."

"I'm pretty sure I did." He grasped her around her waist and cupped her ass, then rolled them over so that she was lying down beneath him.

"Hey," she began to protest.

Before she could get a good head of steam started, Kostya moved down, spread her legs wide and parted the lips of her sex, then swirled his tongue around her clit before sucking it into his mouth.

16

———

BREATHE.

Lark shook her head, gasping for air.

Breathe!

Her right hand hovered over Kostya's head, before landing on the soft gold pelt of his hair.

What was it I need to do?

She raised her knee, then let it fall to the side.

"Good girl," his rough voice rumbled. She could feel his whisper against her secret flesh, then the fiend pushed those wicked fingers into her needy body again.

"Kostya," she wailed. He suckled her clitoris and her head fell back onto the mattress, all thought wiped out of her mind. All she could do was feel.

A wicked tempo increased—in her body, in her mind, in her heart.

"Breathe," he whispered.

"Please?"

Is that my voice? Why do I sound so far away? So weak?

"Please, Kostya, I need you."

Lark sighed with relief as he stood up and unbuckled

his belt. Kostya's every movement caused a different muscle to flex. It was like she was seeing some kind of sensuous performance being played out just for her. When he shoved down his briefs, Lark sucked in a deep breath. Kostya's cock was as big as the rest of him. Her shocked gaze flew up to his face, and he must have read her trepidation.

"Easy, *sólnce*." Kostya walked to the side of the bed and sat down, his fingers sifting through her hair before gently kissing her. This kiss was different; Lark could taste herself, her pleasure, on his tongue. It was sinful. No, it wasn't; it was decadent.

Kostya wrapped his arm around her waist, pulling her onto his lap, giving her the time and reassurance she needed.

"I'm not a virgin," she said grumpily.

Kostya laughed.

"I believe the bill for equal rights for women should be ratified."

"So do I," Kostya said as he continued to chuckle.

Lark hit his arm.

"Fine. You're hung like a horse," she burst out. "Now you know what's bothering me. Satisfied?"

Kostya threw back his head and bellowed out a laugh. "You're killing me, *sólnce*."

"Better you than me," she muttered.

Kostya stroked his thumb over her nipple and she shuddered. He scraped his teeth against the skin behind her ear. "You're gorgeous," he whispered.

Lark twisted on his lap and grabbed his big hand that was resting on her tummy and dragged it between her legs.

"You feel like liquid silk." His whispered words made

her quiver and his clever fingers were sending her to the stars.

The warm duvet cushioned her as she reached up for Kostya. She had to wait as he sheathed himself, then he was there, right there, taking her into his arms. How could she be worried about anything when she felt this safe?

Lark trembled when Kostya parted her folds. When the head of his cock nudged against her tender flesh it felt like the most intimate moment of her life. Their eyes locked and she could swear she saw something far beyond caring, something so much deeper than just affection, but how could that be?

"Are you ready?" His lips brushed against hers.

She nodded.

Slowly he pressed forward, squeezing his girth into her tight channel.

Breathe.

Lark relaxed and started to feel a shivering warmth expanding through her body. The feel of Kostya inside her was incredible, and the deeper he went, the more pleasure she felt.

Heat, she was feeling so much heat. It dazzled her. She gripped his ass. She knew her nails were biting in, she should feel bad about it, but she didn't give a flying fig.

Kostya turned her cheek and she looked up at him, trying to discern all the emotion she was seeing in his eyes.

Apprehension.

Assessment.

Concern.

But then...

But then, underneath everything, there was Kostya and his sparkle of joy. He slowly grinned and Lark's nails unclenched. They slid up his back and she wrapped her legs around his waist and smiled.

"You made it, *sólnce*. You survived," he teased.

"Nobody." She gasped as he slowly pulled out, deliciously torturing her.

"What?" he asked as he pushed back in.

"Ahhhhh," she arched up. The movement sent sparks shimmering up her spine, then boomeranging back down to her needy core. "Nobody likes a know-it-all," she huffed out.

Kostya laughed as he kept himself still.

"Kostya, I might have survived, but you're not going to live long if you don't start moving again."

The laughter faded from his eyes, but before she could worry, she saw his entire visage transform. This was no longer the man that she had laughed and dined with here in the United States. Instead, she was in bed and surrounded by the warrior who had protected her in Afghanistan.

Kostya gathered her close and started a gentle thrust that she felt from her toes to her fingertips. The slow glide in and out soon morphed into a sensuous dance, where he led her like a virtuoso. Lark swayed to music that only they heard, a rhythm known to only the luckiest of lovers.

He drove deep and she cried out her pleasure, loving the open-mouth kisses he delivered along her arched neck.

How can it be like this? How?

"It's you. It's because of you," Kostya answered a question she hadn't realized she'd spoken aloud. When he took her nipple in his mouth, she started to shake so hard she would have lost their connection if he hadn't held her so close.

"Kostya," she moaned.

He lifted his head and all she saw was the blue of his gaze as she shot into a universe of bliss.

"Kostya!" she wailed.

That was all, that was everything. Just *Kostya*.

HE WOKE up as soon as she slipped out of bed, missing her warmth. When was the last time that he had slept this well? Hell, he couldn't remember. He rolled over and picked up his watch and saw that it was four in the morning. He laid back down and thought about what he would do when Lark came back to bed. That's when he saw her move from the bathroom to the door of the suite.

"Lark? Is everything okay?"

"Yeah, everything's fine. Go back to sleep."

Hmmm, interesting answer. She did not say she would be right back.

Kostya threw back the covers and padded out to the living room. Lark was booting up her laptop and she didn't hear him come up behind her. He stood there a few moments. He didn't intend to peek, but he couldn't help but notice that she had a set of headshots on her computer, all men, with their names and titles listed beneath them. It was reminiscent of how Dr. Lord and her team had been displayed.

"Who are they?"

Lark jerked as her head swiveled to look back up at him. "You scared me."

"I didn't mean to. Who are they?"

"They all work for Sanofi Manufacturing and

Analytics. I'm pretty sure that a couple of them, or maybe all of them, are involved in brokering trade secrets."

"Brokering?"

Lark turned away from her laptop so she could give him her full attention. "Kostya, if you want to have a real conversation on what I'm working on, you're going to have to, at the very least, put on your boxers."

"Honey, I wasn't wearing any boxers."

He watched as her eyes widened.

"Seriously?"

"Panty lines," he dead-panned.

"You are kidding me, aren't you?" a blush crawled up from underneath some skimpy piece of froth that she must use as a robe, but it really was nothing more than an invitation as far as he was concerned.

"God, you're easy." He thrust his fingers through her hair and bent in for a deep kiss. Still honey and peaches. Kostya's other hand slid inside her robe, found her taut nipple, and rolled it between his thumb and forefinger. She moaned, and he stored that sound along with every other memory he'd gathered since they'd arrived in her hotel room.

He pulled her up out of the desk chair and carried her back to the bed.

"I need to work." She protested.

"You're not sounding married to the idea," he teased as he fell down onto the bed with her. "Give me some incentive to let you go." Kostya pulled her robe off her.

"Okay. I will." She scraped her fingers through his chest hairs and down his stomach until she circled his cock. Lark squeezed him, but it was too soft. Then she stroked up, then down. "Is this incentive enough?" Her whisper was a purr.

"Lick your hand and do that again," he choked out the words.

As he watched her tongue slide across her palm, pre-cum trickled from the tip of his penis. Then her hot little hand was back, and as if she read his mind, she gripped him harder. Her touch had him gasping for breath.

"Convinced?"

"Huh?"

What in the hell is she talking about?

"Kostya?" She pumped his cock again.

He looked into her twinkling blue eyes.

Game on!

Her plump tits swelled in front of him like a feast. He ducked down and swallowed a tip deep into his mouth, relishing the feel of her satiny, soft flesh as he suckled it. He swirled his tongue around and around her nipple until she cried out his name. He didn't even care that she was working him with two hands and he knew he wasn't going to last. Nothing mattered but the feel of her, the taste of her. Her nipple was diamond-hard, and her cries got louder as he gently bit at her taut peak.

Her hands left him and she shoved him away.

"Fuck me! Hurry. Now!"

Kostya shoved her legs apart and looked down. So pretty, so wet, and all his. He placed his cock at her entrance.

"Fuck me," she groaned as he jerked away from her. "Condom!" He leaped off the bed and grabbed at the strip of condoms he'd left on the nightstand sometime during the night. He bit one open and came back. Lark was writhing on the bedspread. Even through his sexual haze, he couldn't help but glory in the fact that he had Lark

Sorensen waiting for him with as much eager anticipation as he was feeling.

I am such a lucky bastard!

As soon as he knelt down between her spread thighs, she reached for him, pulling him down, but he wasn't having any of it. Lark was a petite little thing; what's more, they'd played hard last night so she had to be sore, so he was damn well taking his time.

She saw him pause.

She drew up her knees and lifted her head. "What part of hurry did you not understand?"

Kostya laughed.

How does she keep making me laugh?

"I understand the concept, *sólnce,* but I'm the man so we're doing it my way." He said it just to piss her off. It was so much fun pissing her off.

She struggled to push up onto her elbows, but before she could, Kostya leaned over and bestowed the gentlest of kisses on her lips. Then he raised his head until her dazed eyes locked with his. "I'm teasing, Lark. In here, in the bed we share, we are always equals. Having you with me is a gift that I will never take lightly."

Her smile was beautiful.

He settled down beside her and lifted her leg over his hip. For long moments, they just hugged, breathing in one another's scents, finding peace as they listened and felt one another's heartbeat.

Kostya finally reached between them and found her slick and ready for him, but he tested her with his fingers, watching her closely for any signs of distress.

"I'm fine, you oaf." She hit his chest and laughed.

Kostya slowly rolled them over and she rested on top of him. "So now I'm in charge, right?" she asked as she raised her eyebrow and positioned her core above his hips.

"If you think you can handle it." He smiled.

The way she fondled his cock as she placed it at the mouth of her vagina had him sweating. Now he was the one wanting to shout, 'Hurry'. But he didn't. He loved watching her enjoy this moment as she slowly slid down, taking just half of his aching erection before pulling back up. Then she pushed back down, taking a little more.

She pulled back up again. Her eyes closed, a blissful smile on her face.

"Why are you punishing me?"

She shoved down harder and her smile got bigger.

"Shhh, I'm concentrating."

I always wondered how I was going to die.

Kostya couldn't take his eyes off Lark. Her expression was rapturous and because of the way her breasts swayed he was sure he was going to start drooling.

Up and down.

Up and down.

Up and all the way down.

"Fucking finally!" he roared as he sat up and grabbed her around the waist.

Her eyes shot open. "What?"

At last, he was completely sheathed inside her warmth. He shoved up with his pelvis and Lark arched backward over his arms. Her breasts thrust up for his delectation, but that wasn't what he wanted. He grabbed her hair and brought her mouth up so he could slam his lips onto hers.

Need.

Kostya couldn't get enough, not close enough. His tongue drove deep into the recesses of her mouth. Like the slick, hot channel that clenched around his cock, her mouth welcomed him.

"Ouch!" he reared back.

She'd bitten his lip.

He saw her wicked grin a moment before her nails dug deep into his scalp and dragged him back for another scorching kiss. Kostya rolled them over, their sweat-soaked bodies twisted on the sheets, he didn't know where he ended and she began.

Lark was moaning but he wasn't worried, not this time. Her legs were wrapped so tightly around him that it was a wonder she wasn't cutting off his circulation. And the way she met his every thrust was like she heard the same melody he did. They matched perfectly.

Her nails scratched through his hair downward, then dug into his shoulders. He'd have marks for days. He loved it.

Lark panted and trembled. He could tell she was close, but he wanted her out of her mind. He kept up his steady thrusts and worked his right hand between their bodies until he found her swollen clit.

"Too much," she cried when he brushed his thumb against her nub.

Bullshit.

Kostya saw her indecision. He pressed down hard on her bud and she whined out his name.

"Too much?" he asked as he thrust in again, and then lightly pinched her clit.

"I don't know," she wailed, her head thrashing against the mattress. "Kostya, I don't know." She hit the back of his shoulder with a fist.

Heat cascaded from the back of his head and sped down his spine. He wasn't going to last. Kostya grabbed her ass with his left hand, tilting her up for an even deeper thrust, then pinched her clit hard.

Lark shrieked his name. Her smile was glorious.

Kostya covered her mouth with his as his head exploded.

Stars.

Snapping, exploding stars. Bursts of white like the first Fourth of July fireworks show he'd ever seen in America. So beautiful.

He'd found freedom.

17

LARK LOOKED UP FROM THE HOTEL DESK WHEN SHE HEARD the room door open.

Kostya frowned when he saw her sitting at the desk. "You know, as soon as you got up, you should have put on the security lock."

"That's a McDonald's bag!" Lark shouted in delight as she shot up from the desk, pulling down the t-shirt she'd stolen out of his duffle bag so it would cover her panties.

"Did you hear me about the locks?" Kostya asked as she grabbed the bag out of his hand.

"Sure, sure. What did you get me?" she asked as she headed back to the desk.

"Look inside. I might not have gotten you a sausage McMuffin and hashbrowns."

Lark started to pull out the contents of the bag onto the desk, but Kostya stopped her. "Easy there, champ, show a tiny bit of decorum." Kostya laughed as he snatched the bag from her greedy hands, went over to the dining room table, and took out three breakfast sandwiches.

After Lark plopped her panty-covered ass onto one of the dining room chairs, he handed her one of the sandwiches.

"Here's yours."

"You're having two?" she asked as she unwrapped her sausage McMuffin and bit into it.

"Three. Already ate one on the way back to the hotel. After all the calories we burned last night, I was hungry."

Lark finished her bite and frowned at him. "Hey, I burned just as many calories as you did, why did I only get one McMuffin?"

He handed her a packet with hashbrowns and she grinned. "That's more like it," but then she grabbed the bag to look inside. She grinned when she pulled out a packet of ketchup. "You know, if there hadn't been ketchup, you would have failed."

"So I was told."

"Dammit, who is your source?" If she wasn't sitting *and* barefoot *and* barely dressed, she would have stomped her foot.

"A good operative never reveals his source." Lark looked down and realized he had already eaten one entire sandwich and was working his way through the second. She drank some of the orange juice he had brought.

"I'm going to figure out who your source is. You know that, right?"

"It would be pretty pathetic if you didn't. After all, you *are* an investigative journalist."

God, he looks smug.

God, he looks good when he looked smug.

Lark savagely took another bite of her sandwich.

Kostya laughed.

Great, now he was a mind reader.

"So what are you working on? Why do you think men from Sanofi are brokering trade secrets?"

"I'll tell you why."

Lark got up from the table, still holding onto her sandwich, and went to her desk. She pushed around papers until she found the half-filled notepad. She came back to the table, chewing and perusing her notes.

"Damn," she muttered when she knocked into the table with her hip as she went to sit down. Kostya caught their coffees before they spilled, then pulled the McMuffin out of her hand and traded it with her coffee. She took a sip, then set it down as she flipped through the pages. Some of the notes were months old; this was the notebook she'd started writing in when she first had a glimmer about this story.

"Are you going to talk to me?" Kostya asked.

"Hmmm?" Lark flipped another page.

"Lark?"

She looked around the table. *Where's a pencil?* She shot up off her chair and rushed back over to the desk and scrabbled through papers, pens, and pencils. When she found one, it wasn't sharp enough. Lark found her computer bag on the floor, blindly reached in, and pulled out the small electric pencil sharpener. She slammed it on the desk then sharpened her pencil and started writing on the notepad.

"How the fuck did I miss this?"

She flipped more pages, and wrote notes in the margins, then went back to the first page and grinned. "You absolute motherfucker!"

All along he'd been acting like the damned martyr. As the SVP of Enterprise Solutions, he'd been defending the hundreds of engineers he managed with his dying breath when really, he was the puppet master of the whole damned operation. Lark would bet her entire retirement fund on it, but how in the hell would she prove it?

"You know, my source never told me that you like to eat graphite."

Lark went to the first blank page in the notepad and started a diagram. If Schroeder really was the one who was organizing everything, then why was he funneling the sales through these chino-pant-half-wits? Lark drew a line between Harkins and Saudi Arabia. With his connections going back to his time working with the petroleum company he was the perfect guy to be selling there. And then there was Stanley, who she'd already—

"Hey!"

Lark glared up at Kostya as he pulled the pencil out of her mouth.

"Lark, you're chewing this more than you're writing with it," he admonished. He leaned against the desk and crossed his ankles. "So what has you so in a twist?"

She grinned up at him. "Nothing has me in a twist, I'm actually untwisting," she bounced in her chair. "Or I'm unraveling. Well not me, I'm fine, I'm sane. It's not me unraveling, I'm beginning to unravel what the hell these limp-dicks have been up to." She lunged for her pencil, but Kostya held it up over his head.

"Tut, tut, tut. No more pencil for you. You have eaten your quota of graphite for the morning."

"Seriously, Kostya, give that back. I need it."

He grinned down at her. "Explain why you need it, and I'll *consider* it."

She stood up to confront him, then immediately realized her error. Her body was damn near plastered against his and if she lifted her arms to try to reach the pencil, not only would she fail, she would be pressing her breasts right against his chest.

"Go for it." His voice was a rough whisper of seduction.

"You planned this," she accused.

"Nope," he shook his head. "But I've been trained to take advantage of situations as they arise."

Lark took a half-step closer and pressed her stomach to his groin. "Yep, I'd say a situation has certainly arisen."

Kostya threw the pencil across the room and grabbed her around the waist. "That's what happens anytime you're around, Woman. Now you have to pay the price."

For just a moment she thought there was something she needed to be doing, but for the life of her, she couldn't remember.

"Kiss me, Kostya."

"Oh yeah."

HIS LITTLE *SÓLNCE* WAS PISSED. Kostya smothered a smile.

"If you blow this for me, I'm ripping your dick off. Do you hear me?" she damn near shouted as she marched her way across the parking garage at the MGM National Harbor casino.

"I hear you, Honey. I also think they did over there." Kostya pointed to the group of retired ladies who were looking at them wide-eyed near the elevator. Lark stopped walking.

"I think we'll take the stairs," she whispered.

Kostya bit back a laugh and grabbed her hand. "Okay, pretty lady, let's get this show on the road."

"Tell me again why your friend had to come?"

"Because it's going to look more natural if Amy has a man with her."

"She's not going to be happy," Lark grumbled as they exited the garage and headed to the casino entrance.

"Yes, she will. Ryker always makes a good impression with the ladies."

Lark glared up at him. When they got into the actual casino, she looked up at the overhead signs. "That way," she pointed. Kostya figured he was going to have to order her a drink, STAT.

"I see you." She squinted her eyes as she gave him a sideways look.

"What?"

"You're planning on getting me liquored up."

How did she do that?

"I don't know what you're talking about," he said innocently. He let go of her hand and put his hand around her waist. He scowled at the two men at the blackjack table who had turned to ogle her. He saw the sign to the Blossom Nightclub up ahead. As soon as they entered he saw Ryker at a table in the middle of the room. There were three women at the table with him.

Figures.

He gave him a chin tilt as he and Lark walked to an empty table cluttered with glasses in the far corner. As soon as they sat down, Lark checked her cell phone.

"Amy said she should be here in twenty minutes. I should have just told her not to come," she muttered.

She'd been saying things along that line since they woke up this afternoon.

"You told me that she was looking forward to a night out," Kostya reminded her. "This way it's safer."

"I don't know what in the hell you're talking about. I

told you—" Lark stopped talking when the waitress came over and started cleaning off the table. "Hi," she smiled brightly. "What's your name?"

The woman looked pointedly at her nametag, then answered, "Andrea. What can I get you two to drink?"

"I'd like a Jameson straight up."

"Reserve?" she asked.

Lark shook her head.

"And you?" Andrea asked Kostya with more of a smile.

"Same."

"I'll be right back." She carried her loaded tray and headed to the bar. Kostya saw Ryker heading toward them. He was relieved to see he wasn't bringing any of his fan club with him.

"Well, hello." Ryker gave a sunny smile to Lark. "I didn't know my lieutenant knew such a stunning woman."

Lark rolled her eyes and sighed. "You must be a baby SEAL. Always with the charm and testosterone, but please don't tell me you're short on the ability to converse."

Ryker's lips twitched.

"Sweetheart, if you're measuring stick is Kostya's conversational abilities, then I'm going to be just fine." He slipped into the chair across from her.

Kostya waited to see how Lark would respond. She didn't keep him waiting long.

"Ahhh, all the misplaced confidence of a newbie."

"I'll pretend you didn't say misplaced, and take the rest as a compliment. As for you calling me a newbie, I guess my skincare regime must be working." He winked at her. "My name is Ryker McQueen by the way." He reached over the table to shake her hand.

Lark gave a resigned laugh and shook it. "Lark Sorensen."

"Hell, I know you." Ryker's eyes widened. "You're the reporter who out-stubborned the Night Storm team and forced them to get Ebrahem Nuri's family out of Afghanistan." His voice changed, becoming sincere and serious. "We really owe you, Lark. Thank you."

Lark dipped her head, obviously embarrassed. "You're welcome," she mumbled.

"Ebrahem was a hero. He really was. It hurt like hell when he was killed." Ryker looked over at Kostya, his eyes dark with pain. He was right; all of their team mourned Ebrahem's passing. He had been essential to Omega Sky when they had done missions in Afghanistan, he had risked his life time and time again. Kostya could think of one time in particular when he would have lost some of his men if it hadn't been for the information that Ebrahem had provided.

"So how long have you been on the Omega Sky team?" Lark asked Ryker when the silence got to be too much.

"I've been with Omega since it formed. Now if you want to talk about wet behind the ears, that was Kostya. How long had you been a lieutenant?" Ryker asked, looking over at him.

"Long enough to demote your ass," Kostya said without heat.

Lark laughed. She reached under the table and stroked her hand along his thigh.

This woman.

The waitress came over and deposited their drinks. This time all of her focus was on Ryker. "What can I get *you* to drink?" Her voice was a low purr.

"What do you have on tap?" he asked. Her eyes lit up.

The way she answered, it was obvious that the first thing she wanted to offer was herself. Kostya and Lark gave each other a knowing look.

"I'll tell you what, Andrea, why don't you decide for me. I trust your opinion."

As soon as she left the table, Lark groaned. "Really?" she asked.

"What? What'd I do?" Ryker asked.

"My God, does that actually work?"

"I'll answer that," Kostya said. "It works far too fucking often."

Ryker smirked. "Now tell me about your friend Amy. What does she look like?"

"She looks like out-of-bounds, that's what she looks like," Lark answered. "For you she is look-but-don't-touch. Got it?"

Ryker threw up his hands. "Whoa, what are you saying? I'm hurt."

Lark shook her head. "You're incorrigible, aren't you?"

"Me? Nah. Actually, I'm all hat and no cattle. The one you need to worry about on our team is Landon. Now he's all cattle and no hat. That poor boy is constantly falling in love. For real, women follow him around in droves, and the next thing you know he's giving one of them the shirt off his back and thinks she's the one."

Kostya snorted. "You're reading him wrong."

Ryker looked at him in confusion. "What do you mean?"

"Sometimes you're right, I'll grant you. But sometimes he can be pretty damned callous. That boy is young and has his head up his ass." Kostya took a drink. He thought about his ex-wife and grimaced. Who the hell was he to talk? He'd gotten married at twenty-seven, three years older than Landon, and look what a mess he'd made of that.

Lark bumped her shoulder into his. He looked down at her, but she wasn't looking at him, just sipping her drink and listening to something Ryker was saying. But it was obvious she'd picked up on his less than pleasant thoughts and was trying to snap him out of it. How in the hell could she be this in tune with him? They'd only been on two goddamned dates!

He sipped his scotch and took another look at her in her silver dress and realized that he'd known her for three years. And for those three years, he'd respected the hell out of her.

He focused in on what Ryker was saying.

"Why do you think Candy is in trouble?" he was asking Lark.

"You mean besides the fact she hasn't shown up to work, and her cell phone is disconnected, and every time I go to her apartment nobody answers?"

"Yeah, besides that," Ryker nodded.

"Well, gee, I don't know," she said sarcastically. "What would it take for you, almighty SEAL, to decide she was in trouble?"

Ryker held up his hands, palms out. "Point taken."

Kostya moved his hand underneath the fall of her hair, rubbing his thumb across the nape of her neck. He wasn't surprised to find her muscles stiff. He began a soft massage as she continued to talk about Candy with Ryker. As they talked, he scanned the bar. When he saw a diminutive brunette sauntering in on the tallest heels he'd ever seen in his life, he was pretty sure he'd spotted Amy. Lark could dress up and take her pretty to sexy, but this woman was pure siren. He would bet his bottom dollar that she'd been attracting boys since kindergarten.

He bumped Lark's shoulder. "That her?"

"Amy!" Lark waved as she scrambled out of the booth.

Kostya was enjoying seeing Lark so excited, then he noticed Ryker. He was sitting stark still. He was looking over his shoulder at Lark and Amy, he was totally motionless. Yep, Amy definitely had powers.

The two women hugged and huddled. Lark stroked Amy's long curly hair and whispered into her ear. It seemed like Lark was the mama-bear of the duo. Amy sidestepped Lark and waved over at him and Ryker. Kostya motioned for her to come over, but Ryker didn't do anything, he sat there like a lump. Yep, he was definitely starstruck.

This could be fun.

18

"SO HOW ARE WE GOING TO GET THIS DONE?" AMY ASKED.

"Before Kostya here decided to horn his way into the action, I figured I'd just ask one of the waitresses to point Dawn out," Lark shrugged.

"And I'm asking you for the twelfth time, why does my presence stop you from doing that?"

"And I'll tell you for the thirteenth time, it's going to look odd for two couples asking. It would have been just fine for two female friends to ask about Dawn. That would have seemed natural."

"You're overthinking this," Ryker chimed in.

Amy cleared her throat as she licked some of the sugar off the rim of her non-alcoholic lemon drop martini. "I say we use pretty boy and have him spin some kind of sob story to our waitress. Of course, he can't say he was romantically involved with Dawn, because that will dash Andrea's hopes of carrying Ryker's love child. But if he bats his eyelashes, I'm sure she'll tell him anything."

Lark thanked all the pixies and fairies of the forest that she hadn't been sipping her scotch when Amy had started talking, otherwise it would have come out her nose.

"Pretty boy? Eyelashes?" Ryker's voice was two decibels lower than normal.

"What? You have pretty eyelashes. I noticed, so did Andrea. Sue us." Amy took a dainty sip of her drink, her pinky poking outwards like she was sipping tea with the queen.

Kostya muffled a laugh and Ryker glared at him.

Lark watched Amy eye Ryker over the lip of her martini glass. What do you know, she was interested in a man. *Hallelujah!* Lark hadn't seen Amy interested in a man in years. Of course, she could have had better taste—Ryker McQueen was a player with a capital 'P'. But Amy's hormones were waking up!

My little girl is growing up.

Kostya leaned in to the center of the table. "Here's your chance. Andrea's at your six."

Ryker leaned back in his chair, and his entire demeanor changed. "My dad's really worried, and I don't know what to do if I can't find her," he said loudly.

"Can I get you another round?" Andrea asked as she eyed their drinks.

"Can I get a glass of ice water?" Lark asked.

"Me too," Amy chimed in.

"And you?" Andrea smiled down at Ryker.

He shook his head sadly. "Just keep refilling my beer. Or you might be able to find me a miracle. Do you know all of the employees here at the MGM?" His chuckle was so pathetic sounding, he really should have been working in the movies, not in the Navy.

Andrea melted. "What's wrong? Is there anything I can do to help?"

Amy winked at Lark, but since Lark was on the booth side of the table facing Andrea she couldn't wink back, so responded the only way she could. She kicked her friend under the table.

"Darlin' I wish you could, but it's a crapshoot and a half. I've done about everything I can. I think I'm going to have to hire one of them private investigators."

God, the man sounded pitiful.

"Seriously, I know a lot of the people who work here. This place only opened six years ago, and I was hired five years ago, so really, I'm considered an old-timer."

"Honey, nobody could ever call you old."

"Ryker," Kostya said with a tight smile. "We don't want to keep this lady all night."

"No, it's okay." Then Andrea looked over her shoulder to the bartender. "Well maybe you're right," she bit her lip. She looked back down at Ryker. "I get off in two hours, maybe I can meet you? Or are you two together?" She made a circle between Ryker and Amy.

"Oh no, he's free as a bird. Nobody's managed to saddle this bronc," Amy cooed. "I could use another lemon drop martini to go with that ice water when you come back."

"Still with no alcohol, right?" Andrea asked kind of snottily.

"That's right," Amy smiled sweetly.

"So where would I meet you, Andrea?" Ryker interrupted their byplay.

"I'll meet you outside the High Limit Slots Area at ten tonight, and I'll be right back with your drinks. Are you sure I can't get you gentlemen any refills?"

Kostya and Ryker shook their heads, and Andrea headed back to the bar.

"Ooooh, Baby, you're getting lucky tonight," Amy said in a sing-song voice.

"Is she for real?" Ryker looked over at Lark. "I mean seriously, she's behaving like a child."

Lark and Kostya started laughing at the same time.

"Like what I said wasn't true," Amy scoffed. "You attract women like honey attracts bees."

Ryker leaned back in his chair and twirled his finger in front of Amy, "and you're saying you're dressing to please yourself? I call bullshit. You're putting on quite the show for every man in this bar."

Amy pursed her lips and blew him a kiss. "I'm glad to hear that you appreciate my efforts. But I hate to be the one to spoil your little daydream. I was coming here as Lark's wing woman, so I dressed the part. If I'd known that I was dressing as part of a couple, it would have been a totally different look."

She took the last sip of her drink, then set it down and pushed it toward the center of the table. "But come to think of it, I guess if Lark had told me about you, I would have no other choice but to dress this way."

"And why is that?" Ryker asked.

"How else would a woman dress who is dating a peacock?"

"Well, Sweetheart, if you wanted to be accurate to nature, you should have dressed down, because the peahen is a lot drabber than the flamboyant peacock."

Amy slammed her palm over her mouth to muffle her laughter, then finally asked, "Is that for real?"

"Absolutely. You can Google it."

Andrea showed up with the waters and Amy's martini, and Kostya asked to close out their tab. She nodded while managing to caress Ryker's shoulder as she left to run Kostya's credit card.

"Yep, she has visions of little Rykers and a picket fence. How many kids do you want?" Amy asked.

"Three," Ryker answered immediately.

Amy's glass stopped midway to her mouth. "For real?"

"Yep. I came from a big family. There were five boys and one girl. That was too much, so I always thought three would be the perfect number."

"Huh, who would have thunk it." Amy took a sip of her cocktail. "So tell me more about this story you're working on," she asked Lark.

Lark's shoulders slumped. She didn't mind talking about her investigation, but she was really worried about Candy. She leaned in and so did the other three at the table.

"There's this company, Sanofi Manufacturing and Analytics. It's fairly new to the game here in D.C. Just started up twelve years ago, but it was started by Senator Alcott's sister-in-law and a guy nobody ever heard of, but he's the money behind the Trusted Allies lobby."

"Oh hell. I fucking hate politics, but even I've heard about those lobbyists running around Washington like little cockroaches. They're everywhere," Ryker said with disgust.

Lark felt Kostya's shift in mood and looked over at him. He looked grim. "What?" she asked.

"Trusted Allies has not made any friends with the Navy."

"In what way?" Lark wanted to know.

Kostya shook his head. "Can't say. But they're big players. Really big. Tell me more about Sanofi."

"Sanofi might call itself a manufacturing company, but it only ever manufactured one thing. That was an innovative retraction actuator for fighter jet landing gear. Everyone was all over it, and it worked, but the truth is, they stole the tech from a company in India and ran them out of business."

"For real?" Ryker wanted to know.

Lark nodded. "I talked to the engineer in Kanpur who built it. He showed me his notes and his e-mails that date back before Sanofi was in business."

"So why doesn't he sue?" Amy asked.

Kostya snorted. "If Sanofi has people tied to the senate and Trusted Allies, that little guy in India would be squashed."

"Yeah, and what's more, now he's working with Airbus and he just wants to put all of that behind him," Lark explained.

"So what does this landing gear stuff have to do with Sanofi, your story, and Candy?" Ryker asked.

"Sanofi just used the retraction actuators as a way to legitimize themselves as a real-live manufacturing company here in D.C. What they really wanted to do was become a consulting company so they could get their tentacles into all the other big manufacturers and defense contractors all around Washington."

"And it worked, didn't it?" Kostya sighed.

"Oh yeah. After just five years in business, they were one of the biggest consulting firms in the Beltway. They had their fingers in every pie imaginable."

"And nobody took exception to the fact that Alcott's sister-in-law was part owner of this company?" Amy asked.

"No. After the second year, she divested all interest in the company. You know, it never ceases to amaze me that someone who graduated from Yale would think that using his sister-in-law as a smokescreen would really fool anyone," Lark sighed.

"You're looking at it the wrong way," Kostya said ruefully as he tugged on a strand of her hair. "It's because he thinks he's so much more above the rest of us, that he underestimates almost everybody. That's his Achilles heel."

"You're both wrong." Amy rolled her eyes. "The people in D.C. don't give a shit about the little people, hell they don't even care about their peers. The players here in Washington give false smiles, stab each other in the back, but then it's all good as long as everyone gets their beak wet. The restaurant I manage isn't good enough for anyone in actual Congress, but it's good enough for their underlings, and trust me, plenty of shady deals get made there."

"So the sister-in-law *was* nothing but a smokescreen, is that what you're confirming?" Ryker asked.

"'Fraid so," Amy nodded. "Didn't mean to spoil all your dreams, big guy."

"It's not until *you* stab me in the back that you'll have spoiled my dreams," Ryker responded with a heated grin.

"Okay, I guess we're all in agreement that the sister-in-law wasn't ever really part of this, but that it was the senator who had his nose in front of the trough." Everyone nodded at Lark.

"So the lobby group, Trusted Allies, and Senator Alcott were just lining their pockets, nothing new there. You can't fool me, that wasn't the story you were working on, was it?" Amy asked with a smirk.

"You caught me," Lark laughed across the table at her friend, her blonde hair getting into her eyes. Kostya tucked it back behind her ear and she shivered at his touch.

"So, what *is* your story?" Kostya asked.

"This is one of those stories that kind of falls into your lap because of coincidence and luck, you know?"

"Lady, I've read your work; I'm never going to believe that what you write comes from anything other than hard work," Kostya scoffed.

"I like. I like you a lot." Amy beamed at Kostya.

"Just listen up you two, okay? So, here's the weird coincidence part. A couple of years ago, there was a tiny start-up in Wisconsin named Sunny-Solar and they came up with some innovative tech in the manufacturing of solar simulation power supplies. This was a big deal, and they had the market cornered. Now they were little guys, so they borrowed all they could get their hands on—friends, family, hell one of the guys even went to people at his church—just to get people on board to launch this. They knew they had something that was going to revolutionize the industry, and they went all-in."

Lark saw Ryker and Amy grinning and nodding, but Kostya had a sour look on his face. She nodded at him. "Yeah, you're getting it, Kostya. It all fell apart. Three weeks before they were going to go live, a Venezuelan company that is backed by their government launched their line that was identical to what Sunny-Solar was announcing. Sunny-Solar was in the announcement stage, but this company already had solar simulation power supplies produced and was ready to take orders, and they did. They took order after order, leaving Sunny-Solar in the dust."

"Sunny-Solar went to our government to see if they had any recourse, but they didn't. The only law on the books for going after this Venezuelan-backed company would be if they were selling to customers in the United States, but they weren't. Therefore, Sunny-Solar ended up going out of business."

"I don't get it, how was this your big coincidence?" Ryker asked.

"One of the three owners, the one who had gotten his parents to invest their entire retirement into the company, decided to alert the press. He had read some of the articles that Craig Hardy had written in different newspapers where he combined tech and finance issues and made them easy to understand. So, Craig agreed to do the story."

"How did you get involved?" Amy asked.

"Hardy's a friend of mine. He knew that I had been in Venezuela recently and wanted my take on just how complicit the government might be about something like this. I said sure, and I gave him a little feedback one night and that was the end of it."

"But not really," Kostya said.

"Nope, not really, because then a year and a half later, something else pops up. Because I was working on a story here in D.C., I ran into another situation. It made headlines. One of our biggest American semi-conductor manufacturers, Rey-Con, had sued a Chinese company for stealing trade secrets. It was all over but the shouting, but there were a couple of rumors on the street that at the time of the theft, Sanofi Manufacturing and Analytics were supplying a shit-ton of engineering consultants."

"So, people were suspecting that Sanofi might have sold the secrets? Was that hurting Sanofi's business?" Kostya asked.

"Hell no." Lark sat back and shook her head. "Not with

the senator pressing people to continue using them. But as soon as I heard about it, I couldn't help but remember Hardy's notes about Sunny-Solar and their simulators. That company in Wisconsin had hired two engineer consultants from Sanofi. It seemed a little too coincidental to me."

"And Candy? How did you meet up with her?" Kostya wanted to know. Lark leaned into him as he pulled her closer.

"I was in a closed online forum that was supposed to be just for engineers to talk about ways to shore up their defenses to make sure that their code couldn't be stolen in the future. There was a lot of chatter about layered encryption tech, and how it just wasn't cutting it anymore." Lark blew out a breath that feathered her bangs upward. "I put in an alert for Sanofi, Sunny-Solar, and Rey-Con, so I could read any chats that talked specifically about them. That's when I found one username that would bring up Rey-Con and Sanofi. No Sunny-Solar, but still..."

"Was that Candy?" Amy asked.

"Yep," Lark nodded. "Now, she didn't know how to block herself, so she was easy to track down. Once I got her e-mail address, I was able to set up a meet."

"She was willing to meet, just like that?" Kostya was skeptical.

"You know, not everybody is as paranoid as you special ops types. But no, not just like that," Lark sighed. "First I had to have her read some of my articles, then she insisted on being able to call into the Vanity Fair office and have the call directed to me, just to make sure I was on the up-and-up."

"Good," Kostya smiled. "I'm beginning to like her."

Lark hit his shoulder. "I told you she was good people, that should have been good enough."

He rolled his eyes.

Lark looked over at Amy. "See? They're cynical as well as paranoid," she huffed.

"Realistic and cautious," Ryker countered.

"Anyway, Candy and I agreed to meet. She laid it all out for me. Her current husband, Jay Jensen, was refusing to sign the divorce papers unless she did some digging on Sanofi. Jay's a janitor at Sanofi, and he discovered some things there. He overheard some conversations and stole some papers. Anyway, he found out that some of the men were using the bank that Candy worked at, so he got the bright idea of having her snoop around at her bank to find out what the Sanofi employees were doing over there."

"And she went for it?" Amy asked incredulously.

"She'd been trying to divorce his ass forever, but he kept refusing to sign the papers. He promised her that if she got him the information he wanted, that he'd sign."

"And did she?" Ryker asked.

"She was still digging around when she and I met up."

"Why was she doing online searches in the chatroom?"

"She figured the more she knew about the Sanofi guys, the easier it would be for her to find out about their banking status," Lark explained. She laughed. "The thing is, after meeting the overbearing pile of stink, I find it hard to believe he could ever be stealthy. Hell, considering how big he is, I can't imagine him ever being overlooked. I sure do understand why Candy was pulling out all the stops to get out of her marriage to Jensen. He's a slime of the first order. I had to take a bath *and* a shower after meeting with him."

"Wait a minute, you met with him? When? Where?" Kostya demanded to know.

"Three days ago. At his apartment. Why?" Lark looked at him curiously.

"You went over there on Thursday?" There was something funny about the way Kostya asked the question. Lark examined his face.

"Why are you asking?"

"Just answer the question, Honey."

"Yes, I already told you, it was on Thursday afternoon."

"So let me get this right. You went to see this guy that you knew was involved in some shady shit the day before you had me fly out here for a date. Am I getting this right?" Now his voice didn't sound funny. Kostya sounded a slight bit perturbed.

"Now wait just a minute, big guy. I go into and have gone into a hell of a lot worse situations than that. Jay Jensen was chump change compared to the crack houses in L.A. And don't get me started on where I had to go and who I had to meet to get the complete story for the shanty-towns in Brazil."

"You mean the favelas?" Ryker asked.

"Yeah, that's the actual name for them in Portuguese, but for the article I used shanty-towns. I stayed there for five weeks, I had six meetings with members of the PCC."

"Goddammit," Kostya growled. "I *knew* it! You never named your sources or which gangs you'd talked to, but in my gut, I knew it had to be *Primeiro Camando da Capital.*"

"And it was. Ergo, meeting with Junkyard Jensen was a piece of cake. Who pissed in your Cheerios?" Lark glared at him.

"Woman, all I'm saying is that you could have called

me one day earlier, or you could have delayed your confrontation by a day, and I could have gone with you. Would that have been such a hardship?"

Lark pushed around in the booth seat so that she was facing Kostya. "Yes, that would have been a hardship. I wouldn't have been able to properly do my job. I needed to see Jensen all by my lonesome. I went in there as Candy's friend, asking for his help. Having you there would not have looked right."

"But you would have been safer."

"I handled myself just fine."

"Lark—"

"You need to back off, Kostya. I don't like where this is going. Do you hear me?"

"Lark?"

Lark turned her head to look at Amy who was holding up her phone.

"I made a reservation at Ginger, but we have to get our butt's over there now."

Lark took a deep breath and nodded. "That sounds good." She looked over at Kostya.

"I agree, dinner sounds great." He gave her a rueful smile.

19

GREAT JOB, YOU ALMOST FUCKING BLEW IT, BARONAVICH! Here's a woman who doesn't need rescuing so there you go trying to force it on her!

Kostya stood behind Amy and Lark as they pressed buttons on the slot machines while they all waited for Ryker to come back with some information.

"Are you sure you don't want to play?" Amy asked again. "Maybe you'll have the lucky touch."

Kostya shuddered. The idea of throwing his money away gambling held no appeal whatsoever. "Why do you keep asking me to play? Aren't you enjoying this?" Kostya asked Amy.

"No. I know Lark likes to play blackjack, but other than that, we're not into gambling."

Lark turned on her stool and gave him a half-smile. "Nope, can't say this turns me on. I like earning my money, and I find my job exciting enough." She slapped her hand against her forehead. "Ah fuck, did I just say that?"

"What?" he and Amy asked at the same time.

Lark reached out and stroked the lapel of his jacket. "I

really don't want to stir anything else up with you tonight. I know you were just concerned, I get that. If we're really going—"

Kostya pressed his finger against her lips. "Stop right there. Yes, we're really going to have something together. Don't doubt it. I fucked up tonight. I know you're more than capable. I admire the hell out of you, Lark. Look, it's my nature to worry. I don't just do it for you, I do it for the men on my team, too. I'm the leader. Do you get that?"

She nodded her head, and he lifted his finger. She grabbed his hand and looked at Amy. "Excuse us." She hopped off the chair and pulled Kostya through the casino to the Felt Lounge. He had no idea how she managed it, but she found a cozy corner on one of the couches and she pulled him down beside her.

Lark brushed an imaginary something off of his shoulder so that she could lean in and look up at him through her lashes. "Did you mean it? You really think that this thing between us is going somewhere? For real?"

Kostya didn't think he had ever heard Lark sound so hesitant before. This woman was always flipping someone shit or throwing down because she thought something should be done a different way, but she was never hesitant. He put his arm around her shoulders and pulled her close.

"You've got it wrong. This isn't going somewhere, it's already gone somewhere, at least from my point of view. And I'm not just saying that because we've had made love. I've known you for three years, and you might have frustrated me a lot of that time with your save-the-world thinking, but I've always been impressed with your accomplishments, been struck by how well you have interacted with the different teams, and then when you stepped up for Ebrahem's family I was awed by your bravery and compassion."

Her eyes glistened silver and a tear slid down her cheek.

"*Derr mo*," Kostya swore in Russian. "I didn't mean for you to cry."

Lark wiped her tears away and made a face up at him. "Suck it up. When you say beautiful things like that, a girl has a right to get all teary. It's in the rule book."

Kostya cupped the back of Lark's head and drew her in for a kiss, but she held back.

"Not here."

He looked around and laughed. Not only was there kissing going on, he saw one woman straddling another woman, and he was pretty sure that the woman on top was not wearing any panties.

"Yes, here." Once again the taste of Lark obliterated every thought in his head. Tonight she reminded him of vanilla, pears, and spring. He wanted to pull her even closer so that her lush breasts could press against his chest, but he didn't. In no way did he want to embarrass this elegant lady.

Lark cupped his cheek. Her fingernails speared through his short hair and he somehow managed not to moan with pleasure. Lark knew precisely how to touch him to provide the most satisfaction.

Kostya reluctantly pulled away and was pleased to see that her eyes glowed with desire, not tears.

"I love the way you apologize," she murmured.

"I'm going to fuck up again, Lark. I'm telling you straight up, it's going to happen."

"Is it because you're a lieutenant?"

"It's deeper than that. I've let people down. People I

loved. It twisted me up, and when I'm around others that I love and care about, I sometimes can't help myself."

It was the most he'd ever admitted to anyone about what happened in Russia. Not even Irina had any idea of everything that happened. About all the ways he'd failed.

"Kostya?"

He looked down. Lark's slim, capable hand was resting on his knee. Her other was on his chest, gliding around in comforting circles. He shuddered.

"Can you talk about it?"

He shook his head. "Not now." He picked up her hand off his chest and kissed the tips of her fingers. "Eventually."

"Is this going to be when we do the deep dark childhood reveals?"

He chuckled. "Will there be alcohol involved? Please, tell me there will be alcohol."

"And laughter," she promised him. "You can't do drama without booze and laughter." Her eyes twinkled and the little minx actually ruffled his hair.

"Did you just do that?" He slid his fingers through the silk of her blonde hair. "You don't mess up a grown man's hair, you do that to a child."

"Nah, you do that when you're having fun with someone."

He moved his hand down and tickled her ribs. Her shriek of laughter had people turning their heads. She tried to jump away from him, but he didn't let her go.

Absolutely, Lark is the woman I can talk to about anything.

RYKER LOOKED like the cat that caught the canary. Or was it the cat who stole the cream? Whatever the hell it was, Ryker looked pretty damned happy with himself. Amy was scowling at him, and her leg was swinging like a metronome as she sat at the bar facing the grinning sun-streaked blond man.

Lark liked the way that Kostya always shortened his stride so that she could keep up with him as she wore these killer heels. They looked great, but her feet were beginning to hurt.

"I think your friend is kind of pissed," he whispered out of the side of his mouth.

"Looks that way," she giggled. "This is kind of fun. I'm still going to use a cantaloupe scoop on Ryker's balls if he tries anything with her."

"You're vicious," Kostya said as they walked up to the two of them.

"Why is Lark vicious?" Ryker asked.

"Trust me, you don't want to know," Kostya answered. "So, what did you find out?"

"Dawn has been a no-show at work since Thursday. She hasn't called in and her shift manager hasn't been able to reach her. She's probably going to get fired."

"That sounds bad," Lark said biting her lip.

Kostya stroked his hand down her back, but even that didn't soothe her. "What else did Andrea say? Or was that all you got?"

"Oh, ye of little faith. I didn't ply her with two drinks and get just that," Ryker scoffed.

Amy rolled her eyes.

"Andrea and Dawn don't travel in the same social circles, so it's not like they were close. According to Andrea, Dawn was a goody-two-shoes. That was an exact quote," Ryker grinned. "Anyway, Dawn started asking for a lot of extra shifts about three weeks ago. That's when Candy went missing, right?"

Lark nodded.

"Andrea called a gal by the name of Rhianna to come meet us over at the Belvedere."

"Where?" Kostya asked.

"That's a bar at the Gaylord hotel," Amy explained. "It's close by."

"That's what took me so long, so now you can retract those claws of yours, Missy." Ryker tapped the end of Amy's nose.

"I have no idea what you're talking about." She sniffed daintily and tossed her hair back over her shoulder.

Lark clapped her hands twice. "Children, keep on topic. What did Rhianna have to say?"

"Rhianna's a sweetheart, and if she's a good friend of Dawn's, I'm betting Dawn is too. She didn't mention Candy, but she did say that Dawn had family in town. To begin with, Dawn was really excited, but by the third day, she was shaky and asking for the extra shifts. When Rhianna asked what was going on, Dawn asked her if she knew of any places out of state that might pay under the table."

"Did she?" Kostya asked.

Ryker nodded. He pulled out his phone. "Rhianna knew about a place in Florida that hired girls and they never looked closely at their paperwork and didn't have any problem paying in cash. This isn't a place we can just call."

Lark looked at the establishment that Ryker had up on his phone and winced. She'd been to Florida, and these types of strip joints littered the sides of different interstates. She hated the idea of Candy having to quit her job at the bank and having to start a job as a stripper just because her sleaze of a husband got her mixed up in some shady shit.

"Thanks, Ryker, I really owe you." She kissed his cheek. "I really owe all of you," she said as she glanced at Amy and then at Kostya. "I guess I have a plane to Florida to catch."

She heard Ryker's laugh and turned away from Kostya to look at him.

"What's so funny?"

"Look back at my lieutenant," he said pointing at Kostya.

She turned back to look up at Kostya. He had a fierce look on his face. She frowned. "What's wrong?"

"I'm going to speak in a calm voice. I will use a respectful vocabulary."

He was vibrating with some kind of strong emotion, but he couldn't possibly be mad, because she wasn't planning on doing anything dangerous. "You're acting kind of odd, Kostya. But I know you can't be upset like you were when I confronted Jay Jensen because now I'm just going to find Candy and Dawn."

She spun around and glared at Ryker when she heard his choked laughter. "Fuck you, Ryker. What is so goddamned funny?"

"Nothing is funny," Kostya damn near roared. He moved so that he was now between her and Ryker. "If you think I'm letting you go chase after Dawn and Candy down to Florida when they're both scared enough to drop everything because they think a bogeyman is after them, you've got another thing coming."

"They're in hiding, it's fine. I just need Candy to

confirm my suspicions that it's Schroeder who's behind everything at Sanofi, and then I can start doing all of my due diligence and write my story. When I'm done, the Feds will come in and scoop them all up, and Candy and Dawn can come home. It's easy."

"Don't you think that if Candy is going to this level of trouble to hide herself it should tell you just how bad it is?"

"Yeah, for her. But they don't know about me," Lark said reasonably.

"God save me from new recruits and neophytes! You are not going down there alone," Kostya growled.

"This is my job, Kostya. You just got done telling me how much you admired my abilities."

"Yeah, I did. Tell me something, Lark—how much money do you think Schroeder is making selling secrets?"

"If he's doing it right, just the microprocessors and memory chip tech that they delivered to China from Rey-Con had to be in the tens of millions of dollars. And that's just one of the hundreds of projects that Sanofi engineers are in on." Lark shrugged.

"People are willing to kill a liquor store owner for fifty bucks," Amy said. "Seems to me that for tens of millions of dollars, traitors at Sanofi would happily murder you and whoever else got in their way. You don't need just Kostya, you need his whole damned team to go with you."

Lark looked from Ryker to Amy and then back to Kostya.

I am so fucked.

20

"I AM SO GOING WITH YOU. YOU CAN'T JUST SEND ME ON some made-up exercise with Jase." Kostya could feel frustration and even anger coming off Ryker in waves.

"This is not made up. This is important, and you know it. Jase is the best tracker we have on the team. We did okay while we were in Russia, but we could have done better. Out of everybody, I think you're the man who could match Jase if he trained you."

Ryker's eyes were still sparking.

"There's some bad juju going on with this investigation Lark is pursuing you and I both know it. You need backup. I'm already up to speed, you need me."

"You're right, I do need you. I need you to train with Jase." Kostya was done trying to convince Ryker; this time it was an order, and Ryker knew it.

"Absolutely, Lieutenant. When and where do I need to report, Lieutenant?" He might be saying the right things, but he was letting Kostya know that he was royally pissed off.

I don't give a shit. Going to a bar with me was one thing, going out of state to help me out? No way.

Kostya told Ryker exactly what he expected, then left his office to go pick up Lark. He knew that he likely had another fight on his hands. Fine, he intended to win that one as well.

―――――――――

"FIRST CLASS? I thought you were mad at me," Kostya said as he looked down at his boarding pass.

"I am mad at you. And what are you talking about?" Lark looked down at the ticket that she'd just been handed. She handed it back to the ticket agent. "There must be some kind of a mistake. I didn't book a first-class ticket."

The man behind the ticket counter smiled at her. "You're one of our premier mileage members, you're automatically upgraded whenever there are seats available," he explained.

"And him?" Lark tilted her head toward Kostya.

The agent looked down at his screen. "Mr. Barona has even more miles than you do, Ms. Sorensen." He looked up at Kostya with an awed look. "It's not often I meet someone who does this much flying with our airline. It's a pleasure to be able to serve you."

Lark saw Kostya catch himself before he argued. Instead, he just gave the man a smooth smile. "What's your name again?"

"Manish Nadella, at your service."

"Manish, I'll let corporate know what a great job you're doing. Thanks again for the upgrade." Kostya grabbed Lark's elbow in a gentle grasp and hurried her along toward security.

"What in the hell was that all about?" Lark demanded to know.

"At first I thought it was you," Kostya admitted. "After all, your mother has more money than God."

"My mom does, not me," Lark laughed. "I told her to leave it to Taja and Nazy, and whichever charity needs it. God knows what will happen."

They stopped at the end of the security line and turned to look at one another. "So, since you know it wasn't me, can you tell me how we're now premiere flyers?"

Kostya pulled out his phone and pressed Gideon Smith's number, but the man didn't answer.

"Who are you calling?" Lark asked.

"My second-in-command. I'm pretty sure you've met him before, Gideon Smith?"

"African American?" Kostya nodded.

"He's your computer expert, right?"

Kostya nodded again.

"I met him once over Zoom, when Kane McNamara from Night Storm was helping me out on a little problem. Kane thinks that Gideon is the cat's meow."

Kostya's lip twitched. "Cat's meow, huh?"

"Yeah, that's what I said. Kane said he's just the kind of man he would have liked to have running a division of his software company."

"I thought Kane had to sell that?" Kostya said.

"Yeah, even though he was the one who started it, and he was the CEO, he sold it to the three men under him who he really trusted. He has it worked out that when he retires, he has an option to buy back in, but I doubt that he will."

"Why not?"

"He's not the type," Lark said as they got close to the front of the line. "He's always thinking, like my mom. Probably like your guy Gideon too. My guess is that Kane will have something new up his sleeve when he retires from the Navy. So you think Gideon is responsible for our upgrade?"

"That's my bet," Kostya sighed as he ushered her up to the TSA agent.

THEY HAD ALREADY STARTED the boarding process by the time they arrived at their gate, but even so, Kostya and Lark were still two of the first people to board the plane. Kostya grinned when he immediately saw Gideon at the window in first class. He held up his glass of champagne in salute.

"And you're here, why?"

"Because you need me," Gideon smirked.

Kostya watched as Lark looked at her ticket and started to sit down next to Gideon. He then looked at his ticket and saw that he was seated two rows back.

This was a no-go.

"Hold on a second, *sólnce*," he said as he pulled Lark back into the aisle. "Gideon is sitting in the wrong seat. He's back two rows."

"I'm sure you have it wrong, Lieutenant," Gideon said as he held up his ticket between two fingers. "This ticket says my place is right here, and this lovely lady is my seat companion."

Kostya gave Gideon a feral smile. "And I'm sure *I* have it right, and your ass is planted in the wrong seat. Do you know how I know this?" Kostya ignored the line that was forming behind him.

"How?" Gideon's smile got even wider.

Kostya leaned in real close and started speaking in a low voice. "Because if it isn't me sitting next to Lark in the next twenty seconds, then I'm telling your brother Mike that you taught Felix how to hold out for bigger payouts on his Roblox hacks."

Gideon normally had a good poker face, but Kostya had been hoarding that little tidbit of blackmail for just the right moment, and by the look of horror on Gideon's face, it looked like he'd hit a home run.

"My God, man, you sure do play dirty. And here I was letting you and Lark live the high life in first class." Gideon gathered his backpack and scrambled out of his seat, but not before he gave her shoulder a squeeze and hauled ass two rows back.

Lark gave him a quizzical glance. "What was that all about?"

"Long story. I'll tell you about it during the flight," Kostya smiled. He watched as she sat down, enjoying the way her jeans molded to her curvy bottom. Had it really been only eighteen hours since the last time they'd made love? It seemed like months.

They buckled up.

"What can I get you to drink?" The flight attendant asked.

"Nothing for me," Kostya answered.

Lark took a moment to consider. "Water is fine."

"I'll be right back."

"Okay, tell me what's going on. Why's Gideon here? How did he know we were going to Florida?"

"Ryker has a big mouth, and Gideon probably thinks because there's something to do with computers, he should be involved."

The flight attendant gave Lark her water and she took a sip. "That's really not a bad idea. But aren't the two of you going to get in trouble? I mean, you're working on a project that is in the United States, after all. SEALs are only supposed to operate outside America's borders."

"Me going on vacation with my girlfriend is not a mission, it's me going on vacation."

"And Gideon?"

Kostya shrugged. "He's going on his own vacation."

"Okay," she said slowly. "You know the rules. Who is it for me to question?"

"Exactly."

After she finished her water, Kostya grabbed her hand and slid his fingers through hers. She looked at him through her eyelashes and gave him a shy smile. A loving smile. It warmed his heart.

Damn right he was going on *vacation* with her. Lark might not realize it, but he would do anything in his power to keep her safe. It didn't take long for her to push back her seat and close her eyes. When he finally heard her breath take on the soft cadence of sleep he allowed himself to follow.

"I LIKE a woman who packs light. She's definitely a keeper," Gideon said under his breath. "Of course, there's the whole thing with you being in the rescue mode again." He flagged down the Uber and Kostya looked over his shoulder to where Lark was still on her phone.

Kostya snorted. "Lark is the last woman on Earth who needs rescuing. She's been everywhere and done everything and came away with not a scratch. I had to cajole, push and plead for her to let me come with her on this trip and even then it didn't work."

"So what did?" Gideon asked as the Uber pulled over to the curb.

Kostya gave his friend a wicked grin. "A gentleman never tells."

"Way to go!" Gideon said as he laughed.

"What's so funny?" Lark asked as she came up to them.

"Everything," Gideon answered. "Your Uber has arrived. You're going to love your accommodations."

Kostya shook his head. God only knew what Gideon had up his sleeve. By the time they checked in he realized what Gideon had done. Kostya and Lark were checked into the presidential suite at the same room rate he'd originally signed up for.

"Are you kidding me?" Lark said when she walked into the room and immediately toed off her shoes so she could revel in the plush feel of the carpet. "Just how much do they pay you in the Navy?"

"Sorry to burst your bubble, but this is just another little gift from Gideon, so if you're all into me for the money, you're going to have to rethink things."

Lark dropped her purse on the floor and sauntered up to him, twining one arm around his neck and slowly gliding one hand down to his crotch. She got onto her toes and whispered into his ear.

"No, Baby, I'm all about the dick." She squeezed his cock.

Kostya shouted out a hoarse laugh as she molded her hand around him, taking him from zero to sixty in less than three seconds. She leaned back and gave him a mischievous grin as she felt his erection swell.

"You're loving the effect you have on me, aren't you?" he choked out.

"Oh yeah," she whispered.

He pulled her hand away from his engorged flesh.

"Hey, I wasn't done," she whined.

"*Sólnce*, we haven't even gotten started."

Kostya bent and pushed his shoulder into her stomach and lifted her over his shoulder.

"Hey, wait just a damn moment," Lark yelled. "What are you doing?"

Kostya swatted her ass, and she kicked her legs against his stomach as he strode toward the door to the bedroom. "If you keep up with kicking I'll swat you again," he threatened.

Lark stopped kicking for a moment as he went through the bedroom door, then she started kicking him even harder. He laughed and gave her another slap before tossing her onto the middle of the king-sized bed. She had a big grin on her face as she looked up at him.

"We should be going over to the strip joint; you realize that, don't you?"

"It's thirteen hundred hours, I'm pretty sure there's not much going on yet," Kostya said grinning back at her. He climbed up on the bed and was soon perched on top of her, his hands lightly holding Lark's wrists so that her hands laid flat on either side of her head.

"What do you think you're doing, Lieutenant?"

"Well, if you're not impressed by my money, I thought I would impress you with my dick."

Lark sighed. "Yes please."

God, when she spoke in that breathy voice of hers, he thought the top of his head would blow off. Never in his entire life had a woman excited him more.

"Unbutton your blouse," he ordered as he released her wrists.

Her eyes turned liquid silver as her fingers went to the top button. He could see that she wasn't quite steady. Kostya studied her face to make sure that she was okay with their play, and when he saw her flushed cheeks and the way she licked her lips in anticipation, he knew she was with him.

It seemed like it took forever for her to finish unbuttoning her blouse, but when she was done he was rewarded with the prettiest piece of frothy white lace he'd ever seen. The only thing better was when he would see her breasts. Kostya put his forearm under her blouse and lifted her up off the bed. He easily divested her of the garment, then laid her back down.

"You're gorgeous."

"You're biased," she scoffed.

Kostya took a moment to ease both of her breasts out of the cups of her bra so that they were presented up to him for his enjoyment. "No, Honey, not biased, I'm telling you the God's honest truth." He traced both nipples with his index fingers, circling around and around, collecting every one of Lark's whimpers into his memory so that he could relish them later.

She arched up, pushing her breasts toward him, looking for a firmer touch.

Kostya watched her eyes as he pinched her tight nubs.

"Eeeeh," she whined, then reached up and gripped his shoulders. Her nails dug into his flesh through his t-shirt. It felt good. He pinched and rolled her now-swollen buds even harder.

"Yessss," she hissed. "So perfect." Her nails dug in even deeper.

He was going to die if he didn't get inside her, but there was no way he wasn't going to amp things up. He regretfully let go of her luscious flesh and scooted down her body until he was resting on her thighs.

"Unbutton your jeans, then lower your zipper."

"Kostya, there's no time for this. I need you now." Lark shouted out the last sentence and he grinned. His woman wasn't even thinking about any of the other hotel occupants and he loved it.

"Lark, do as I say." He used his command voice.

She lifted her head off the bed and gave him a fierce look. "Just remember, paybacks are a bitch, Barona."

She unbuttoned her jeans, yanked down the zipper then pushed them down as far as she was able with him sitting on her thighs. "Satisfied?" She growled out her question.

"Not even close, *Sólnce*."

"Fine." She put her thumbs into the sides of her panties and started to tug, and he stopped her with his hands.

"Now, did I ask you to do that?" Kostya asked as he raised his eyebrow.

"Kostya, you're the one who got me all worked up. Come on already, please?" she wheedled.

He gave her a slow smile as he shook his head. He put her left hand on his chest and splayed her right hand down onto her tummy. "You're all worked up, huh?"

"Yessss," she wailed. She looked down pointedly at his jeans where it was obvious that his cock was doing its best to claw its way past the zipper.

"I'll make it good for you," she promised.

"First I want to know how needy you are."

It was a crapshoot if he could keep this up, but she was so damned sexy writhing underneath him. Even her pissed-off pleading was more erotic than any striptease he'd ever seen. He could listen to her voice for days and never be bored.

"I'm needy," Lark whispered, her left hand kneading his chest. "I'm so damn needy," she purred.

"Prove it," he whispered. He caressed the back of her right hand, the one lying on her stomach. "I want you to slowly, ever so slowly, slide your hand underneath your lace panties. Then I want you to touch yourself, I want to know if you're really as desperate as you say you are."

"I am, I really am. I don't need to prove it to you, you can trust me. Please, make love to me."

She was panting and arching into his body.

"And Lark?" He didn't say anything else, he just waited.

"What?"

"After you're done touching yourself, I want you to bring your wet fingers to me and prove just how badly you want me to fuck you."

She let out a long moan. It was exactly how he felt, but seeing her this worked up, this on edge, and knowing that he had done this for her? It made him feel ten feet tall.

"Come on, *Sólnce*, just this one more little thing, then I promise, I'll give you everything you never knew you wanted."

She bit her lip, her chest heaving. "On your honor?"

"Yes. On my honor."

He leaned down and touched his lips to hers. She tasted so good. This time she reminded him of cherries, cinnamon, and passion. She bit down on his lip, hard. He grinned and continued to kiss her. Kiss after kiss, until this time she was moaning not with frustration, but with pleasure. Kostya finally lifted his head. "Are you ready now?"

"Huh?"

"Just one last little task, Lark."

"Why don't you just touch me, you'll see how ready I am for you," she coaxed.

Kostya moved her hand so that her fingertips were just under the lace of her barely-there panties. He watched in fascination as she moved her hand. He could see her fingers touch her mound and when she gasped, he knew that she'd just touched her oversensitive clit.

He changed positions so that he was kneeling beside her, then he pushed apart her legs. Kostya could see Lark's fingers stroking herself, her toes clenched and her body trembled. He hissed when he saw two of her fingers disappear into her channel.

I'm such an idiot! Why did I ever think I would be torturing Lark, she's totally torturing me.

He saw her draw her fingers out, then stroke them over her clit and begin to circle that bundle of nerves. God, he wanted those panties gone! He looked up at her face. Lark's eyes were closed and he saw that same glowing look of concentration and need that she always had just before she was about to climax.

"Oh no, you don't." Kostya grabbed her wrist and tugged her hand out of her panties, then brought her hand up high so he could see the glistening moisture coating her fingers.

"Now. You promised," she panted out.

He looked at her softly. She was heartbreakingly beautiful. Kostya brought her wet fingers to his lips and sucked them into his mouth, savoring every bit of her flavor.

She shuddered, "Oh. My. God."

He smiled. "You taste like honey. I think I might need another taste."

"You said on your honor," she whispered.

On his last lick, he caressed her cheek with his other hand, his thumb stroking her lower lip. "That's true, and I keep my promises."

21

I'm melting. No, I'm losing my mind.

Lark looked up into Kostya's navy blue eyes and felt like she was falling.

Hell yeah, I'm falling. I'm falling in love.

From the time she heard her first fairytale and was told about Prince Charming, she knew that it was all a hoax. Her father was dead, and she saw up close and personal that there were no happily ever afters. So she shook her little head, hardened her heart, and avoided every rom-com ever written and Disney movie ever made.

But here she was, looking into Kostya's eyes and dreaming of so much more, hoping for a bright, shiny future when she should just be concentrating on the now.

She nuzzled her cheek into his big warm hand. Kostya swooped down for a deep kiss and she tasted the tantalizing mix of Kostya and herself. He thrust his tongue deep and the vibration of his growl made her head spin.

When he lifted away from her and got off the bed she was in too much of a daze to even protest. Then he began to shed his clothes and she drank him in. She couldn't imagine a time when she wouldn't be spellbound by his beauty.

"If you keep looking at me like that, the first round will be over before it has a chance to really get started." His accent was pronounced as his gaze burned as he stared down at her.

"First round? You promise I get more than one?"

"On my honor," he grinned.

At last, he was naked. He pulled condoms out of his pants pocket.

Condoms.

More than one.

Thank God.

HIS EYES SNAPPED OPEN. Kostya knew exactly where he was and exactly who he was with. Lark's breathing was rapid, and she was whimpering.

What the hell?

"Lark," he whispered gently as he stroked his hand firmly down her arm. "Lark, Honey, wake up. You're having a bad dream."

She shrank away from his touch, and it reminded him of her reaction in the casino parking garage. He stopped touching her and spoke louder.

"Lark, Honey, it's me, Kostya. It's time to wake up, can you do that for me?"

She stopped moving and she opened her eyes just a fraction. He knew what she was doing; she was trying to hide the fact that she was awake. She wanted to survey her environment before showing herself.

"Honey, it's just me." He put a smile in his voice, trying to coax her back to him.

She opened her eyes and looked around. He saw her relax her shoulders but it wasn't real, she was forcing herself to do it. Then she forced a smile. Damn, she was good at it.

"What happened? Why did you wake me up?"

"You were having a nightmare."

"That's weird. Maybe I ate something that didn't agree with me."

Kostya gathered her up in his arms. He knew what was wrong. "Lark, you told me that there was a problem with your step-grandfather. That he was a big guy. I think the way we played tonight brought up some bad memories. Can we talk about it?"

Lark looked up at him, then her eyes started to dance. "Oh, Kostya, you've got it all wrong. I'm sorry if I made you think that I was sexually abused. I wasn't. Harris was a lot of things, but he was not a pedophile."

Kostya felt a huge weight lift off his shoulders.

"Look, this is something I should have just talked to you about a week ago. It's really no big deal."

Kostya stroked back her hair and gave her a soft kiss. Even a kiss that he meant only to give for comfort, shook him. Lark tasted different each time. Tonight she was strength, moonlight, and raspberries and he wanted more, but he pulled back. Smiling, he tapped the end of her nose.

"Even if it isn't a big deal, tell me about it."

Lark snuggled closer to him. "First, you need to know that Harris got gone the moment Mom saw what was going on. I've never seen her flip her shit like she did that day."

Kostya had no doubt that Beatrice Allen would have ripped the head off anyone who was abusing her daughter.

"Tell me about it."

"Looking back on it, it wasn't so bad. He never even hit me. Not once. The fact that I cringe or flinch pisses me off. You know?" She rolled her eyes.

Lark relaxed into his caresses as he cuddled her closer. "That's looking back on it, *Sólnce,* but you know better than that. What matters is how you were feeling back then."

She let out a deep sigh. "You're sounding like Amy."

"Didn't a psychologist tell you this?"

"Again, you're sounding like Amy. Mom dragged me to one after she booted Harris. I went for a year. It was a waste of time."

Kostya tucked that little nugget away. If something big ever happened, it would take quite a bit of finessing to get Lark to go into counseling.

"So, you've talked to Amy about this? Can you tell me?"

"Again, I repeat, it's not a big deal. Harris Evans only ever got out of line with my grandmother. I know he hit her, but almost always it was in some other room where I couldn't see."

"But sometimes you did see, right?" Kostya interrupted.

"Sometimes," Lark reluctantly agreed. "But only a few times. Mostly, I only heard it happen. I also heard him yell that if she didn't do what he said he'd hurt the brat." Lark gave a weak grin as she looked up at him. "That'd be me, I was the brat. Imagine that."

Yep, that was his Lark, hiding her pain behind humor. Kostya hated the way she was minimizing all of this.

"Kostya, you're getting that Navy SEAL protective look on your face. This was a long time ago. Harris is in some old-folks-home now, eating mush and he can't remember his name. He's nothing. Seems to me he got his comeuppance."

He eased his fingers underneath her hair so he could massage her scalp and tried a different tack. "How's your grandmother doing now?"

"She's doing great. These days she's hiking with her friends, but mostly she's focused on Mom's philanthropic foundation. Mom did a good thing when she put Nonnie on the board."

"So no men on the horizon for your grandmother or your mom?"

Lark shook her head. "That's not true. Nonnie might actively avoid men, but Mom dates sometimes. Look, I get what you're trying to say, Kostya. But I've mostly worked my way through this, okay?"

He sighed, then smiled down at her. "Okay."

She rubbed her nose against his chest. "But things are looking up for me, aren't they? Or am I reading too much into things?"

"Are you asking if I mean to be a big part of your future? If you are, then you can count on it."

Her eyes shimmered liquid silver. "I'd like that. I'd like that a lot."

"Wait for me to come open your door," Kostya said.

"You're kidding, right?"

Kostya gave her a look that said he wasn't kidding.

Lark rolled her eyes at him but planted her ass into the hard seat of the truck rental as she waited for him to open the passenger side door for her.

"You know, this wasn't really necessary," she grumbled as she took the hand he held out to her.

"Normally it wouldn't be, but with a bunch of horny men around, I think it's good to let them know early on that you're taken."

He had a point.

"Where's Gideon?"

Kostya shrugged. "He's around."

It took them more than a minute to weave through all the big pickups parked on the uneven parking lot, many of them not bothering to park within the designated white lines. Yep, they were in for a fine time tonight. Lark wished she could say that she would have felt just as comfortable without Kostya's presence, but she made it a habit not to lie to herself. She looked up at him out of the corner of her eye. He looked good in his black jeans, cowboy boots, and the white t-shirt that lovingly molded across his chest.

How in the ever-loving hell can I be thinking of sex again? Down, girl!

Kostya shot her a knowing grin. Lark flipped her hair and turned her head away from him, and of course, she heard him chuckle. She rolled her eyes yet again but had to grin. The damn man got her. It was nice. Another reason that she might, possibly, could be, a little bit, in love with him.

Kostya opened the door to the strip club and the sound was loud enough to almost push her backward, but Kostya was right behind her to hold her steady. It was dark as she stepped inside, but not dark enough to miss the bouncer who looked her over and leered. Then he looked up behind her and his expression immediately changed.

"Forty bucks," he said to Kostya. Lark started reaching for her purse, but Kostya put his hand over hers.

He chuckled at the man. "You're charging her a cover? You're kidding me, right?"

"With you standing over her all night, hell yes," the bald behemoth said.

Kostya handed the man a twenty-dollar bill over Lark's head.

"I said forty." He glared at Kostya.

"Do you really want to do this?" Kostya sounded bored. Lark had no idea what kind of expression he had on his face, but whatever it was, the man took the bill and stepped aside for them to pass by.

Lark didn't bother to ask what had happened; she was too busy combing the room for any sign of Candy. She had no idea why she thought it was dark when she had first walked in because it wasn't. There were lights all over the place. Scratch that. There were lights all over the stage. She looked at the three girls currently gyrating around the poles, wearing the tiniest thongs that had ever been created, and wondered if one of them was even old enough to drive.

Kostya led her around many tables until she found herself being lifted up on a tall stool at a high-top table.

"When are you going to stop staring?" Kostya whispered in her ear.

Holy hell, Lark realized how it must look, and her blush had to have turned her entire upper body fire engine red. Kostya was out and out laughing at her when she turned to face him.

"They're putting on quite the show, aren't they?" His eyes were dancing.

"Yes, they are. I've seen this in movies, hell even on TV shows, but never in person."

"So is this something you're thinking about as a backup job if journalism takes a dive?" Kostya asked with a twinkle in his eyes.

"Ah, no. First, I'm not young enough. Second, I'm not flexible enough. Third, and most importantly, I'm not brave enough."

"You forgot number four," he said as he stroked his hand down her arm, and she shivered.

"What's number four?"

"Your man wouldn't allow it."

Wouldn't allow it.

Lark let those words simmer for a while, watching Kostya study her. He'd definitely thrown down, but she didn't feel annoyed in the slightest. As a matter of fact, she really liked Kostya's caveman attitude...about *this one thing*.

She grinned up at him.

"Thank fuck," he breathed out.

Lark laughed. "You are such a neanderthal."

"Can I help it if I don't want my woman having money stuffed down her G-string while she's shaking her body in front of strange men?"

"That sounds perfectly reasonable to me. Just know it goes both ways, hot stuff."

"That's a deal."

Lark clapped her hand over her mouth before a giggle escaped.

God, what is my life coming to?

She pulled her phone out to change the course of the conversation and pulled up the pictures of Dawn and Candy. "Gideon has these pictures too, right? It's too bad we couldn't have met with him before we got here." Lark bit her lip as she laid her phone down on the tabletop.

"I've got them right here," Kostya said as he put his phone down next to hers. "As for Gideon, he has them, don't worry. I hope to hell he has a lot more than that," he grumbled. Lark saw him scan the room again and this time he looked back at her with a satisfied smile.

"You saw one of the women?"

"Nah, but I finally found my second-in-command. He's charming two of the waitresses."

"Geez, is that some kind of mandatory skillset for your team members?"

"After looking over how the Coronado teams operated, I absolutely *did* make it a part of the recruitment process." Lark watched as he started texting. Hell, Kostya was so serious in how he answered, that she couldn't tell if he was serious or not. He looked up from his phone and winked at her.

"You're an ass," she muttered.

"I had you going, didn't I?"

"I don't want to talk about it," she huffed. "Were you texting Gideon?"

"Yeah," he responded.

Lark saw a waitress at the table next to theirs and flagged her over. She nodded as she was finishing up with the other customers.

"What did Gideon say?"

"He found out that there was a new waitress named Candy. She started two weeks ago."

Lark felt a ten-ton weight lift off her shoulders. "Thank God. Is she working tonight?"

"She comes in at nine. Apparently, she and her sister got jobs at the same time. Her sister works as one of the bartenders."

Lark looked down at her watch. It was eight-thirty. "Should we flag them down in the parking lot before they come in?"

"*You* should," Kostya said. "I'll wait nearby until you call me over. We don't want to scare them off."

The waitress walked up to them. "What can I get you?" she asked.

Lark gave Kostya a lascivious look and slid her hand from his knee up to the top of his thigh. "I think we're going to skip drinks and go back to our hotel."

"Honey, that happens more than you would think." She grinned at the two of them.

Kostya put a twenty-dollar bill on her tray and helped Lark down from her seat. They grabbed their phones and headed out. When they got outside they looked at one another.

"Where should we wait?" Lark asked.

"Gideon said there was an employee entrance around back. Let's move the truck back there so you're not just standing next to the door waiting to pounce. How does that sound?"

"Sounds good."

Soon they were one row back from the employee entrance, watching for vehicles that entered this side of the lot. It didn't take long before they saw a Ford Prius pull up three spaces away from them.

"That's them." Lark damn near squealed. She jumped

out of the truck and started walking over to the economy car.

The driver's door opened and Candy got out. She jolted as she spotted Lark.

"Lark? How did you find me?" Candy looked around the parking lot.

"I've been worried as hell, Candy. I knew something was up as soon as you told me that Sanofi had liquidated its assets from your bank. Then you disappeared. What's going on?"

A cute little redhead came up beside Candy, then pushed her behind her back. Dawn glared at Lark. "You're that reporter. You need to leave Candy alone. And if you know what's good for you, you need to quit butting your nose into things that could get you killed. Now go away."

Lark was floored. What was she talking about, people getting killed?

Lark turned her attention back to Candy. "Candy, I can help."

Candy stepped around Dawn. "No, you can't. This has gotten way out of hand." Her bottom lip trembled and Lark saw that she was fighting back tears.

Lark stepped forward and grabbed her hand. "What is it? You know you can tell me. We've been through so much, you can trust me."

Candy shook her head and looked back at Dawn. "I can't tell you this," she mumbled.

Lark looked back at Kostya. He'd come closer so she knew he'd been listening. He shrugged his shoulders. He didn't know what to make of things either.

"Candy, I want to help you. If we put a stop to Schroeder, then it's done." Lark took a step closer and put her hand on Candy's arm and gave it a comforting squeeze. "You know this isn't what you want for your life. This isn't the future you intended. Let me help you."

"They killed Rick," she spit out. "They killed him." She shook off Lark's hand. "I heard it. I heard the whole thing."

Dawn came up and wrapped her arms around her sister and pressed her cheek against the side of Candy's head. "It's okay. It's going to be all right," she crooned.

"No, it's not. It's never going to be okay. Rick is dead." Candy covered her face and started to cry.

Lark knew that Candy had to be talking about Rick Turner. He was one of the sales execs who worked for Schroeder. If she was remembering right, his two big projects were two government contracts. One with the FDA and one with the Missile Defense Agency.

"How do you know someone killed Rick?" Lark asked. "I mean, all you've been doing is watching how Schroeder and the men deposit money into the First United bank where you work."

Candy looked down at the ground. She didn't answer for a long time. "He wanted to set up a college fund for his daughter. That's my department, so he was assigned to me. That was two and a half months ago."

Lark's whole body began to tingle. Holy hell, two and a half months ago?! "Candy, what happened? Are you saying you met with Rick Turner?"

Candy's eyes were pleading when she lifted them up to look at Lark. "Lark, Rick is, I mean *was*, such a nice man. He showed me pictures of his daughter, and he wanted good things for her. That's the only reason he was involved with Schroeder and his scheme."

"How often did you meet to discuss this college fund?" Lark asked suspiciously.

"Pretty often. He asked me out to coffee that first day. After two weeks I invited him to my apartment for the night."

Lark remained silent, waiting for her to go on.

"I fell in love with him."

Lark felt her entire body slump. "When did you tell him that we were investigating him and the others?" Her voice was resigned.

Candy looked back down at the pitted asphalt. "Three days before he died. I told him if he turned himself in now and agreed to provide evidence to the Feds, he might get out of this without serving any time."

Candy's eyes grew wide as she stumbled two steps backward. Lark didn't have to turn around to know that Kostya was now right behind her.

She glanced over her shoulder, then turned back to the women. "This is Kostya Barona. He's one of the Navy SEALs who is going to help us. I promise you, Candy, we're going to be safe. We're taking Schroeder down."

Candy was trembling. "You don't get it. They're willing to kill. I was there."

Lark frowned at Candy. "What do you mean, Schroeder?"

"Maybe. I don't know. Maybe somebody working for Schroeder. All I know is that they will kill."

Kostya put his arm around Lark but it didn't help. "You saw them kill Rick?"

Candy nodded. "Three men came to his house in the middle of the night. I was in the bathroom. I hadn't wanted to wake Rick up, so I'd closed the door and kept the light off."

Lark nodded for her to continue.

"I was still, you know, tinkling, when I heard Rick

shout. Then I heard another man yell at him to shut up. He sounded foreign. I got up and hid in the tub, behind the shower curtain. It was loud out in the bedroom."

Candy was crying and Dawn was staring daggers at Lark. She didn't care. She needed to know everything that happened.

"What did you hear?" Lark coaxed gently.

"It lasted for hours. Again and again, they asked Rick where the code was. Rick said he didn't have it, he said he'd never had it. They didn't believe him, because he'd shown him some of it. Whatever it was had to do with missiles."

Lark shivered. That was bad, really, really bad.

"Sometimes they would talk to each other in a different language. I'm pretty sure it was Arabic because I've heard it on TV, but I'm not a hundred percent sure."

Kostya's grip got tighter on Lark and she was glad he was with her.

"Candy, can you tell me what else you heard?"

"I heard Rick scream, and cry and beg. I heard him tell them about every other person he worked with at Sanofi. He even mentioned me. I thought for sure he'd tell them I was in the house somewhere, but he didn't. Instead, he..." She covered her face.

"What did he do?"

"He told them I was on vacation. Las Vegas with my sister. He protected me. I told you, he was a nice man." Candy sobbed.

"Did he ever tell them how to get their hands on the code?"

"No, he didn't. He would have if he had it. Rick couldn't have withstood that kind of torture."

"How did you get out of there?" Lark wanted to know.

"Rick eventually quit crying and it got quiet. I knew they'd killed him. I still didn't leave the bathroom for a long time."

"But when you did?" Lark prompted.

"All the bedding, including the sheets were gone. So was Rick. I saw a little bit of blood on the carpet, but Rick had been screaming about a knife, so I know they'd been cutting him. There should have been a lot of blood. That's why they took the covers and sheets when they took his body."

"You should have told me as soon as you left the house," Lark admonished. "I would have been there for you. I would have helped you."

"No, you would have taken me to the police. There is no way the police could have saved me against these guys. Even though Rick told them I was out of town, they still went to my apartment."

"What?"

Candy nodded. "I went home and I heard noises inside, like they were tearing the place apart. I had to run. So I called Dawn."

Lark wanted to deny Candy's words, but she couldn't. She stepped forward and pulled her away from her sister, then wrapped Candy in a hug. "Please don't ever disappear on me like that again. You scared the hell out of me. You're my friend."

Candy gave her a dazed look.

"It's true, you are. You *are* one of my friends, Candy. Believe it. Please stay in touch. As soon as this is over with, I will get back in touch with you, I promise."

"What will you do?" Candy asked.

"We're going to stop them," Lark said emphatically.

"No more selling secrets, and the men who killed Rick will pay."

"Do you promise?"

Lark pulled Candy in for another fierce hug. "On my honor."

22

"A Waffle House?" Kostya asked for the fifth time.

"Quit your bitching and eat. This is the shit," Gideon grinned.

"You're from San Jose, California, they don't have Waffle Houses there," Kostya protested.

"Kostya, you're sounding like a big baby, what is your problem?" Lark demanded. She was sitting in the booth across from him, next to Gideon. For the last hour, they'd been acting like long-lost friends. "Seriously, these are the best waffles on the planet, but it's the sausage, egg, and cheese bowl that's the real treat."

Kostya looked at the congealed heart-attack-inducing heap in the bowl sitting in front of her and shuddered.

"I'm fine with my over-easy eggs and bacon."

"Then for God's sake, eat it," Gideon said as he started in on his second waffle.

Kostya started eating, not even noticing what he was putting in his mouth, too astounded by the amount of, and type of, food that Lark was consuming.

"Dude, pay attention. We need to talk about the next steps," Gideon said as he snapped his fingers in front of Kostya's face.

"The next steps are that Lark is going to go home with me for a couple of days."

"I am?" Lark's head popped up and her fork stopped mid-air.

"You are. First, we'll talk to the authorities. After that, the story can wait for a minute or two now that we know that Candy is safe. I want us to have a little time together. I want to show you where I live."

"You mean you're not all excited to see my little one-bedroom apartment in Manhattan?" she teased.

"Damn, girl, I thought your Mama was a gazillionaire."

Lark grinned over at Gideon. "I'm pretty sure she's a multi-gazillionaire. But as I've told Kostya, that's her money, not mine. Therefore, I live in a one-bedroom apartment in Manhattan. But to be fair, I'm betting my apartment costs more than your house in Virginia Beach." She wiggled her eyebrows at Kostya.

"I wouldn't take that bet if I were you, Lieutenant."

"Lark?" Kostya asked quietly.

She put down her fork, pressed her napkin against her lips then rested her hand against the table, palm up. He grabbed it and tangled his fingers with hers.

"I would like nothing better than to see your house and spend some quality time with you, Lieutenant Barona."

"Shit, I would have thought you'd all quality timed enough already." Gideon was smiling despite his sarcasm.

"You're just jealous," Kostya said without heat. "Wasn't

the last time you quality timed was at Sebastian's wedding? How is Jada Harlow? Have you been keeping in contact?"

When Gideon didn't answer, Kostya forced his gaze away from Lark's and looked at his friend. Gideon was frowning.

"What?" Kostya asked.

"It's complicated."

"Complicated how?"

Gideon gave Lark a considering look, then shrugged his shoulders as if to say he trusted her. He set down his fork and leaned back against the booth.

"She's young."

Kostya nodded. "And?"

"I mean *young*. She's twenty-four."

Kostya laughed. "Serves you right for making fun of my age so damned often."

"How old are you?" Lark asked.

"He's thirty-seven," Kostya answered for Gideon.

"So, I'm thirty-one. There are ten years between the two of us," Lark said, tipping her head toward Kostya. "There'd only be thirteen years between you and Jada. What's the big deal?"

"Think it through, Lark. Think about what you've accomplished in those seven years between twenty-four and thirty-one." Gideon rubbed the top of his head.

"What about your feelings?" she asked.

"Feelings?" he asked.

Kostya snorted. Yep, that was his man, the techno geek.

"Yeah, emotions. You know, *les passions*," she said the last two words with a French accent.

"Those are overrated. Well, maybe not the passion part. But she's too young to toy with. What's more, she's Sebastian's wife's best friend."

"What went on between you two at their wedding?" Kostya asked. He had a pretty good idea, but he needed to know to get the full picture.

Gideon glared at him. "It doesn't matter. Look, this is a stupid conversation. Just let it go, okay?"

Kostya held up his hands, palms out. "You got it."

"So what are we going to do about Lark's little problem?"

"I'll call Ryker tonight, then when we fly in tomorrow morning we can circle up. How does that sound?"

"Sounds like a plan," Gideon said as he waved down the waitress.

Yep, the man sure did like his waffles.

———

RYKER WAS WAITING for them at baggage claim. "I took the liberty of bringing your SUV, Lieutenant."

Kostya scowled. "And how did you manage that?"

"I hot-wired it," Ryker grinned.

"Dammit, that's not good for the engine. I've told all of you to quit doing that."

"The others don't know how to do it right," Ryker said as he led them toward the parking garage. "I have a light touch."

"And here I was nice enough to put your Harley away before our mission. Last time I do you a favor," Kostya grumbled. "Give me my keys," he demanded as they walked up to his Bronco.

"I hot-wired it, remember?"

"For the love of God." Kostya fished his wallet out of his pocket and pulled out a spare key, and glared at Ryker who now had his arm around Lark's shoulders.

"How are you doing, beautiful?" Ryker asked Lark. "Are you going to make stripping your second career?"

"No, she's not," Kostya bit out. "And get your hands off of her."

Ryker and Gideon laughed. Kostya took Lark's elbow in a gentle hold and guided her to the front passenger seat.

"I can sit in the back, I have shorter legs."

"No way. You're sitting in the front," Gideon stated. He opened the back of the Bronco and started throwing their luggage in.

"We're going to my house," Ryker informed them. "I have lunch set up. I want to hear everything."

"In that case, swing by my condo, I want to grab my other laptop too," Gideon told Kostya.

Kostya gave Lark a quick kiss, then shut her door and got into the driver's seat. It was good to be finally driving his vehicle. By the time he made it in front of Gideon's place, he felt settled. The smell of the ocean surrounded him along with the subtle scent of Lark beside him. Life was fucking perfect.

"Be back in a second," Gideon said as he hefted his duffel out of the back and hot-footed it up the walk to his place.

"Are you going to fill me in?" Ryker asked as he leaned forward.

"Let's wait until we get to your place," Lark said. "Today is Amy's day off; she's been texting me for updates, so I want to call her up and put her on speaker."

Kostya laughed at Ryker's sour expression.

"She's already played her part, why does she need to be involved?"

Lark looked at him curiously. "I would have thought you would have liked that idea."

Ryker was slow in responding. "She hasn't returned any of my calls, so yeah, normally it would be nice to hear her voice again. I just don't want her wrapped up in anything dangerous, and something tells me that this is."

"At least your close in age," Kostya smiled at Ryker.

"Huh?"

"Don't mind him," Lark said as Gideon climbed into the car.

"Let's get going, I have some ideas." He tapped the back of Kostya's car seat, and he started up his Bronco.

It took them forty minutes to get to Gideon's, have him gather what he needed, then get back to Kostya's bronco. Then it was twenty minutes to Ryker's place, a small rambler.

"I've got steaks," he said as soon as they got into the house. "The baked potatoes and corn are wrapped and they're going onto the grill too. In the meantime, fill me in." He opened his fridge, and handed out beers, then headed out to his back patio.

Kostya watched Lark easily fit into the situation. He'd seen her do that in every situation they'd been in and he loved that about her. No matter what, Lark could blend in.

"So?" Ryker asked as he lit the coals.

"Hold on, let me call Amy," Lark said as she gave Ryker a sly grin. She pulled her phone out of her purse, put it on speaker, then set it down on the picnic table.

"Yo," Amy answered. "You didn't start without me, did you?"

"Yes," Ryker answered. "It's all figured out, you can hang up now."

"Blow me," Amy said.

Gideon, Lark, and Kostya laughed.

"No, we're just starting to go over things. Some of them are up in the air," Lark answered.

"Well, now you have me," Amy said with satisfaction.

Kostya sat back as Lark started talking. First, she filled in Ryker and Amy about what they had found out from Candy.

"What about work? Hasn't Sanofi done a welfare check on him? It's been what, four weeks since he's shown up to work," Amy said.

"That's definitely strange," Ryker agreed.

"Aren't you putting the steaks on a little early? You just put the potatoes on the grill."

"My house, therefore my grill. No comments from the peanut gallery."

Kostya rolled his eyes, then turned his attention back to Lark.

She'd brought her laptop in as well as her many notepads. It was damned cute how many pencils she had lined up. He and the other guys had smothered chuckles when she'd pulled out her electric pencil sharpener. At his question, Lark grabbed one of her notepads and started leafing through it.

Gideon looked up from his laptop. "I checked the employment records at Sanofi, and Rick's down for short-term disability. Apparently, he had gallbladder surgery."

Kostya watched with a smile as they all frowned. "Apparently, none of you have had to fill out paperwork on behalf of one of your employees. Schroeder must have phoned that in and handed it to HR."

"Wouldn't he be trying to get ahold of Rick?" Amy asked through the phone's speaker.

"Definitely," Lark answered. "What's worse, I think that these men with accents might be visiting the other Sanofi employees. Gideon, can you check to see if any of the others have gone on short-term disability?"

Ryker flipped the steaks and Kostya's stomach growled as they waited for Gideon to answer the question.

"Got it," Gideon looked up from his laptop, his brown eyes gleaming. "Guy named Mel Stanley had a pretty traumatic skiing accident. It really fucked him up. Broken bones and lots of lacerations. He's been in the hospital for two weeks. Then there's Donald Harkins. Supposedly he was in a car with a friend, but he was thrown during the crash and the friend left him for dead and drove off. This was ten days ago. He's not expected to make it."

Lark shivered.

"Enough of this shit. I need to bring in my friend from the FBI. Rick Turner was in charge of engineers who were working for the Missile Defense Agency. I would bet my bottom dollar that whoever is doing all the killing and maiming is after code from that project."

Kostya nodded as did his two men.

"Amy, honey, I'm going to have to cut this phone call short. I have to call Trevor over at the FBI. This can't wait another minute."

"Understood. Be safe, Lark. Make those idiots take care of you. Just because they're all brawny military types doesn't mean they have this in the bag. Especially any goof with the last name McQueen; that shit just sounds made up to me."

"Listen here, pipsqueak—"

Lark cut the connection before Ryker could say anything more.

"Dammit, Ryker, I think I smell my steak burning," Kostya grumbled.

23

JUST WALKING UP TO KOSTYA'S HOUSE WAS A PLEASURE. Kostya took her in the side door and she got to appreciate the two-story home, with the cantilevered roof that extended out over a cedar deck at sunset.

"How often do you sit on this deck and drink a beer?"

"Not often. Now, if you want to know how often I savor a glass of whiskey, that's another story," Kostya said with a smile. He guided her through the door that led into the kitchen. She was met by warm granite countertops and stainless steel appliances.

"I have to ask again, how much does the Navy pay?"

Kostya chuckled. "I bought this house after my divorce. It was a real fixer-upper, but it had good bones. I've been working on it for years. It all came together last year."

"Divorce?"

"Yeah, Debra and I split nine years ago."

"I'm sorry, Kostya. Divorce is rough."

He paused as he was opening the refrigerator. "It can be. But it was definitely the right thing to do, at least for me. Gideon pointed something out not so long ago, and I realized why we hadn't worked out." He opened the freezer. "I have homemade lasagna that I can warm up, how does that sound?"

"It sounds like a lot. The steaks at Ryker's were more than enough."

Kostya grinned as he closed the freezer. "What do you think of some fruit, cheese, and crackers?"

"That sounds wonderful." She watched him start to pull things out of his refrigerator, then meandered to the big window overlooking the bay. This sure as hell beat her view back in Manhattan.

I wonder if he needs this? If it keeps him sane when he comes back from the field.

She grinned when she saw his bookcase. It was bigger than hers! She couldn't resist checking it out. Lots of biographies on military commanders—no big surprise there—but seeing Mark Twain, Louisa May Alcott, and Jules Verne tickled the hell out of her. She looked back at the kitchen and saw that he was cutting something up, so she continued to peruse. On the bottom two shelves were books in Russian. She recognized some names, like Dostoevsky, Chekhov, and Solzhenitsyn but it was the very bottom shelf that caught her attention. She pulled out two tiny books, obviously well-worn children's books. The first one had a cat on the front, and when she opened it up it showed the cat watching over a sleeping boy in his bed. It went on to show more animals with the little boy; there was even a picture of a rabbit playing the violin. When Lark looked closely, she could see that there were jam fingerprints made by a child on the cover. It was definitely a much-loved and treasured book.

The second book was for an older child because it was

mostly text, but it showed two little boys on the front. One boy was carrying the other boy in the snow.

"What do you have there?" Kostya asked from behind her.

"Books," Lark smiled up at him. "You must have read them as a child. She held them up. The one with a cat on the cover was on top.

Kostya smiled as he motioned for her to follow him to the couch. He set down a platter along with two glasses of wine.

"I remember that book. When Irina and I first came to America we were sent to a temporary foster family. There were lots of other kids. The people there were nice, but it was so different than what we were used to. Nobody there spoke Russian, and it seemed like forever before I could understand English. But one of the social workers who checked in on us found a couple of movies in Russian and that book in Russian to make me feel more at home." He handed her the glass of white wine.

"There are two books," Lark corrected him. "Here's the second." She pulled the book with the two little boys from underneath the other and handed it to him. "It doesn't have any pictures. How old were you when you came to America? Were you able to read it?"

As Kostya took the book from her, his hands were visibly trembling. "Yes," he said hoarsely.

Lark waited. He didn't say anything more.

"Yes what?" she asked gently.

He traced the picture on the front. "I was able to read it."

Kostya didn't look up. He was staring at the book, not moving. It was eerie. She needed to get him talking.

"Did you read it to Irina?"

He shook his head.

She put her hand over his. "Honey? What's the matter?"

He looked up at her, and his eyes were filled with more pain than anybody should ever have to feel. She gasped at the sight.

"Kostya, sweetheart. Talk to me."

"I don't know if I can," he choked out. "I was weak. So weak. I failed him." His voice trailed away. Again Lark waited for him to continue.

"Who did you fail?" Lark eventually asked softly.

"Roman," Kostya whispered.

Lark tried to grapple with his answer. She knew he couldn't be talking about his nephew; his nephew was fine. She looked down at the book in his hands.

"Who's Roman?"

"My brother. My older brother. It was my job to keep him safe, and I failed." Kostya started to tremble. Lark set her wineglass down on the coffee table and didn't care when it toppled over. Instead, she launched herself at Kostya, pulling him into her arms.

"I've got you," she crooned. "I've got you."

He grabbed at her like she was the only solid thing in a world gone mad. Lark hadn't the slightest idea what she said to him, she just knew that she kept talking, soothing him, almost as if he were that child on the cover of the book. When Kostya had regained control, he stiffened. She could feel him begin to draw inward, but there wasn't a chance in hell she was going to allow it.

"Booze."

"Huh?"

She released her hold on him and pushed up from the couch. "Booze," she gave him a saucy grin. "I've already spilled my wine, so it's time for the good stuff." She strode to the kitchen. "Where's the Jameson?" Lark opened the cabinet above the stove.

She felt him behind her. "For God's sake, woman, I would not store my good whiskey above something that heats up." He reached up to the cupboard over the refrigerator and pulled out an unopened bottle of liquid gold. "So, my meltdown drove you to drink, did it?" he asked as he pulled out two highball glasses. "How much do you need?" He broke the seal on the bottle.

"Dial it back, big guy. This is the part where we agreed to share dysfunctional childhoods, share some booze, and laughs. Don't go all broody Russian on me." She took the bottle out of his hands and poured herself a finger of whiskey.

He stared at her, befuddled. She had to fight back a smile. She pulled the paper towel roll off the holder, took her drink, and went back to the sofa. When she started to clean up the spilled wine mess, he took the paper towels out of her hands and took over.

"Sit down and tell me how in the hell I went from having a nervous breakdown all over you to having laughs over our childhoods."

"Well, maybe not laughs. After all, you were all gentle, sweet, and nice to me about the big bad step-grandfather crap..." Lark sighed. "So I guess I need to shove some compassion your way."

Kostya chuckled.

Lark sat back and crossed her legs, enjoying the fact that he immediately stared at them, even if they were in jeans. Good, the man was definitely back in the moment and he wasn't going all deep-freeze on her. Now she should be able to get him to share with her.

"So?" Lark asked as she patted the seat cushion next to her.

Kostya nodded and sat down. He took a healthy swallow of whiskey. "There's really not much to tell about my childhood."

Yeah, sure.

Lark plucked his glass out of his hand and carefully deposited both of their drinks on the coffee table. She didn't want a spillage repeat. She got up off the couch and unbuttoned the first two buttons of her blouse. Kostya's eyes turned navy blue. Lark swung one leg over his lap, then straddled him, shimmying down so that both knees rested comfortably along each of his hips.

"There now, I'm holding you as you held me. Fair's fair."

"Lark, I never talk about this." His words were a plea. But she couldn't allow it, he desperately needed to talk.

"Kostya," she breathed out his name as she curved her hands around both sides of his neck. "Tell me about your brother. What was he like?" She kept her voice soft.

His eyes searched hers. She tried to give him all the empathy and understanding he would need for his story, and he must have seen it because he answered her.

"He was smart," he said solemnly. "Roman was so much smarter than me. At school, he was the smartest in his class, even smarter than all the older kids."

Lark nodded and waited.

"But he never made me feel stupid. We were a team. Roman was sick a lot. Mama said it was lung disease, so I was bigger than he was and kids tried to bully him."

Lark loved his ferocious expression. "You protected him, didn't you? Even though you were younger. How much younger were you?"

"He was two years older, and yes, I protected him. That was my job. In my family, everyone knew that I was the protector. It was my duty."

"How old were you then, Kostya?" Lark stroked her thumb along his jaw.

"It was always that way."

She glanced over at the book. "Did you ever have to carry him? In the snow?"

He tried to turn his head away from her, but she held strong. "Kostya?"

"I couldn't. I had to carry Irina," he whispered. "Roman had to walk by himself, and I couldn't help him." There was a wealth of pain in his voice.

"How old were you then?"

"Seven." For a moment she saw tears in his eyes, but he closed them. "I was seven years old."

24

LARK CHOKED BACK A WHIMPER. INSTEAD, SHE KISSED HIS cheek. "Why were you in the snow together?"

He opened his eyes and cleared his throat. "This is not an unusual story, Lark. Russia was a hard place back then. Bad things happened. People were killed. You just had to find a way to survive. You had to be strong." His jaw tightened and he swallowed. "You had to be brave."

She nodded, holding his head still so that he was forced to look her in the eyes. "I get it. But you were just seven years old, Honey."

"Age didn't matter, it was who you were. I was me. It was my job to take care of Irina and Roman. It. Was. My. Job."

"Where were your parents?"

"That night they were killed. I didn't understand at the time, but it was KGB. Mama was…"

She lost him. His eyes faded away to a long-ago time in a faraway land. Someplace that was filled with agony for a little boy named Kostya.

"Honey?" The one word could barely be heard.

"Lark." His eyes focused on her. "My mother. There was so much blood, but I couldn't go to her. I had to stay hidden. I had to stay with Roman and the baby."

"Of course you did. Of course, you did." She stroked his cheek, his jaw, his neck.

"The monsters dragged Papa away. When we were trying to sleep in the tent one night, Fedor told us the KGB had killed him."

"Fedor?"

"A pig. He needed to die, but I needed him, and I didn't know how to kill back then."

Her fingers involuntarily tightened on his neck as she bit her lip. "Tell me more," she urged. "How did you escape?"

He pulled her in for a hug, sucking in a deep breath. Lark knew that he was taking in her scent because she'd taken comfort from his smell often enough. "They seemed like monsters to me. They were dressed in black and had black ski masks. They set our home on fire after they killed Mama. They wanted to kill whoever was left. I made Roman take Irina out the window and wait at the church while I found grandmother's diamond brooch in the mattress. We needed it to pay Fedor to take us across the border into Poland."

"How old was Irina?"

"She was three. The snow was deep that winter, she had to be carried. Fedor guided two other people to Poland that month. It was a very old husband and wife. They could barely help themselves, they couldn't help us. I had to carry Irina."

"But surely this Fedor man could have helped."

Lark managed not to squeak when Kostya tightened

his hold on her—so hard she thought her ribs might break.

"*Ublydudok!*" Kostya roared. He started to rise from the couch, but Lark pushed down on his shoulders.

"No, stay with me. I need you to hold me," she cried out, begging him to stay on the sofa. Kostya hovered over the cushions, then finally slumped back down.

"I'm sorry, Lark, did I hurt you?"

"No, Honey, of course you didn't. But Fedor did, didn't he?"

Kostya's breaths became choppy. "I'd gotten all of the coats we had before I escaped from the burning house, but we were always cold. At night, Fedor would only build a very small fire to cook whatever rabbit or rat he'd caught during the day. Even deep in the forest, he said the soldiers might find us, so we had to be careful and a big fire might draw their attention He kept telling us how lucky we were to have tents, but the one we slept in had a tear in it, and snow came in at night. I made sure that I slept under that part, not Roman or Irina."

Of course, you did.

He was breaking her heart; she didn't know how much longer she could listen and not cry. But she had to keep it together.

"By the second week, Roman's coughing got really bad. The old lady had brought medicine with her. She gave it to Roman, but it didn't work. He kept getting sicker and sicker. He was having trouble walking. Fedor said we had to leave him behind."

Lark knew that Kostya wasn't aware of his tears.

"What happened?" Lark choked out the question.

"The old couple gave Fedor more money so we could

rest an extra day, but that next morning, Roman couldn't get up, no matter how hard I tried to help him."

Lark lifted herself high up on her knees so that she could hold Kostya against her breast. She barely contained her sobs.

"Honey, what happened next?"

"Fedor packed up the tent, and there was Roman lying in the snow, with no blankets, no nothing. Irina was crying and even the old *babushka* and *dedushka* told me we had to leave Roman."

Kostya stopped talking, and Lark didn't want to know the rest of the story. She didn't. But she had to. Kostya had been living with this for thirty-four years. He needed to share this.

"What happened next?"

"Roman grabbed my hand and yanked me hard. I didn't know he'd have that much strength, but there I was with my face in the snow right next to his. He used every swear word we'd ever learned and told me I had to leave him. I had to take Irina and go."

Lark felt Kostya's tears as they trickled onto her breasts. "And?"

"I begged Fedor to carry Irina with him. To please take her. He refused."

Lark was shaking. One sob escaped her.

"Even though I was responsible for my baby sister, I couldn't leave Roman, I just couldn't." Kostya's arm's gripped her even tighter. "I held Irina on my lap and rocked her. I sang every song I knew until I was hoarse. I have no idea when he died, but when I finally stopped singing, his arms and legs were stiff and his lips were blue. I couldn't save him, Lark. I couldn't." He looked up at her, so lost and bewildered. It was as if it had happened yesterday.

Lark couldn't stop sobbing. How had this little boy survived?

"But you left? You caught up to them?"

Kostya nodded. He gave a wet chuckle. "I'm pretty sure that the old couple walked really slow so that I could catch up. Fedor was furious."

"I hope he burns in hell."

Kostya looked up at her. His eyes didn't contain any shadows.

"I do too."

Lark wiped away his tears and kissed his forehead, his cheeks then finally his lips. The salty taste of despair eventually morphed into soft pleasure.

"Will you come into my bed with me, Lark Sorensen?"

"There is no place on Earth that I'd rather be."

THINGS HAD CHANGED after that night.

Lark fell into an easy rhythm in Kostya's home. She knew that she was in love, totally and utterly in love with the best man in the world. She had no idea where the future might lead, but being with him was the happiest she had ever been.

She checked in with Trevor Simmons daily, ensuring that Schroeder and the rest of the men at Sanofi would eventually be arrested. Currently, the FBI was still gathering all the evidence they required to arrest them, but they had no leads on the mysterious foreigners. They were leaning hard on Mel Stanley to see what he could remember. Trevor knew that Lark was holding something back, but she refused to give up Candy. Trevor was just going to have to work the case without her.

Lark cuddled up on one of the deck chairs with a thick wool blanket and a mug of tea. Kostya would be back from work in a few hours, and she was contemplating calling Amy to figure out something to cook him for dinner, but she highly doubted that would be happening. Lark believed in cooking like she used to believe in love. Which meant she didn't.

She swiped through her phone to see what could be delivered. They'd already gone through all of his frozen meals, so she had to figure out something different.

Her thumb hovered over Amy's number when her Mom's picture popped up. Lark grinned and accepted the call, so happy to see that she was calling via Facetime. She really wanted to see her mom's face.

"Hi, Mom. I've missed you." She snuggled back into the deck chair and pulled the blanket over her legs.

"If you missed me so much, you might have called me," her mom countered with a twinkle in her eye.

"Oh I'm sorry, did I miss some voicemails and texts?" Lark teased.

Beatrice Allen chuckled. "It's been kind of busy around here. How about with you?"

"I'm not conquering the technological universe, so my world is easy."

Her mom snorted. "I don't believe that for a minute. Who's going under the microscope next? Is it one of my peers? Is it some banana republic? Is it our government? Is it me?"

"Aw, Ma, I'd give you a twenty-four-hour heads up if I was going to publish something about you," Lark promised.

Her mother let out a loud laugh. "I appreciate that, Honey. Now tell me how you're really doing. I talked to Amy and she said you had a new guy in your life who wasn't pathepic."

Lark shook her head and gave her mom an exasperated look. "Why are you checking up on me through Amy? You obviously have my phone number."

"Honey, you know I love Amy. Her mother is a blight on mothers everywhere. I worry about her, so I like to check in."

Lark sank deeper into the lounge chair. Hell, she almost melted. This was why she adored her mother. It was her big heart.

"So tell me about this man," her mom persisted.

"You know him."

"Please dear God, tell me it's Lieutenant Barona."

She sat up so fast that she almost dropped her phone. "Wait a minute, how did you know that? Did Amy tell you?"

"No, but I met him when he was visiting the Nuri family, and he's stunning."

"Mom, there's more to him than his looks."

"I wasn't talking about his looks," Beatrice protested.

"What else could you have meant?"

"Honey, how he was with those girls, took my breath away. Then the way he handled Samira and coaxed smile after smile out of her was enchanting. I was so impressed. Then when we went to dinner, he had me laughing so hard, that I could barely take a breath. Plus I was impressed by the depth and breadth of subjects he could talk about."

"Not tech, though."

Again her mother laughed. "Nope, he's as technically

inept as you are. More's the pity, I was always hoping that you would find somebody who could even you out in that regard."

Her brow furled. "You thought I might find a man?"

"Once you pulled your head out of your ass and stopped dating those pathepic men. God, I love that word. Your friend Amy is fabulous."

"Yes, she is. But let's get back on topic. Are you saying I had my head up my ass?"

"Yep. I've tried to coax you into counseling a few times, but you're a stubborn little so-and-so."

Lark snorted. She knew her mom was really calling her a stubborn bitch, but she was okay with that. *If the shoe fits...*

"Did you love my dad?" Lark suddenly asked.

"With all my heart. With all my soul." She watched as her mother's eyes went dreamy. "Why are you asking, baby girl?"

"You know I never believed that was in the cards for me. Love, I mean."

"I know. It broke my heart. Your grandmother still beats herself up for that."

"Mom, no. Please say she doesn't. I hate that."

Beatrice's face took on a stormy look. "Yeah, well I hate the fact that she let Harris Evans anywhere near you." She paused and her face crumpled. "But I hate myself more for not realizing what was going on. You should have been my first priority. Your father would have been so angry with me if he'd known what I had done."

"Mom, as soon as you found out, you had Harris behind bars."

"Yeah, but he was out in two days. The bastard never even stood trial. I couldn't get Mom to testify."

"Hey," Lark touched her phone. "Stop it, it's all water under the bridge, and, and, I've pulled my head out of my ass."

"More like someone got out a crowbar and unstuck it for you," Beatrice grimaced.

Lark scrunched her nose. "Thanks, nice imagery."

"So, Kostya, huh?"

"Yeah," Lark sighed. "Kostya. I love him. Mom, I always knew he was a hero, I'm serious about that. But how he got there? The road he's traveled? I just don't know how he came out whole."

"Do you want to talk about it?" Beatrice asked quietly.

Lark shook her head, knowing her mother would respect that.

"So he's it, huh? He's your forever after?"

"Oh yeah."

"What did he say when you told him you loved him?"

Lark stiffened and her mother laughed. "So my daughter who makes her living with words has forgotten to tell the man she loves that she loves him."

"I am such a fucking idiot." Lark pushed the blanket off and rushed to the sliding glass door.

"Honey," Beatrice called out. Lark pulled the phone back up to her face after she was in the house.

"Mom, I have to go."

"It's going to be all right, Lark, I promise. He knows you love him."

"I've got to go."

SHE RUSHED to Kostya's closet where she'd hung up some of the clothes that Amy had sent to her. There it was, the silver dress that wasn't hers. Trust Amy to send one of her slinky little bits of fabric. It was perfect!

Lark threw it on the bed, then headed for the shower. She was midway through the shower when it occurred to her to call Ryker for the name of a restaurant to take Kostya. She wanted to pull out all of the romantic stops for tonight. She tried to think of all of the shoes that Amy had sent.

She ran naked into the bedroom and grabbed her phone so that she could call Ryker as she started to slather on lotion.

Where is my vanilla lotion?

She ran back to the closet. She'd been trying to be careful not to junk up Kostya's bathroom, so she'd been keeping a lot of her things in her suitcase in the closet. Whenever Kostya had noticed, he'd pulled it back out of her suitcase and put it back on the counter. He was a total stinker. But he hadn't found her lotions yet.

As she grabbed the tube of lotion she heard her phone ring. Hopefully, it wasn't Kostya saying he was coming home early. She frowned when she saw Candy's number on the phone. Lark put a smile on her face when she answered the phone, hoping the smile would come through in her voice.

"Hi, Candy, how are you?"

"Lark?"

Lark didn't recognize the voice on the phone.

"Is this Candy?"

"Lark, it's me. Candy." Lark still couldn't place her voice, it sounded both gravelly and weak.

"You don't sound like Candy. I need to confirm it's you. What are the names of your two sisters?"

"Rosie and Dawn." This time it sounded like she was crying. But at least she finally knew it was Candy.

"God, Candy, what's wrong?" She pulled the towel tighter around her naked body.

"I didn't know what else to do. I'm so sorry. They were going to kill her. I couldn't let them kill her." Her words came out garbled and fast, but Lark got the gist of it. Candy was sorry and some 'they' were going to kill someone.

"Slow down, Honey. Who *is* they? Who was it who tried to kill someone?"

"They broke into our apartment in the middle of the night."

"Who did?" Lark asked again gently.

"They were after the code that Rick sold them."

Oh God, not them. How had they found her?

"Tell me what happened, Candy."

"They cut me. They said Rick had gotten money from them. He had shown them part of the missile code, so they knew he had it, and I must be hiding it to sell to a higher bidder." Candy started panting and coughing.

"Take your time."

"They didn't believe me when I said I didn't know anything." Candy whimpered. "They kept cutting me. Then they started cutting Dawn. They had duct tape over her mouth. They told me if I screamed, they would slit her throat."

Candy started crying so hard that Lark couldn't understand a word she said next.

"I need you to calm down. Slow down and explain it to me," Lark coaxed.

"They wouldn't believe me. No matter what I said, they wouldn't believe me," Candy wailed.

"Jesus," Lark murmured. "This happened last night?"

"No, two, maybe three nights ago. I was in surgery, this is the first time I've really been awake."

Lark looked up at her reflection. She looked as scared as she felt.

"I kept telling them I didn't know what they were talking about. I tried to fight them off, but they kept cutting me. But I had nothing to tell them, Lark. I couldn't even think of a lie."

Somehow, Lark kept ahold of the phone.

"I'm so sorry you went through this. How's Dawn?"

"Dead," Candy whispered. "Even after I told them about you. Even after I lied and thought it was over, they shot her in the head. Then they left me for dead."

"What do you mean, told them about me?"

"When they put the gun to Dawn's head, I had to tell them something, anything, to get them to believe that I knew something. I told them that you had the code. That Rick was working with you to write an exposé."

"You *what*?" Lark couldn't wrap her head around what she was saying.

"It's all I could think of to save Dawn's life," Candy said fiercely. "I would have said anything."

"It's okay, Honey, I understand."

"Can you forgive me?" she pleaded.

"Of course I forgive you. Were they the same men in Rick's house?"

"They were foreign. They spoke the same, Arabic. This time I saw them. They were big, like your guy." Candy started panting for breath again. "Your guy, Barona, he can keep you safe, right?"

Lark's mind was buzzing wildly. She could think of three or four Middle Eastern terrorist organizations who would love to get their hands on the United States missile defense plans because once they knew the US defense plan, it was easy enough to figure out ways to get around those defenses.

"Lark, I promise, I wouldn't have told them your name. But I thought I could save Dawn." She started to cry. "Please tell me that SEAL can protect you. He can, can't he?"

"Are you sure they came to your apartment two or three nights ago? Monday night?"

"What day is it today?" Candy asked.

"It's Wednesday."

"Oh God, this happened on Saturday. They came on Saturday."

A chill ran up Lark's spine.

I need to call Kostya.

"Candy, I've got to go. I'll call you soon." Lark hung up and called Kostya. She got his voicemail. She hung up. She keyed in a text.

BAD GUYS GOT TO CANDY. KILLED DAWN. WE NEED A PLAN. CALL ME.

LARK LOOKED in the mirror and studied her pale face and red-rimmed eyes. Thinking about the tiny red-headed firecracker, she wanted to scream. How dare someone kill her! She had been so fiercely protective of Candy. Lark shut her eyes and took a deep breath and wondered if it was her fault that Dawn had been killed and Candy had nearly died. Maybe it was. She probably should have told Trevor about Candy's involvement with Rick.

Lark clenched her hands into fists and dropped her towel before heading to the bedroom. Not even seeing Amy's pretty silver dress spread out on the bed could make her feel better. She took a deep breath.

Get it together.

First things first, she needed to get dressed. It was time for the Wild Bunch to circle up and go out for a ride.

Lark's lips tipped up at the thought. Gideon with his computer and her with her electronic pencil sharpener probably didn't fit in with the Wild Bunch analogy, but what the hell? She shrugged. She went to the drawer that Kostya had insisted she use. Actually, he wanted her to take over half of his dresser, but at the time that had made her feel kind of hinky, so she had limited it to one drawer. She pulled out underwear, jeans, and a long-sleeved Henley then threw it on. She'd forgo the vanilla lotion. The lotion and make-up would be for later when they weren't in investigative mode.

When she was clothed and her boots were on, she went into the kitchen to make herself a protein drink and think about the next steps. The only saving grace in all of this was that the men who'd hurt Candy and killed Dawn wouldn't know to find Lark here in Virginia Beach. She rested her elbows against the granite countertop as she sipped her drink and stared out the windows into the horizon.

"Shit!"

She slammed down the glass and picked up her phone. She scrolled through her recent calls, found Trevor's number, and called it.

Voicemail!

"Jesus, isn't anybody answering their phone today?"

"Trevor, call me. It's Lark. It's urgent! I mean now!"

As soon as she hung up, she texted the same message to him. Who in the hell actually listened to their voicemails these days? But they sure as hell reacted to their goddamn texts. Lark ignored her protein shake as she pulled up Gideon's contact and tried him.

"Of course," she muttered. She left a voicemail for him to call her as soon as he could, then she texted him the same damn thing.

"Where are you guys? Soaping up each other in the shower?"

Of course, the same thing happened when she called Ryker, so she texted him too. She was too hyped up to sit on her hands and do nothing. It wasn't in her DNA. She grabbed her computer bag, carefully pulled out her laptop, and rested it on the kitchen table, then upended all of her papers onto the table.

"Time to get to work."

If she could figure out who these assholes were, then maybe they could backtrack and hunt *them* down, instead of always being hunted by them.

Lark tidied up her notepads into two piles, the 9x11 in one pile and the 5x8 in another. She went to the last page on each of the purple pads.

Her phone rang, and she answered it, "Kostya?"

"This is Trevor. What do you have for me?" he asked brusquely.

"You're going to be mad, but suck it up."

"I'm not liking this already."

She could picture him rubbing his hand over his shiny bald head.

"I have a source who was dating Rick Turner. She saw him being killed. The people who killed him managed to track her down to Florida and killed her sister last Saturday, and almost killed her too."

"What the fuck?" Trevor roared. "Are you fucking kidding me with this? Jesus Christ, Sorensen, you're supposed to be smarter than this! You're behaving like a rank amateur!"

Lark shivered. Shit, maybe she really had screwed up. She'd just been trying to protect Candy. She'd been so sure she was doing the right thing, that Candy would be safe, but...

"Where the fuck are you?" Trevor demanded to know.

"I'm in Virginia Beach. I'm here with Lieutenant Kostya Barona."

"Well, that's something. Keep your ass planted there; at least they don't know about you." He heaved a heavy sigh.

"Well, actually they do. Candy gave them my name."

The silence that came over the line was deafening.

"Lark, you're fucking kidding me. Please to fucking God, say you are kidding me. Right now."

Lark swallowed. "I'm not."

"Is he with you?" Trevor spat out the question.

"No. I'm alone."

"Get the fuck out of there. Now!"

Lark looked around the living room. Suddenly she imagined ninjas swinging through the plate glass window on nylon ropes with Samurai swords.

"Trevor, you're freaking out. They don't have any idea I'm in Virginia, let alone at some random guy's house on the beach."

"Call Barona, tell him to meet you somewhere, and get the hell out of there. You do this. You do this, this very minute. Are you hearing me? Do you have a gun?"

"Uh, no."

"Barona will. Call him, find out where his is, and get it. Then leave the house. You got me?"

Lark nodded, caught herself, then answered. "Yes, I got you."

"Call me the minute you're on neutral ground. Then call me again when you're with Barona. Got it?"

"Got it."

The line went dead.

25

SHE CHECKED HER PHONE, BUT NEITHER KOSTYA, GIDEON, or Ryker had responded back to her, and she was too freaked out to think about them showering together. She'd never really considered the fact that Kostya would have another gun, or guns, around his house. She'd only seen him with the one that he always wore and took to work.

But first things first. She needed to fill him in, which meant leaving a voicemail.

She called his phone again, hoping he might actually answer, but no such luck. After she heard the beep she left the best, most coherent message she could.

"Kostya, long, complicated message ahead, so keep up. Candy called from Florida. The bad guys who killed Rick got to her, tortured her, then killed Dawn. This was on Saturday. She tried to keep them from killing Dawn by saying I knew something, so she gave them my name. There were four of them, and she thinks they were Arabs. I'm thinking they're probably part of a terrorist group that wants a code from the Missile Defense Agency. Couldn't get ahold of you, Ryker, or Gideon, so I called Trevor. He went batshit crazy and told me to find a gun of yours and leave. That's what I'm going to do. Call me and I'll tell you where I ended up."

Lark sucked in a deep breath and started to hit the 'end' button.

Then stopped.

"Dammit."

"Kostya, I wanted to do so much better than this. I wanted to do a dress with fuck-me heels and everything. I will too." She looked up at the ceiling, noticing the stainless steel ceiling fan for the first time.

"Kostya? Everything's going to be fine. Trevor's just acting like an old lady. But still. I'm so sorry I haven't said this before now. I love you," she said softly. "I believe in fairy tales now. I believe that you're my Prince Charming." She scrubbed away a tear and cleared her throat. "Okay, next time there will be a short dress and fuck-me heels."

She hung up. Now to find a gun. She needed to think about this calmly. Her man would definitely be responsible about this.

He'd have a gun safe!

She twirled around the living room, her eyes taking in everything. Nothing stood out.

Where?

She went back to their bedroom. She narrowed her eyes at the doorway and scoped out the entire room. He'd want it close to him. He always had his Sig Sauer in the nightstand near the condoms. The man had his priorities.

Quit with the naughty thoughts and think!

Wait a minute! She rushed over to the closet and pushed back the clothes on hangers near the back of his side of the closet. There it was. A huge safe. It took her a moment to figure out that it opened with some kind of finger or thumbprint.

"Fuck me!" she yelled and spun away.

"Next. What's next. Goddamned Trevor." She checked her phone again. Nothing from the guys, and here she was all in a tither because the old man at the FBI has his panties in a twist!

She stomped back to the living room.

I need a drink.

Lark looked over to the cabinet above the fridge, then grimaced in disgust. Okay, there was only one vehicle and that was the Bronco which Kostya took to base. She went back to the kitchen counter and called up her Uber app. She tapped in her address and scheduled her ride.

"I'm pissed at you, old man," she growled as she thought about Trevor. She started to load up her computer bag.

"Dammit!" She gritted her teeth when pencil shavings spilled all over the table and the floor. It never occurred to her to leave the mess, or to leave without her pencil sharpener.

Fine, I have a little bit of OCD, sue me.

She looked at the clock on her phone. It was still going to take another fifteen minutes before the Uber got here, not that it mattered. Trevor was out of his mind. But if he was this over the top, she shuddered to think what Kostya would be like, so she figured leaving was probably a good idea.

She went to the laundry room and grabbed the vacuum cleaner. She came back and vacuumed up the pencil shavings. She straightened up the table, made sure she had everything she needed in her bag, and that the top on her pencil sharpener was closed tight. Then she put that in the bag as well.

"Looking good."

Her phone buzzed. "Finally," she grinned.

Her shoulders slumped when she realized it was just the Uber driver outside, and not Kostya or one of the others. She hustled up and took the vacuum back to the laundry room, grabbed a coat, her purse, and the computer bag, then left the house and locked the door.

Why does every Uber driver drive a Prius?

"Hi!" she shouted as she bounced down the front steps.

The driver didn't even look up from his phone, not even when she opened the back seat door and got in.

"You're going into town?" he mumbled into his phone.

Lark rolled her eyes. "Yeah, Starbucks."

KOSTYA LOOKED around the room at all of his men. It was damn near five weeks since all fourteen members of Omega Sky had been together in one room. If he had to guess it wouldn't be fourteen members much longer. He would bet his bottom dollar that Sebastian Durand would not be signing his next contract. Kostya grinned. He knew the man wasn't planning on getting into Louisiana state politics, that was for damned sure, but he also knew who was trying to recruit Sebastian and he didn't think that Durand would be able to hold out much longer. Especially since it would allow Sebastian to live anywhere he wanted and that would mean he and his wife Gianna could move closer to her family.

"Okay, you're dismissed. I want everyone back here at

oh six hundred. Some of you are looking a might sickly, so I'm thinking a couple of tours around the obstacle course in the morning might just be the pick-me-up you need."

There was the obligatory groaning, then there was the jesting as to who would fare better. Kostya unbuttoned the pocket on his cargo pants and pulled out his phone. It had gone off a couple of times, but he knew if it was a true emergency, his Commander would have found someone to come down the hall to the ready room.

His blood froze as everyone started filing out of the room. He re-read the text, then saw that Lark had left him a voicemail.

"Lieutenant, I got a text from Lark," Ryker said as he came to the podium.

"So did I," Gideon came up from behind Ryker.

"Shut up." Kostya waved his hand at the two of them. He ignored both men and a couple of others who had remained when they saw Kostya's demeanor change.

Kostya listened to Lark's voice, and the acid in his stomach turned to lava. After the first two sentences of her complicated story, he turned to Gideon.

"Call Lark," he barked.

Kostya continued to listen to Lark's voice. His heart clenched when she mentioned fuck-me heels, but then... but then, she said she loved him. He knew she did. He just didn't think she realized it.

"She's not answering," Gideon said.

Kostya ended the call and tried calling her from his phone. It rang and rang until it went to voicemail. He looked around and saw Ryker, Gideon, Nolan, and Jase surrounding him.

"I want two vehicles, and you on your motorcycle," he said, pointing to Ryker. "We're going to my house. I can't get ahold of Lark. It's possible that we've got a terrorist group after her. If we do, know that they have had no problem torturing and killing people for what they want. Gideon, you're riding shotgun with me, bring whatever comp or tablet you can. You're going to find Lark, these terrorists, and the fucking president if I need you to, got it?"

"On it," Gideon answered.

Kostya stormed out of the ready room with his men on his heels. *Gideon better fucking hurry with his electronic toys.*

THEY'D SHOT HIM. They'd just shot that kid in the head like he was nothing. Lark still had some of his blood splattered on her.

When she'd seen the big Escalade roaring down the driveway toward them, she'd shoved her phone into her shirt, deep in her bra until it hit the underwire. She knew that it was on silent because she'd felt it vibrate, but no sound had blasted. Gideon would be able to track her from her phone, wouldn't he?

"Where are you taking me?" she asked again. She hadn't been pestering the men because they were scary, and they had killed Dawn. She was stuck in the backseat between two of them.

"Don't talk," the one on the right of her rumbled.

Lark shut her mouth. Never in her life, not even in those dark cages in Afghanistan, had she been this scared. At least then, there had been Nic, Cullen, and Kostya with her.

The man on her left spoke to the driver in Arabic. She caught the words money, woman, and plane. Did they plan to take her on a plane? That didn't make any sense. Why hadn't she bothered to learn more Arabic? She'd always meant to.

"Uhm," she started.

The man on the right yanked her hair and twisted her head so they were face to face. "No talking, unless you want me to start cutting you right now. Or maybe I will anyway." He grinned. He pulled a knife out of his suit jacket and drew it down Lark's arm, slicing through the fabric of her Henley, and cutting deep into her skin.

She whimpered and clamped her lips shut.

"That's better."

He settled back in his seat but kept the knife held loosely in his hand as it rested on his lap. Lark tried to ignore it as she stared out the window. They weren't taking her into the city, they were going along the coast. She prayed they would be driving for a long time. Wouldn't that give Kostya more time to rescue her? Isn't that what Prince Charming did? Rescue people?

She couldn't say how long they'd been driving when the vehicle pulled off the road and parked near some kind of storage facility. She saw trees. Lots of trees. Was that a gate? Lark looked down and saw that her jeans were soaked with blood, so they must have driven a long time for that cut to have bled that much. She frowned when she realized how disjointed her thinking was.

"I said get out!"

She looked up and realized all four doors were open and all of the men were out of the SUV. The man who had cut her grabbed her injured arm and yanked her out of the car. Her screams echoed into nothingness. Was it nothing?

"She's going to pass out. How badly did you cut her? We need her awake to question her."

The man holding her started yelling back in Arabic and darkness swirled around her head just before Lark slumped to the ground.

26

"I TOLD YOU I HAVE HER."

"If you have her, then why haven't we found her?" Kostya roared. All he saw in front of him was open highway.

"Kostya, you need to calm down, we need to take the next exit."

"Is her phone still moving, or has it stopped?

"It's moving, but it's slowed down," Gideon answered.

"Gideon, can you give me the coordinates? I'm going to go in first and reconnoiter," Ryker said into their comm system. All of the men had their communication units on.

"Negative," Kostya answered. "Gideon and I are going in first."

There was no response, and Kostya could feel Gideon's eyes on him. He took his eyes off the road to glare at his friend. "What?" he practically yelled.

"You're not thinking like a commander. You know that Ryker is correct; he's on his bike and he needs to go in first," Gideon said.

Every single emotion, good, bad, ugly, hateful,

passionate, and terrified roared through Kostya's system within a millisecond.

Get your shit together, Baronavich!

He blew out a jet of air through his nose. "You're right, Ryker. Gideon, get him the coordinates. And Gideon, let us all know when Lark's phone comes to a stop."

"You got it," Gideon nodded. Then he gave Ryker the coordinates.

Kostya came to a rolling stop at the end of the off-ramp, then took a right onto the farm road. "Where in the hell are we?" he asked Gideon.

"Between Frederica and Little Heaven."

"Come again?" Kostya said.

"It's true," Nolan said over the comm. "A girl I once dated was from around here. She thought it was cute to say she was sent from heaven. It got on my nerves."

"Jesus, Nolan, the first time I heard her say that I would have—" Jase started.

"Shut up!" Kostya growled into his mic. There was silence.

Now all he could hear was his rapidly beating heart. That was fine. He needed all of his concentration on finding Lark and making sure that she stayed alive.

"They stopped," Gideon said.

"I'm fifty meters away from a black Escalade that's stopped in front of the storage facility. They're pressing in the code to open the gate."

"That's them."

"I've got wire cutters in my truck," Jase volunteered.

"That'll work," Ryker said.

Kostya pressed down on the accelerator.

By the time the storage facility was in view, the gate was closed and there was no sign of the Escalade or Ryker.

"We've got a problem," Ryker whispered.

"What?" Kostya demanded.

"The good news is that I had eyes on Lark and she's alive. The bad news is that she passed out as soon as she stepped out of the vehicle."

Kostya shut his eyes, then opened them. *She's alive.* That's what he had to focus on, she was alive.

"Where are you?" he asked.

"There's a road that goes a little way in, with a chain across it that says no trespassing. I parked my bike behind there. I jogged back behind to the south side of the facility. It's nothing but woods back here. In order not to be seen, you're all going to have to hoof it. The storage unit doors are facing to the north, so they won't see us."

"Got it." Kostya saw Jase's truck coming in behind him. He turned left onto the road that Ryker had described, and Jase followed him.

They all scrambled out of their vehicles. Both Jase and Kostya pulled out identical bolt cutters that were used by fire and rescue teams. They did have different assault rifles; Jase had a MK 16 SCAR, while Kostya preferred the M4A1 Carbine. Jase tossed out one more SCAR to Nolan.

"What, none for me?" Gideon bitched.

"Here," Kostya handed him his second Sig Sauer.

"Fuck that noise, I've got my own," Gideon sniffed. "Give me the bolt cutters."

"Shut up and start running," Kostya said as he tossed Gideon the bolt cutters, then turned around and headed for the storage unit. He wasn't even breathing hard by the time he met up with Ryker.

"What was wrong with her? How was she looking?" he immediately asked Ryker.

"I was looking at them from the east side. I didn't

have binoculars or a scope, so I couldn't get a good look. One of the guys dragged her out of the SUV. She was standing on her own for a moment, then she slumped over. She would have hit the ground if he hadn't caught her."

Kostya grit his teeth.

"Which unit?"

"The second one from the west end."

Jase, Nolan, and Gideon were there listening to Ryker's report.

"I want cuts on the ends of both sides of the south fence. Then I want Jase to go in on the east side, followed by Nolan. Ryker, you're with me on the west side."

"And me? Am I just chopped liver?" Gideon asked.

"You're coordinating. If you hear anything that doesn't sound right, I want you orchestrating the action."

Gideon nodded.

"Go." Kostya started toward the end of the south fence that was closest to Lark's storage unit. He had to get to her, but he had to stay sane about it.

Ryker ran around to the west fence, then came back to where Kostya was beginning to cut.

"The storage unit is open at the bottom, maybe five inches. I don't hear a sound coming out. The Escalade is parked in front."

Kostya nodded, continuing to cut, wincing with every snap the cutters made.

When he'd cut enough fence away, he and Ryker pulled at it so they could make their way through.

A scream rent through the glorious calm of the Southern night.

I hear nothing. Nothing.

Kostya was no longer there. He had disappeared. He

was no longer human. He had one mission—to destroy. To kill.

There was an occasional buzz in his ear as he strode around the side of the storage units. He felt his man at his back. He looked up for a moment. Two others were coming at him.

"Are you all in position?" It was Gideon.

"We're at the unit, on either side," Jase answered in a barely-there whisper.

Another buzz, louder this time. Longer, high-pitched. Kostya forced it out of his mind. There were men inside this unit who needed to die.

He looked across the unit to Jase and Nolan. He gave them a signal and they nodded. He looked over his shoulder at Ryker who nodded as well. They all knew what to do.

Kostya held up his hand, three fingers up.

Three.

Two.

One.

A fist.

They all dropped and rolled in front of the unit. They shoved their gun muzzles under the open door of the unit and took aim. Buzz after buzz after buzz pierced through the air as bright bursts of blood and bone exploded from men's feet, ankles and calves.

Kostya shoved up the rolling door with his shoulder. He felt someone help him. They shot at the men until only one buzz remained—and turned into Lark's screams.

He saw her. She was duct-taped to a chair in the middle of the unit. There were remnants of a blue shirt and a pink bra hanging off her body. There was blood. So much blood.

He dropped to his knees in front of her, not knowing if she was alive or dead.

He took her tattered shirt and used it to wipe away the blood. So much blood. He couldn't see.

"Lieutenant, you need to move. Let me see her." Was that Nolan?"

He saw a hand try to touch Lark and he violently shoved it away.

"Kostya."

It sounded like Lark saying his name.

"Kostya," Lark said his name louder.

"He saw a cut on her upper breast, but it was shallow."

"Kostya, Honey. I'm okay."

He gently wiped away some blood on her stomach.

"Kostya, come on, Honey, you told me you didn't want me stripping in front of a bunch of guys, remember?" Was that Lark laughing? "Next thing you know I'll have to buy a G-string."

His head shot up.

She was gritting her teeth. He could see the pain she was holding back, but his girl, his woman, there she was, doing her best to keep it together, somehow there was a twinkle in her eye, just for him. She was being brave. Being strong.

Kostya closed his eyes for just an instant, then opened them and smiled. "Then I better cover you up."

He ripped his shirt over his head while Ryker used his knife to cut her free. She hissed as the circulation came back to her arms. Kostya took her hands into his and started rubbing them.

"Clothes first," she whispered. He could see how upset she was. Her humiliation. Not so much because of his men, but from before. He wanted to kill the monsters all over again.

Kostya gently helped her put on his blue t-shirt.

That was it, then she launched herself at him, hissing in pain.

"I'm all right. I'm fine."

Again, she was trying to soothe *him*. Trying to comfort *him*.

"Enough, *Sólnce*." As softly and tenderly as he could, he lifted her up into his arms, pushing her hair off her forehead, and planting his lips there. "You're safe now. I have you. You're safe."

"Promise?"

"I love you, Lark. I'm always going to keep you safe."

"On your honor?" she asked as he walked out into the evening dusk.

"On my honor."

"You know you're my Prince Charming. I'm sorry I said I love you on the phone. I should have said it sooner." His gut clenched when he saw her first tear.

"*Sólnce*, I'll tell you a secret. As soon as you told me you loved my dick, I knew you were telling me you loved me."

Lark's laughter could be heard across the sky.

EPILOGUE

"He looks good with a bit of a beard," her mother said as she bumped her shoulder. Lark looked over to where Kostya was sitting cross-legged on the grass with little Nazy. She was putting a tiny crown on his head and he was sitting up straight and smiling, just like any good princess would.

Irina handed Lark a cupcake. "Eat this. You've been running around all day. You need nourishment."

"After the meal that we had last night, I couldn't eat 'til now," Lark said as she started peeling back the cupcake wrapper. "Mmm, red velvet. Mom, whoever you have to cater these events, you should double their wage. Did you know red velvet is Kostya's favorite?"

"Yep, I sure do. Irina told me. I love it when I can spoil people with things they like."

Lark had her cupcake up to her lips for a second bite when it hit her. "Oh my God, you're Kostya's source!"

"Huh?" Irina asked. "What do you mean source?"

"Kostya has been spot on from the start, making sure he has taken me to every kind of restaurant that I would love. Hell, he even knew about my love for sausage McMuffins! You told him, didn't you, Mom?"

"You are such a good little investigative journalist," her mother teased as she pinched her cheek.

Irina howled with laughter. "You two remind me of me and Lexi."

Lark turned to Irina and mouthed the words, 'I told you so.' Kostya's sister had been nervous about meeting her mother, somehow thinking that because Mom was a billionaire she'd be all snooty. But she wasn't. She was just Mom.

"Let's go sit down in the shade," Beatrice suggested. "I don't know about you two, but the kids have wiped me out."

"I'm sorry," Irina said as she winced.

"Are you kidding, I enjoyed every minute of it," Beatrice said. While Irina and Beatrice settled down under the pergola, Lark went to pour them all some lemonade. "I've got to say, Irina, I adore your children. And your daughter Lexi? She is wonderful with those two girls. They are going to want to be just like her when they grow up. Taja is already wearing those cute pink jeans she brought for her."

Irina smiled with pride as she looked over at her daughter with Taja.

"Are you getting me a glass?" Kostya asked as he wrapped his arms around her waist.

"There's also strawberry lemonade, iced tea, or beer for you to choose from." Lark arched back and kissed his neck. He smelled good, but...

"Is that cream cheese frosting on your neck?"

"Probably. I'm betting it's in my hair and beard too.

Nazy was eating one of the cupcakes and the frosting got everywhere," Kostya laughed.

"So, what would you like to drink? I think that the iced tea would make a nice pairing with the cream cheese," she teased.

"I'm sold."

She finished pouring the lemonades and Kostya picked them up. "Are these two for Irina and your mom?"

"Yep."

"I'll take them. Why don't you go grab that swing over there before Lexi steals it."

Lark looked over at the cushioned swing that had been hanging from the old weeping willow for as long as she could remember. "She's too busy playing with Taja, but I'm definitely going to claim it." She nodded and took her lemonade and his iced tea across the lawn. It was perfect because she could still watch Lexi and Roman play with the girls. Roman had taken Kostya's place and was now having a tea party with Nazy. He was holding one of her stuffed animals and helping it hold its teacup. He was almost as adorable as Kostya.

Kostya sat down beside her and took his iced tea.

"Look, Samira is sitting next to your mom and my sister. There is no way that would have happened a few months ago."

"You're right about that." His voice drifted off and Lark saw that he was watching Roman. She loved the fact that in the last few months since she had moved in with him, he had talked about his brother Roman with fondness. He'd even brought up some good memories of his mother and father.

Kostya wrapped his arm around her shoulders and Lark leaned into his side. Hell, a few months ago it never would have occurred to her that she would be plastered against a big man, here in the sun on her mother's estate, but here she was, and she reveled in it.

"Are you having a good time?" he asked.

"The best. I'm so glad we were able to do this. I'm just sorry that Tony wasn't able to make it. I can't believe how much that man travels."

Kostya chuckled. "Yeah, but when he's home, then we're forced to go over to the Romanos for their small family get-togethers. How have you been fairing with those?"

Lark looked up at him and punched him in the arm. "You know I love those. All that family, all those kids."

"Yeah, and all those babies," he let his voice trail off.

"What are you saying?" she asked. She didn't like his tone of voice. He was being too serious all of a sudden.

Kostya pulled the glass out of her hands and set it down on the ground with his. He cupped the back of her head and kissed her. It must have been their thousandth kiss, but it was still a magical kiss. Kostya stoked her passion, she felt it rising and she squeezed her legs together, trying to assuage her ache. But from the way he stroked her hair, she could tell that's not what he was after. He was weaving a soft and sweet kind of magic this afternoon.

Kostya lifted his head.

"Your eyes are silver," he whispered.

She rested her hands on his chest and felt his steady heartbeat. It gave her comfort.

"Your eyes look like the sky. Filled with endless possibilities."

Kostya's lip tipped up. "You say pretty words, Lark."

She grinned. "I write for a living."

He hesitated and she wondered what was going to come next. "I bought you a ring last month."

Her breath stopped. Then her heart stopped when she realized he wasn't saying anything more.

She eventually let out a long burst of air. "And?"

"I couldn't give it to you."

Lark nodded. "Okay."

I'm not going to cry. I'm not going to cry.

"Do you know why I wasn't going to give it to you?"

She shook her head.

"Yes, you do. It's because I didn't trust myself with a family. I didn't trust that I could keep my whole family safe. And I knew…"

Lark closed her eyes. She ached for him. "What did you know, Honey?"

"I knew you wanted babies."

"I want you, Kostya. I want *you*."

"But I finally realized something."

Lark opened her eyes and saw that blue sky of possibilities. "What did you realize?"

"It wouldn't just be me keeping our babies safe, it would be both of us. And with you by my side? We can do anything."

He pulled the most beautiful ring she had ever seen out of his shirt pocket, picked up her hand, and slid it onto her finger. "Marry me, Lark."

"Oh yes. Absolutely, yes."

"And babies?" he asked.

"We're naming our first son Roman."

ACROSS THE COUNTRY in Virginia Beach, Gideon's phone rang and he frowned when he saw whose name was on the screen.

"Hello?"

"Gideon, it's me, Jada."

"I know." He really hadn't ever expected to hear from her again. Not after the way they'd left things.

"Gideon, I'm in trouble. Big trouble. I stumbled across something when I was..."

"When you were what, hacking into some system you shouldn't have?"

"Anyway. I was checking some things out, looking into a couple of systems, and I noticed an anomaly. But Gideon," Her voice was shaking. "I don't know who else to turn to, and—"

"Jada? Jada?" Gideon looked down. Their connection had been lost.

DON'T FORGET to pick up your copy of Gideon and Jada's story in Her Unflinching Warrior.

ABOUT THE AUTHOR

Caitlyn O'Leary is a USA Bestselling Author, #1 Amazon Bestselling Author and a Golden Quill Recipient from Book Viral in 2015. Hampered with a mild form of dyslexia she began memorizing books at an early age until her grandmother, the English teacher, took the time to teach her to read -- then she never stopped. She began re-writing alternate endings for her Trixie Belden books into happily-ever-afters with Trixie's platonic friend Jim. When she was home with pneumonia at twelve, she read the entire set of World Book Encyclopedias -- a little more challenging to end those happily.

Caitlyn loves writing about Alpha males with strong heroines who keep the men on their toes. There is plenty of action, suspense and humor in her books. She is never shy about tackling some of today's tough and relevant issues.

In addition to being an award-winning author of romantic suspense novels, she is a devoted aunt, an avid reader, a former corporate executive for a Fortune 100 company, and totally in love with her husband of soon-to-be twenty years.

She recently moved back home to the Pacific Northwest from Southern California. She is so happy to see the seasons again; rain, rain and more rain. She has a large fan group on Facebook and through her e-mail list. Caitlyn is known for telling her "Caitlyn Factors", where she relates her little and big life's screw-ups. The list is long. She loves hearing and connecting with her fans on a daily basis.

Keep up with Caitlyn O'Leary:

Website: www.caitlynoleary.com
FB Reader Group: http://bit.ly/2NUZVjF
Email: caitlyn@caitlynoleary.com
Newsletter: http://bit.ly/1WIhRup

facebook.com/Caitlyn-OLeary-Author-638771522866740

twitter.com/CaitlynOLearyNA

instagram.com/caitlynoleary_author

amazon.com/author/caitlynoleary

bookbub.com/authors/caitlyn-o-leary

goodreads.com/CaitlynOLeary

pinterest.com/caitlynoleary35

ALSO BY CAITLYN O'LEARY

OMEGA SKY SERIES

Her Selfless Warrior (Book #1)

Her Unflinching Warrior (Book #2)

Her Wild Warrior (Book #3)

NIGHT STORM SERIES

Her Ruthless Protector (Book #1)

Her Tempting Protector (Book #2)

Her Chosen Protector (Book #3)

Her Intense Protector (Book #4)

Her Sensual Protector (Book #5)

Her Faithful Protector (Book #6)

Her Noble Protector (Book #7)

Her Righteous Protector (Book #8)

NIGHT STORM LEGACY SERIES

Lawson & Jill (Book 1)

THE MIDNIGHT DELTA SERIES

Her Vigilant Seal (Book #1)

Her Loyal Seal (Book #2)

Her Adoring Seal (Book #3)

Sealed with a Kiss (Book #4)

Her Daring Seal (Book #5)

Her Fierce Seal (Book #6)

A Seals Vigilant Heart (Book #7)

Her Dominant Seal (Book #8)

Her Relentless Seal (Book #9)

Her Treasured Seal (Book #10)

Her Unbroken Seal (Book #11)

BLACK DAWN SERIES

Her Steadfast Hero (Book #1)

Her Devoted Hero (Book #2)

Her Passionate Hero (Book #3)

Her Wicked Hero (Book #4)

Her Guarded Hero (Book #5)

Her Captivated Hero (Book #6)

Her Honorable Hero (Book #7)

Her Loving Hero (Book #8)

THE FOUND SERIES

Revealed (Book #1)

Forsaken (Book #2)

Healed (Book #3)

SHADOWS ALLIANCE SERIES

Declan

Made in the USA
Columbia, SC
07 June 2022

61378439R00186